Spring Fever

M. J. Rutter

© Copyright AuthorMJRutter2018

Acknowledgements

Alas, we have come to the end of this amazing journey. I want to thank each and everyone of you who has recommended this series, shared this series and read this series.

I couldn't have completed this journey without my crew, my girls, the awesome team known as my Beta Readers. Some new along the way and some who have been here from the start.

Denise Mitchell, you work all the hours God sends, a mum and Scout leader and you still find time to read my books. I cannot thank you enough for all you have done and the support you have given me, we definitely need more coffee mornings, I know that much.

Susan Scott, my lad of the Highlands, studding at Uni and still reading with three boys to keep in check too. You are amazing, and I adore you for all you do and all of the support you give. Thank you for being my northern star,

Elin Wester, my Smiley Swedish girl, I miss you so much and am so grateful for everything you have done for me. You were with me back in Windham N.H. USA when I would let you read my appalling writing back then. A friend, a diamond and a true gem who makes me smile. Thank you.

Michelle Robinson, once again you have found time to read this series. I miss you so much, but always there when I need you. Working full time and looking after that old man of yours, (Love you Kenny). Thank you so much for all you have done.

I couldn't have written a word without the continuing support of my wonderful husband Franie and my patient children, Mackenzie and Brodie. I owe you a big day out, promise, no writing.

A special thank you to the wonderful **Sassy Queens of Design** for creating the amazingly beautiful covers for this series and the support they give me. Seriously, they are not just cover designers, they go above and beyond for all of their authors. They can be found on Facebook if you are looking for covers, book trailers or swag, tell them Melissa sent you.

To all of my readers, family and friends, thank you for your support and encouragement, this road is hard and arduous at times, but you keep me going, without you I wouldn't have a reason to write. I love you all, keep with me, I have so much more to give.

All rights reserved. No part of this book may be reproduced or distributed in any form, including digital and electronic or mechanical, including photocopying, recording, or by any information storage and retrieval system, without the prior written consent of the Publisher, except for brief use in reviews.

This book is a work of fiction. Characters, names, places, and incidents either are the product of the author's imagination or are used fictitiously, and any resemblance to any actual persons, living or dead, events, or locales is entirely coincidental.

One

Kelsey

"Can you please confirm your full name for the court?"

"Jeremy Harrison Buxton," he answered not taking his eyes off me. I smiled slightly. Not because I found this funny, nothing could have been further from the truth. He looked petrified and I smiled to reassure him that I still stood by him.

From behind I could see that her hair had grown and needed a colour. I could see that she had lost weight and that she was shaking, but did I feel sorry for her? Absolutely not. Natasha Mason was paying for her crimes, her lies had unraveled and now she had to answer to the law.

"May I call you Jeremy?" her attractive, blonde haired solicitor asked.

"You may," he confirmed.

"So, Jeremy, how did you and my client Natasha Mason meet?" she then asked.

"Her company approached The Press, where I work, for us to copy edit some of their work. I am now the copy-editing manager, but at the time, I was assigned to the job of writing up the official contracts and ensuring that Miss Mason's requests were met as far as work went."

"We'll come back to that. So, you have worked at The Press for…?"

"Three and a half years. It will be four years in July."

"And already a manager, I am impressed," she smiled at him and looked around. "So, you had a number of professional meetings to discuss the contracts?"

"Four work related meetings, yes."

"That's right, and at the last meeting you made it known to Miss Mason that you were attracted to her."

"No," he frowned, "never. I never told her I was attracted to her because I wasn't."

"Really," she smirked and turned around to look at me. "Are you saying this because your heavily pregnant wife is here?" *Heavily pregnant, my arse!*

"I am saying this because it's the truth." He affirmed angrily.

"Objection, Your Honor, Mrs Buxton's condition is not a matter for snide comments and insinuations." The prosecutor, Andrew Prescott, protested.

"Miss Kendal, please keep to your questions and opinions to yourself. Mr Buxton is not on trial here." The Right Honorable Judith Hayes stated.

"Of course, Your Honour. So, Mr Buxton, when did you learn of Miss Mason's attraction to you?"

"On Friday, October the eleventh."

"And how did she tell you?"

"She sent me an e-mail blackmailing me into meeting her, you must have seen the e-mails."

"I have, but anyone can hack into an e-mail account if they know how."

"Well, I don't."

"So, against your better judgement you met with Miss Mason, after only one threat?"

"At the time I left the office, I had no idea of what she truly wanted until she actually told me in my car."

"Please remind us of what she actually said to you."

"Her actual words?" he checked.

"Yes."

"She said that she wanted to feel my hands on her, she wanted me to uh… to uh fuck her to kingdom come." He fidgeted in his seat as the court erupted in mumbles.

"I find it hard to believe that someone of Miss Mason's stature would use such derogative words, I'm shocked."

"Believe me, so was I," he muttered.

Miss Kendal tried her hardest to bring Jeremy down, but every time she shot a smart remark or question at him, he answered her. "Tell us about the alleged incident." She goaded.

"After she showed me the pictures on her phone, I drove her back to the Crown. I ordered her to get out of my car and instead she uh, she grabbed me."

"Grabbed you, where?"

"On my uh, on my penis," he replied awkwardly.

"Was your penis out then?"

"No, she did it through my trousers."

"Are we to believe that you have brought a sexual assault charge against Miss Mason for grabbing you through your clothes?"

"Yes. If it was the other way around and I was on trial for groping her, would you still want me prosecuted even if I only groped her through her clothes?"

"Did you grope her through her clothes, Jeremy?"

"Objection!" Andrew bellowed, his voice echoed out making me jump.

"I'll withdraw the question." Miss Kendal announced. "Okay, so she *grabbed* your penis through your trousers and then what?"

"She moved her hand," he shifted slightly in his seat, I could see sweat had formed across his forehead. My poor baby, how could she put him through this?

"Moved her hand, how? You need to give us a clear idea of what happened, Jeremy." She pressed. He looked at Andrew who in turn nodded his head.

"She moved her hand up and down on my penis."

"And while this was happening, did you try and fight her off?"

"Yes, and I told her to stop."

"Are you sure?"

"Yes," he frowned and rubbed a shaky hand over his forehead.

"Did Miss Mason say anything to you?"

"She said 'You want me; you know you do.'"

"And then what happened, did she just stop?"

"Not um, not until I um... Well not until she made me ejaculate."

"So, she made you ejaculate, which says to me that you enjoyed yourself." She turned around and smirked, right until she saw me glaring at her. *Bitch!* She turned away and faced an extremely embarrassed and red-faced Jeremy.

"Steady now," DCI Hollins whispered, "we don't want you to go into labour."

"No, but I can get off with diminished responsibility, right?" I muttered as the court settled.

"No, I did not enjoy it at all. You can't stop these things happening, I tried not to let her have that on me, I fought until the pain became too much and I had to let go."

"With all due respect, Jeremy, you can stop these things."

"How would you know? You are not a man; how could you possibly know if we can control whether or not we ejaculate?"

"You are right, Jeremy. But ejaculation after a sexual act usually confirms enjoyment though."

"Your Honour," Andrew interrupted and stood. "We have medical evidence proving that even when a man is not enjoying a forceful sexual act, should his penis be rubbed in such a manor, he will, in fact, ejaculate, though it causes pain rather than enjoyment. Whether Mr Buxton did or did not ejaculate, the fact remains that this act was carried out on him, regardless of the outcome, against his will. Miss Kendal would not treat a rape victim this way and in the eyes of the law, Mr Buxton said no and meant no. Miss Mason continued anyway, this should not be deemed as a double standard act and he should be treated with the same amount of compassion as any other victim of a sexual act regardless of gender."

"I agree," Judge Hayes nodded. "Miss Kendal, I will give you one last chance to question Mr Buxton respectfully and without passing comments on his answers. We are here to establish the facts. You cannot inflict your personal opinions on this court to better your defence, no matter how much the Masons are paying you."

"Yes, Your Honour. I am sorry, Jeremy."

Jeremy nodded in acknowledgement of her thin gesture. She continued her line of questioning, though a little tamer and calmer than before. Jeremy answered and looked relieved when she announced she had no more questions. He had held it together and I knew it couldn't have been easy for him to sit there and tell everyone in the room in great detail of what that bitch had done to him.

Andrew asked him a few more questions and after he finished the judge sent the jury away to consider their verdict. Natasha looked concerned, but I couldn't pity her at all. She almost destroyed us and for the first few months after everything came out, it was not easy, not by any means.

I remembered back to the night when it all came to a head. Jeremy and I had been to his cousin Seb and my best friend, Jude's, engagement party at Buxton Manor. Natasha had sent me all of these messages with pictures of Jeremy having sex with other women in an attempt to split us up, she almost succeeded. I honestly don't think my heart could take another beating. We had a fight, but we sorted things out and in the end, we realized that nothing and no one could tear us apart.

    I confronted her the day after, I needed to see her for one thing and I needed to let her know that she had lost, that nothing she had done to us could destroy us. I was adamant that nothing she said was the truth, okay there was the pictures, but each of them were dated around the times we hadn't been together. I couldn't punish him for what he did, it seemed he had been through enough.

Discovering I was pregnant after such a stressful few months was not easy. Not only were Jeremy and I trying to rebuild our relationship, but we had a very poorly little boy to look after and I'd be lying if I was to say I was over joyed at becoming pregnant again. With less than ten weeks to go until the baby arrived, the timing couldn't have been worse when the paperwork came through requesting that Jeremy gave evidence at Natasha's trial. She had denied the charges even after all of the evidence was stacked up against her and now here we were sat in Bournemouth Crown Court awaiting the jury's decision.

We left the court and headed, next door to Tesco's for a drink, his lips were white, and I really needed some fresh air. The early spring sun shone when the clouds moved enough for it to beam out its much-needed golden rays. The winter wasn't particularly cold, but it was drawn out and spring seemed to be taking forever to get here.

I sat at a table while Jeremy got us some tea. He looked so tired, I knew he had been dreading this day ever since the letter arrived asking him to appear and provide evidence. He had barely eaten either, even after five months, Natasha Mason still seemed to be affecting our lives and I had had just about enough of her and her shenanigans.

"I got extra milk for you, love," he said as he set the tray on the table. He sat opposite me and frowned.

"You did well, Jeremy. Don't worry. I watched the faces of the jury, they all believe you."

"This is why I didn't want to press charges, knowing that she did that to me was bad enough, but having to admit it in public, well, that has just about destroyed me." He sighed tugging at his tie. "I don't think I have ever done anything so belittling, so humiliating before in my life."

"I know and that is why the jury don't doubt you, sweetheart. They know how hard it must have been for you in front of everyone and you told her lawyer straight. I think she may actually go to prison for this."

"I bloody hope not," he shook his head. "Her father would want my blood if she did."

"She almost destroyed your life," I retorted angrily. "She could have cost you your job and your marriage and you still worry what punishment she'll get?"

"This is going to be in the papers, Kelsey. The whole sodding world will know what happened and it will be ten times worse if she goes down for it."

"So, if it was me, if it had happened to me, let's say I had Sam or Kyle charged and it went to court, would you want me to worry what punishment they got?" I snapped.

"No," he sighed, "I'd have them castrated."

"Hormonal woman here, believe me, the nights I have led in our bed and thought about the pain I would happily inflict on that woman." I smiled slightly. I reached across the table and placed my hand in his.

"That can't have been easy for you, love, I am so sorry you had to watch that." He sighed.

"I am more concerned about you at the moment."

"I'm okay," he lied, I could see he wasn't. "Well, I will be okay." He corrected and smiled slightly.

"We will be okay together," I stated. He squeezed my hand before letting go to drink his black tea. Just the thought of black tea or coffee in my condition made my stomach turn.

At least I was alright around fish this time. With our toddler, Harrison, I couldn't go near fish at all. This pregnancy was different, and I was able to eat what I wanted, but drinking black tea was just yuk. Poor Jeremy had no choice. He couldn't have anything with milk in it, he couldn't even have breast milk as a baby.

We thought about finding out what we were having, but both of us liked the idea of a surprise, so decided not to ask. Boy or girl, we would be happy and with the weeks winding down, we didn't have long left anyway.

He received a text message asking us to return to the court, it seemed the jury had already made a decision. This time Jeremy stood beside me and DCI Hollins while the judge asked the foreman of the jury to reveal their decision. He stood, a tall man with hardly any hair, he wore a white shirt with a brown tie, he handed a piece of folded paper to the bailiff who passed it to the judge. She frowned at the paper and looked up.

"Will the defendant please rise?" she asked. Silently, Natasha stood, for about a split second, I felt sorry for her, only for a split second though.

"For the charges of blackmail, how do you find the defendant?"

"Guilty."

"And for the charges of Sexual Assault on Jeremy Buxton, how do you find the defendant?"

"Guilty."

"Finally, for the charges of Perverting the Course of Justice, how do you find the defendant?"

"Guilty."

"Natasha Mason, you have been found guilty on all of the charges brought against you. Therefore, I can see no reason to drag this out further, I will pass sentence today so everyone, especially Mr Buxton, whose life you very nearly destroyed, can get on with their lives and move forward. For the nature of the crimes, I cannot allow this sort of behaviour to go under punished, the punishment must fit the crime regardless of wealth or background, you simply cannot do this and get away with it. That being said, your father has promised to take you away from this town, unfortunately, because I feel there is no remorse for your actions I have no choice but to issue a custodial sentence.

"For the charges of Blackmail, considering these charges are not involving money, I will give you a two-year suspended sentence. For the charges of Perverting the Course of Justice, I am sentencing you to four months in prison with no time off for good behaviour and finally for the charges of sexual assault, I sentence you to a further six months in prison to run concurrent with the previous sentences. I hope that these sentences give you time to think about your actions and confirms to you that no amount of money gives you the right to destroy someone's life. Mr Buxton is an honest and hardworking husband and father; you have no right to move in on someone for your own pleasure. I hope while away you seek some sort of psychiatric help, because frankly, Miss Mason, I feel you definitely need it. Take the defendant down." She ordered with a bang on her gavel.

It made me jump, but it wrenched my heart to see her as she looked at her father, tears streaming her pale face, maybe she was sorry. I felt that right until she glared at my husband, her eyes showed nothing, no remorse or anything and I didn't care, she was going to prison, and I only hoped that would be the end of it.

I took hold of Jeremy's sweaty hand, his lips were pale and the colour had drained from his face, as was the sheer dis-belief expression covering it. I lightly squeezed his hand,

"Are you okay, sweetheart?" I asked him.

"I can't believe they locked her up," he muttered.

"Considering what she did, the judge was very lenient on her Jeremy," DCI Hollins stated.

We stood with the detective and he pulled his car keys from his suit pocket.

"I suggest you have a couple of stiff drinks tonight, Jeremy." DCI Hollins said as we readied to leave. "After this week, you have earned it."

"Thanks for everything," Jeremy said and shook his hand.

"Just doing my job," he nodded and looked over our shoulders, Mr Mason, Natasha's father, a short man with silver hair, approached us. I honestly expected him to start, but he held out his hand to Jeremy who had sort of braced himself for an altercation.

"I am sorry she did this to you, Jeremy." He said, "Please accept my sincere apologies."

"Thank you," Jeremy said and shook his hand. "I never expected…"

He shook his head, "She has to learn the hard way," he frowned and looked at me. "I am also sorry to you, Mrs Buxton, I can only imagine what she has put you through."

"Well, maybe she'll get the help she needs," I nodded rubbing my hand over my swollen stomach.

He followed my hand and smiled slightly, "Perhaps," he agreed. "Best of luck to you both," he then left with the sour looking solicitor hot on his heels.

"Well, that was not what I expected," DCI Hollins smiled. "Good luck, Jeremy, with a new baby on the way, your future is already looking brighter."

"It is now." Jeremy agreed and squeezed my hand.

Two
Jeremy

I heaved in a deep breath of fresh air as we left the courts and headed to my car. Still holding my hand, her heels, clip clopping on the tarmac as she walked beside me, was my beautiful wife. If nothing told me more that she was a keeper it was the past few months. She had been so supportive, so understanding and was with me every step of the way.

The nights I sat up over a cup of coffee she sat beside me, sometimes we would talk and other times we just sat in silence. Our relationship had turned a corner, this could have destroyed us and all we had, and it very nearly did, but it only made us stronger.

    She held me when I woke shaking and sweating from nightmares, she hugged me when I had had a tough day and she always seemed to know what was on my mind. Okay, so Natasha only handled me as such, still, the thought of it made me shudder. A million men would have just enjoyed it, but not this man, it proved that my wife was my one and only, not that I needed confirmation of that.

The weeks leading up to the assault had been strenuous at home, Kelsey and I had had more bumps in the road than any other married couple I knew. Regardless, we survived, and it appeared we were one of those couples who triumphed over adversity, instead of allowing it to destroy us we grew closer and stronger together.

We climbed into the car out of the early spring sun and closed the doors. I turned in my seat and watched as she pulled the seatbelt over her tummy.

"What?" she asked with a little smile.

"I have never said thank you." I said.

"Thank you for what?"

"For this, for being here beside me, for being not only my wife, but also my best friend, for loving me and trusting me. I honestly don't know how I would have coped over the past few months without you by my side." I lifted her hand from her lap and pulled it to my lips. "So, thank you, thank you for believing in me, in us. Thank you for being my wife." I leaned towards her and pecked her lips, "I love you, Mrs Buxton."

Her eyes welled with tears, "I love you too." She said and kissed me back.

"I didn't want to make you cry…" I frowned catching a tear on my finger.

"That was one of the most beautiful things you have ever said to me," she explained. "Plus, I am an emotional, hormonal wreck at the moment." She sniffed, "Let's go and get Harrison."

"Yes, my lady," I winked and started the engine.

Kelsey's parents, Jane and Dave, were thrilled with the outcome of the case. Natasha had somehow made her way into all our lives and now I just wanted to put her and all the mess she created behind us. Kelsey was six and a half months pregnant and I was so excited to see what we were having this time. She wouldn't find out again, I suppose a surprise is nice, but I was literally burning to find out. She wasn't as big as she was with Harry, she certainly didn't crave anything weird this time either, so secretly I hoped we were having a girl, but to be honest, a healthy baby is all I really wanted.

Harrison had a good winter with only one cold, so we didn't spend the best part of it at the hospital as we did the previous year. He was talking, running around and potty trained. He had a mouthful of teeth and such a little character about him. He was hot headed like me and stubborn like Kelsey, he was perfect, well, aside from the ticking time bomb that was his heart. No one would ever know how truly poorly he was just by looking at him. He looked like a normal, happy toddler and I prayed every day that he would have the operation to fix his heart and come through it okay.

His new doctor was amazing, and we had a good relationship with him, it was the waiting that seemed like hell. Every letter we received from the hospital caused the colour to drain from Kelsey's face, she was petrified of losing him like she did her little brother. Even though the doctors told her Harrison would survive, it still put the fear of God in her to open those letters.

When we got home all I wanted to do was get a take away, have a few beers and spend the evening with my wife. Sebastian, my ever loving and loyal cousin, had other ideas. He and his fiancé Jude, were waiting in their car when we got home.

 Jude lifted Harry out of the car and Seb carried his bag. I told them I would explain everything when we got inside, and they followed us in. Jude went to the kitchen to help Kelsey make some coffee and I sat in the living room with Seb.

 "So?" he asked sweeping his blond hair out of his light blue eyes.

 "They locked her up." I replied.

 "Shit, really?"

 "Yes," I frowned and fidgeted.

 "Wow, I thought with all of her money, they would have given her a slap on the wrist and banned her from Dorset, but prison, bloody hell." He shook his head.

 "Don't you think she deserved it?" Kelsey asked as she brought in two mugs of coffee.

 "Of course, she deserved it, Kelse, I just didn't think they'd believe him."

"Well, your recordings helped put her behind bars." I stated.

"I am glad they did help," Seb grinned. "So, what are we doing to celebrate?"

I frowned and shook my head, "I am absolutely knackered, mate, can't we wait till next weekend?"

"That's my stag night," he responded.

"Exactly," I smiled.

"Are you going to tell me where we are going yet?"

"Not a chance," I replied smugly, I had something over him for a change and it felt good.

I think he was expecting strippers and a weekend of pure, alcohol fuelled fun. I had other plans, I mean yes, we were going to get drunk, we had to, it's practically the eleventh commandment, but strippers were a definite no.

I knew Kelsey had organized going to a show in Southampton for Jude who refused to allow Kelsey to pull out of Maid of Honour duties and brought the wedding back by a month, so she could be in the wedding. My brother and sisters were coming down for the weekend and couldn't wait to spoil their nephew.

Jude and Seb stayed for dinner, the girls talked table decorations in the kitchen while Seb and I drank a few cans of lager as we watched a movie in the living room. I'll be honest, I said I wanted Natasha out of my head, but I couldn't stop thinking about her, locked up in a prison cell, dressed in a grey uniform, lights out at nine. But I don't think it was pity, I think it was more about the fact that it could have been me. The thought of it made me shudder.

"Are you alright?" Seb asked.

"Yes, why?" I lied.

"You look like you are going to throw your guts up."

"No, I think I am just tired, mate." I shrugged and sipped my warm beer.

"I have work tomorrow, so we'll make a move in a bit."

"Since when do you work weekends?" I frowned.

He looked at the door and leaned towards me, "Since I want to buy a house and not live in that dingy flat for another year." He replied. "My parents are giving us enough money for a deposit as a wedding present and I am working all the overtime I can to pay for the legal fees. But don't tell Jude, it's going to be a surprise at the wedding."

"Wow, secrets from the misses already," I smirked.

"Technically, we have been together longer than you two and let's not forget about the shit pile of secrets that blew up in your face last year."

"Good point." I agreed.

"What are you two whispering about?" Jude asked as she came into the room.

"Sex," Seb smiled and sat up. "Are you ready, princess? I have to start at seven."

"That's what I was coming in to tell you." She smiled slightly. She had dyed her hair brown again, personally I preferred the bright red she had usually, but apparently it clashed with the blue bridesmaid dresses.

"I'll use the loo then," Seb stood and hurried out of the room.

"Are you okay?" she asked me.

"I am now it's over." I answered and stood. "Thank you for being here for Kelsey, Jude, she has really needed you these past few months."

"She has, but she would have stood by you all the way no matter what the outcome." She smiled. "So, what's happening next weekend?"

I ginned, "My lips are sealed."

"Well, as long as you remember I still have my meat grinder and I am not afraid to use it."

"Duly noted." I winked and hugged her.

"Bloody hell," Seb said from behind, "he's at it again, Kelsey. Get your whip out, love, you need to teach your man to leave my woman alone," he called out. She came from the kitchen, her cheeks flushed and her blue eyes sparkling, smiling from ear-to-ear. "I caught him red handed."

"It must be Buxton blood or something." She stated and playfully patted my backside.

We waved them off from the doorstep and almost said together, "Can you keep a secret?" I turned to her and said. "You first."

"Jude's five weeks pregnant."

"No, really?" I grinned. "That's fantastic news."

"Yes, now you," she goaded.

"He's buying her a house as a wedding present."

"Oh my God, she will love that." I wrapped my arms around her and pulled her close to my body, obviously as close as I could anyway. "I love you so much," she declared.

"I love you too," I smiled and pecked her soft lips. "Fancy an early night?"

"It's a date," she said taking my hand and leading me inside.

I don't know what it was, but nothing could turn me on. I was crushed, completely. She said it was probably because I was tired, I don't know about that, but the thought that my insanely, sexy wife couldn't even get me jump started, I wanted to die. This had never happened to me before, not even thirty and I couldn't get it up. WTF?

I led there listening to her breathe as she slept not feeling the *man* I should have been. How could this have happened to me, never, in all the women I had slept with, had I suffered from this, from… I can barely say it, limp dick, shit!

Kelsey told me not to worry about it, but I knew it upset her. I knew she would think it was because she didn't turn me on. She already felt that she had gained weight and I was losing interest, as if, I mean, her boobs were amazing. Anyway, I sighed loudly in the dark thinking she was asleep.

"Sweetheart, I told you, its fine."

"And I have known you long enough to know that fine means it's anything but." I retorted. "What if it's a sign, what if there is something wrong?"

She turned over slowly, "And what if you had to go through something hugely humiliating today and the last thing on your mind is sex right now?"

"But…"

She flicked on the light, my eyes burned with the brightness. "I love you, Jeremy Buxton, so what if you can't get it up for the first time ever, so what?" When my eyes finally adjusted I gazed at her, she looked incredible with her rosy pink cheeks and soft looking lips. I smiled and pushed her hair back out of her face. "Maybe we need a little fun to spice things up."

"What do you mean?"

"Well, outfits…" she frowned at her bump, "maybe not right now, but I don't know, something to help get your motor running."

"Kinky stuff?" I asked loving the sound of the lengths she would go to, to turn me on.

"Maybe, but no rubber and no whips."

I smiled, "I am liking the sound of whips," I joked.

"Huh, you are not turning my arse fifty shades of pink, that's a dead cert."

I began to laugh, giggling at first, then all out, stomach cramping laughing. She joined in with me as we lay there in the middle of the night trying to calm down, but every time I replayed her words in my head, I just burst into hysterics. Only my wife could take something that could be potentially serious and turn it into a joke.

"Fifty shades of pink," I chuckled with tears streaming my face, "I can just see you strapped to the bed now. God, I love you so much," I smiled. She beamed a smile at me and kissed me tenderly. Her warm hand rest against my chest as her fingers began to circle my nipples.

"I could get some nipple clamps on these babies, maybe burn you with some candle wax, I could even…" her hand moved lower, my insides warmed, "Oh, hello," she grinned, and she took me in her hand. I don't know what it was, the playful banter or the thought of whips, but it did something. Sliding her hand up and down, I closed my eyes and moaned, "No you don't, Mister, not yet." She stopped her hand and kissed me deeply, pushing her tongue inside my mouth. I pushed my hand into her hair and held her face against mine, my insides burning like a white-hot fire. She climbed onto my waist and lowered herself slowly. "That's better," she said and lightly scratched her nails up and down my thigh muscles. This drove me crazy and she knew it, I wriggled until she moved forward and began rocking her pelvis, moaning as she moved. I caressed her breasts as everything began to tighten. This was not going to take long for either of us, I could feel her clenching around me as she moved, pushing deeper and deeper while on top of me. Her rocking sped up and my heart raced, in a sudden rush of warmth, I felt the pressure in my testicles relax as I let go inside of her with a moan. She groaned loudly and bit on her lip, her nails embedded into my chest as she stopped moving almost instantly. She opened her eyes and smiled.

"So," I grinned. "I think red will work."

"Red?" she frowned.

"Red, rubber knickers."

"You can get on your by-cy-cle and peddle it, love, no bloody way." She beamed.

"Well, will you at least consider a maid's outfit, lace and frills have always done it for me?"

"Maybe," she shrugged and leaned forward to kiss me, "but only if you grow your hair a bit longer on the top and stay out of the sun," she winked, I frowned. "I've always had a thing for that sparkly vampire, you look a little bit like him, I suppose."

"And all this time I thought you married me for my charm and sophistication." I smirked.

"Actually, I married you for your money, your car and that gorgeous arse of yours." She grinned as she climbed off me.

"I do not have a gorgeous arse." I protested playfully.

"It is from where I look at it." She winked.

"Right, so, as well as my arse, its biting you are into then? I think I can do that." She smiled knowingly and stood from the bed, "Kelsey, thank you, you know, for not making a big thing of this." I said pointing to my groin.

"You never have to thank me," she frowned slightly lifting her robe and pulling it over her naked body, "I love you and I'd do anything for you."

"Except rubber and whips," I checked.

"Most definitely, no rubber or whips" she nodded and left the room.

When she returned to our bed, she climbed in beside me and rested her head on my shoulder. I moved her hair away from her face and kissed her forehead. A few moments later she was breathing deeply, and I knew she was asleep. I flicked off the light and allowed the darkness to carry me away.

Three

Kelsey

I woke feeling cold and felt beside me looking for my hot water bottle of a husband to warm me up, but Jeremy wasn't there. It was Saturday and I knew he hadn't planned to work, so I got up to go and find him. Wrapping my bath robe around my body, I pushed open the door and could hear snoring. I knew Stuart wasn't in the house as he had planned a weekend away with Elliot. So, it could only mean one thing, Harrison was bad in the night and Jeremy was sleeping with him.

Slowly, I pushed open Harrison's door and discovered I was right, cuddled up together, snoring their heads off, lay Jeremy and Harrison. His curly hair pressed against his father's face, the sight brought tears to my eyes. As I went to step out of the room, the squeaky floor board let rip and Jeremy jumped awake.

"Sorry," I whispered.

"He had a bad dream," he whispered back.

"Stay there and I'll make you a cuppa." I smiled and left him in bed.

I put the kettle on to boil and prepared the cups as two arms folded around my tummy and warm lips pecked at my neck.

"Good morning, wife." He said into my hair.

"You didn't have to get up," I said.

"I needed the loo, besides, our little angel up there, almost pushed me out of the bed. He is still soundo," I turned to face him. "About last night…" he frowned. I pulled him into my body.

"I know, it was incredible." I was not going to allow him to beat himself up over something so unimportant. I moved back to gaze into his eyes, "Now, are you making me breakfast or what?"

"I could make us an omelette," he suggested.

"Sounds good." I returned his smile and let him go to finish making our drinks. It was rare that Harrison slept in and we were going to make the most of it before our toddler awoke and wreaked havoc wherever he could.

Not only did we get to eat our breakfast and drink our tea in peace, we were able to shower and get dressed before Harrison finally woke up. I was sat on the sofa when little thuds came down the stairs.

"Hello, mate," Jeremy said in the hall. "You okay?"

"Yes," Harrison answered. "Where's mummy?"

"In the lounge, I'll make you some toast." A few moments later, Harrison came into the living room with a huge grin.

"Good morning," I greeted him as he climbed up beside me and cuddled my tummy.

"I had a bad dream," he told me.

"Did you?" I asked, and he nodded, "What about?"

"Monsters under my bed."

"Well, I bet Daddy scared them away," I said kissing the top of his head.

"Daddy snores," he sighed.

"I know, sweetie, but don't tell him." I chuckled and squeezed him.

"Harry," Jeremy called out, "toast is ready." He sat up and ran out to the kitchen. I clumsily got up from the couch and headed up to his room.

The spring sun shone brightly through the crack at the bottom of his blind. I opened the window to let in some air and made his bed before sorting out his clothes. Barely three and already dry at night and during the day. I was amazed how easy he was to train over Christmas.

"Are you okay, love?" Jeremy asked.

"Yes," I smiled, I had drifted off again thinking about Seb and Jude's news.

"I was thinking about getting some rose bushes for the garden…" he began.

I shook my head, "I want to move." I said.

"What? Since when?"

"I want us to have a fresh start and I think with the way the market is, we could get a really good price for the house." I explained.

"Where do you want to move to?"

"I don't know, just out of Bournemouth."

He frowned, "I am not leaving Dorset, Kelsey. My job…"

"No, not out of Dorset, maybe Wimborne or Corfe Mullen, somewhere in between your job and mine."

"Are you going to still work after the baby is born?"

"I am thinking of changing to evenings, although, I can't stay in Complaints, I'd have to go back into Service or something," I nodded.

"Is this because of Natasha?" he asked warily.

"I just think that because she knows where we are, she might never leave us alone." I replied.

He stared for a few moments, "Okay, if you want to move, we'll contact an agent and get the house up for sale."

I smiled, "Thank you," then hugged him and felt warmth as his arms folded around me.

He pecked my neck lightly and breathed warmly against my skin, "I'd move anywhere as long as we're together."

After dressing Harrison, we had to go food shopping, something I hadn't done since the trial began and we were low on everything. Jeremy found a trolley that had been made to look like a car, anything to keep him occupied and not throwing tantrums, shopping had become the one thing Harrison detested. Jeremy strapped him into the trolley car and told Harrison to drive us around the supermarket.

I began looking at baby stuff, I had kept most of Harrison's things, but feared that if we were having a girl, we'd turn her into a Tomboy with all of the neutral and boyish looking baby-grows and onesies. I dared to touch anything pink though, as tempted as I was, I didn't want to jinx it, those cute dresses and pink dungarees, they were so pretty. I pulled myself away and caught Jeremy and Harrison up.

When we got to the till we were behind a man in a wheelchair, and you know those times when you pray to God that your toddler, who asks questions about everything, either doesn't notice that the man had a missing leg, or at least thinks it might upset him if he mentions it, I tried very hard to concentrate on Jeremy loading the shopping on the conveyor belt as Harrison stared at this poor man.

My prayers were not answered that day, "Where is your leg?" Harrison asked out of nowhere.

"Hey, Harry…," Jeremy tried to distract Harrison.

"Oh no," the man said, "don't tell me that naughty leg has got away again." He looked up to me and winked. "Did you see a spare leg around the shop?"

"No," Harrison frowned shaking his head.

"Well, Harry, if you see my leg in the carpark, tell him John is looking for him and he is in big trouble, alright?" Harrison nodded his head.

"I am so sorry…" I muttered.

"It's okay, love, he is observant, nothing wrong in that."

"Thank you." I smiled slightly. My face must have been blood red, I could feel it burning so much.

"Can I help you pack your shopping?" Jeremy asked.

"No, thanks, son. I have my missus here somewhere, she'll no doubt come back with a few more bits we've forgotten." He smiled. True to his word, a flustered woman with a warm smile hurried towards us. "Finally, Maggie, what did we forget?"

"T-bags." She replied and moved towards him. After she paid she began loading the bags into her trolley, John turned around and smiled again,

"Remember, Harry, keep an eye out for that pesky leg of mine."

"Okay, bye." Harrison nodded and waved goodbye.

"Bye." he said and wheeled away.

"That could have easily been very awkward." Jeremy sighed.

"I almost snapped at Harrison, how embarrassing?" I blushed.

We popped in to my mother and Dave's on the way home. I was a bit worried about her, she had looked so poorly the day before, so I wanted to check that she was okay. She was fine though, greeted us with a smile, made us a cup of tea and cut us some of her dairy free cake. She looked after Jeremy and spoiled him rotten, when I thought about it, she always had.

We told her of what had happened in the supermarket, she chuckled lightly, but it seemed to hurt her to laugh,

"Mum?" I frowned.

"I pulled my side yesterday, I'm alright, it's just a bit sore." I looked at Dave as he entered the kitchen. "I'm okay, love, honestly."

"I knew something was wrong," I sighed, "you were too pale when we collected Harrison." Then it hit me, "It wasn't lifting him, was it?"

"No, of course not, I pushed the side board in the lounge and it got stuck on the floor." She explained. I didn't know if I truly believed her, but at least she looked better.

"Jane, if you need things moved again, just let me know and I will help Dave, okay? Don't try it again."

"Okay, Jeremy," she smiled and squeezed his hand.

That night we had been invited to Felix and Nicki's for dinner, I hadn't seen her for a while as she had been off work sick then with Jeremy's court hearing, time seemed to run away from us. I was actually looking forward to catching up and seeing their new bungalow in Ferndown. Felix had left the pub he was working at where Jeremy had taken me on our first date and now worked running the kitchen at a hotel in Wimborne, a small town not far from where they now lived.

We arrived at seven as arranged and the door opened, Felix hugged Jeremy and I before we could even get into the house. He made a huge fuss of Harrison and lead us inside. The front door opened in to a large open planned living room and dining room all in one. The walls were painted cream and they had a Purbeck stone fireplace.

 On the wall behind the large brown leather couch, hung a wedding picture of Nicki and I. I gazed at how empty and sad my eyes looked and remembered painfully why. Jeremy and I weren't even talking, I was desperately trying to hide the bump I had because I didn't want him to feel obligated to be with me. I couldn't believe the pain I had inflicted on us both back then and wondered how he ever found it in him to forgive me.

 "Kelsey," Nicki said and broke into my thoughts, I turned around, standing with a familiar bump herself, she grinned. I couldn't see Jeremy or Felix; Harrison was sat on the floor eating pretzels out of the bowl on the coffee table.

 "How many weeks are you?"

 "What?" she asked.

 "You are pregnant, right?"

"That's why we invited you over, to tell you face to face, not only am I pregnant, but its twins, Kelsey, bloody twins."

"That's amazing news." I grinned and threw my arms around her. "Two for the price of one," I sniffed as we parted. She frowned as she gazed into my eyes, "Pregnancy emotions." I smiled.

"Plus, with everything you have been through this week."

"I know." I rubbed my hand over my bump. "At least she's locked up now and we can move on. Actually, we have decided to move as well. We are putting the house on the market."

"Well, I don't blame you, to think that hoity-toity cow came into your home and sprayed her cat scent every-bloody-where, I would have scratched her eyes out."

"I wanted to, believe me, but then I went to see her that day and I could see how pathetic she was, that her life was a mask for the shallow, insensitive yet insecure girl inside." I agreed.

"Well, thank God they believed you and showed that money doesn't always talk." I nodded. "Okay, let's get the kettle on, dinner won't be long. Would you like juice, Harrison?" she asked.

"Yes, please," he said, still munching on pretzels.

"Aww, he is adorbs." She gushed. "You take a seat, Kelsey, I'll be back in a minute."

Jeremy and Felix returned shortly after with beers in hand. They joked and talked while waiting for dinner to finish cooking and Nicki and I talked baby, pregnancy tips and stretch marks of all things. I was lucky enough not to get them with Harrison, so was hoping that my skin would be the same with this one, six months gone and not a mark in sight. I suppose the fact that I practically bathed in Bio oil helped matters.

Dinner was delightful, and I expected no less. It felt good to be waited on again and especially since it seemed we had our own private chef as a friend, we were extremely spoiled with roasted gammon and pineapple juice sauce with sautéed potatoes and char-grilled vegetables. Harrison had chips with his and ate every bite. After we had hand-made, dairy free black cherry roulade. It was incredible and the company just as much. This was just what we needed, and I was sad the perfect evening had come to an end.

Just before leaving Felix offered to cook us an anniversary meal, I hadn't even thought about it, but we were only weeks away from celebrating our fourth year of marriage.

"Actually, I have something organized, mate, but thanks for the offer." Jeremy said tapping Felix's shoulder. A flutter of excitement tickled my tummy from inside as Nicki grinned and hugged me goodbye. I didn't want to pry as we drove home, I liked the idea of a surprise.

The weekend flew by and we were soon back in the routine of work and rush hour traffic. Honestly, it was getting worse, it seemed more and more people were driving than ever before. I had arranged to meet with Shawna and Lou, we had promised it since I finished work to go on maternity leave. They wanted to know the ins and outs of a cat's backside in regard to the trial and were so shocked to hear that they had actually locked Natasha up. I was just relieved that it was finally over, and we could now move on.

For once in my life I didn't have to worry, and it felt weird. Harrison was doing so well and the last time we saw Harrison's doctor and my friend from Majorca, Martin, he said that we might be able to avoid surgery until he was older. Jeremy and I were getting along amazingly well, he couldn't make it up enough and apologised so much for putting us through the strain the previous autumn. We were about to embark on a new adventure, a new home and a new family member, but what is that saying, never count your chickens until they hatch? Yep, never saw this coming in a hundred years…

Four
Jeremy

Walking back into that office the following Monday, I felt ten feet tall. A huge weight had been lifted and I was again excited by life and the changes that were approaching fast. Natasha was gone, out of my life and I felt I could truly breathe again. Seb's wedding was approaching fast and I could now concentrate on my best man duties and get some sort of stag night organized.

I smiled at Amanda, my new assistant, as I entered the office. Yes, I now had an assistant. She came with my promotion and I have to say, I was completely shocked when they told me. After everything I had been through, my wife trusted me again, I got a promotion and life was good again.

I no longer had to spend my days copy editing, now I got to distribute the work throughout my team and overlook their work, and I loved my job. My manager, Mark, had been so supportive in the torturous weeks leading up to the trial and now she had been found guilty, it showed other perspective investors, that you can dangle as much money as you like at us, but if you at inappropriately to our staff, we will take action.

He had told me from the start he believed me, but I always wondered if that would change after the trial if the outcome had been different. We invited Mark and his husband, Steven, to our home to celebrate Christmas day with us and they spoiled Harry rotten. Stuart got to meet them, and it showed Stuart that being openly gay was not a bad thing. That you could love whoever you wanted and be proud of it, not ashamed and feel the need to hide.

Elliott also joined us for lunch that Christmas day and although they tried very hard to behave themselves, no one could miss the chemistry between them. Mark and Steven chatted with them that evening and I think Stuart finally turned a corner, he seemed more confident in himself, something I would never have believed unless I had witnessed it myself.

"Jeremy," Mark called out before I could sit at my desk in my small office, "I need a word," he added sternly. I placed my bag on my desk and headed towards his office.

"Is everything alright?" I asked.

"Come on in," he frowned furrowing his dark eyebrows together.

My throat dried instantly as I entered the room. "So…?"

"I thought you might have called to tell me what happened last week at court." He said as he closed the door and walked towards his seat behind his desk.

"Well, to be honest, I was a bit shocked and thought Seb might have told you."

"Oh, he did, but I thought we were friends and you would have called to tell me." He sighed sitting.

"Sorry, Mark, I never meant…"

"So, they locked her up," he said cutting me off.

"Yes," I swallowed.

"Well, the magazine is demanding story rights and wants you to go to London for an interview." He scoffed running his fingers through his dark hair.

"What?" I frowned as I sat opposite him.

"They're worried it will damage their reputation and want to show they are supporting you. So, they are sending a car for you tomorrow to take you to London for a few days."

"No," I snapped. "I am not going. I don't owe them anything and the last thing I need right now is some sordid story released in an international magazine."

"I doubt it will be sordid, Jeremy," he reasoned. "Trust me, I'd rather you didn't go, but I don't think you have much of a choice. You know what Mason is like."

I rubbed my hand over my face feeling sick to the stomach, "Can we get a gagging thing, you know, like they put on the press to stop a story releasing? It's over with and I just want to move on from it."

"I can ask Brian to look into a gag order, but Mason is…"

"Not going to get his own way on this. I swear, if they breathe a word of what happened, I will sue." I insisted. "I don't want my father to read of this or anyone else for that matter, it's embarrassing enough to have that defence solicitor rip into me and make it sound like I was a pervert."

"Okay, I'll speak with Brian. I suppose no one can force you to go."

"Thank you," I sighed. "I am sorry I didn't call, Mark. I do think of you as a friend and I would hate for this to ruin that."

"Don't worry about it, I just felt like I was the last to know and then Steven and I had a huge fight about it and well, he's not talking to me at the moment."

"Send him some flowers," I smiled slightly.

"We don't do flowers, but I might get him something nice on the way home." He nodded. "Anyway, are you all ready for the big stag night?"

"Can I let you in on something?" I asked with a frown, he nodded. "I haven't got a ruddy clue as to what to do. Seb is expecting this alcohol infused extravaganza and I don't know where to start."

"Well, I can't make it, but you set something up and I will put some money behind the bar, so you can all get sloshed on me," he grinned.

I shook my head, "Mark, I can't let you do that."

"Yes, you can and that's the end of it. You have been to Hell and back this past few months, Jez, it's about time things went your away for a change."

"I could use a bit of luck," I agreed. "Thanks, Mark."

"Right, now get back to work," he grinned and winked.

Work was slow, I am not sure how many times you can read something over and see anything wrong, especially when the words all merge together. I got myself a fresh cup of coffee and began searching on venues around Bournemouth and Poole for a stag night.

Every bar and pub in the town centres said no *all-male parties*, so we were stuffed. How do you go out as a group of around twenty and get in to these places? I looked at paint balling and go carting, I even looked at casinos. The rules were strict, and I doubted I would find anywhere. But I didn't know the area like Kelsey did, after all, she was a native. During my lunch hour, I went to my car and called her.

Leaving it with her, I returned to work. As I entered the building I could hear Seb on his phone.

"Of course, I am being serious; would I lie to you?" I held back out of sight because I didn't want him to think I was ear wigging on his conversation with Jude, I am no gooseberry. "Well, I think the blond one suits you the best, it brings out those incredible blue eyes." He continued. Now, I was concerned, Jude's eyes were brown, I was certain of it. I began to feel uneasy, was Seb cheating on her only weeks away from their wedding? He began to laugh, "I'd like to see that, send me a picture tonight, don't worry, how will anyone notice your boobs when they won't be able to take their eyes of your sexy bum?" That was it. I stepped forward, he blushed as soon as his eyes met mine. "Right, well, I need to go. I will speak to you soon, okay?" he ended the call and licked his lips anxiously.

"Please tell me you are not screwing some bird behind your fiancé's back."

"What sort of bloke do you think I am?" he snapped.

"Once upon a time, I would have called you a slut, but if you are cheating on her…" I warned.

"I am not cheating on Jude." He insisted.

"Who were you talking about boobs and bums to then?"

"None of your fucking business, just stay out of this, Jez," he barked and walked away.

I stood there, not quite sure I had heard right, Sebastian rarely spoke to me like that and I think I was in complete shock if I am honest. Then anger began to filter through my veins, if he was cheating on Jude, I did not want to be in his shoes. Only days before he told me he was buying her house while all along he was possibly shagging some girl's brains out. And Jude, shit, she was carrying his baby and I knew it was meant to be a secret, but this changed everything.

If I was wrong though, and I prayed I was, I knew what it felt like to be wrongfully accused and to be honest, Seb stuck by me, he had my back, almost suffocating trying to help me get evidence of Natasha bribing me. He stood up for me and I owed it to him to give him the benefit of the doubt, for now.

Over the next few days, Sebastian avoided me like the plague, all showing me that perhaps I was right to be concerned. I didn't tell Kelsey, the last thing I wanted was for her to worry and tell Jude, ending the wedding right there. I wanted Seb to feel he could trust me and tell me anything, but by Friday, we had hardly shared a word. He was meant to be having his stag night on Saturday, not that I had organized much, the Smuggler's Run Artisan Ale House, it was known as a free pub in Parkstone and sold all locally made ales, beer and cider. It was the only place we could go to as a group. I popped in there one evening and got chatting to Denise, the bar manager. She was lovely and said we could spend the evening there, allowing us to use the back room.

 I wrote down the details and just before leaving at four-thirty, I slammed them down on Seb's desk in front of him making him jump.

 "It's the only place I could get, nowhere else will allow a stag party. You can come, or you can go wherever you like. I really don't give a toss anymore." I snapped. "I'll be there at seven." I added and left.

I drove home praying that my temper calmed before I got back. The last thing I needed was for Kelsey to start asking questions. I knew I was hiding stuff from her again even though I had promised her faithfully that I wouldn't. I couldn't tell her anything until I knew for sure and with Seb not talking to me, I doubted very much that I would find out a thing anyway.

Arriving home, just after six, I stared at our house. It held so many memories and now all Kelsey wanted to do was pack up and move. I'd be lying if I said the last year had been the best, and I knew why she was so desperate to move. She wanted to put it all behind us, to start a fresh and for those reasons, I wanted to move too.

    I wondered for all of five seconds if Kelsey would consider a clean break completely. I had said I didn't want to leave Dorset, but I knew I could get another job and I couldn't just stay behind for the sake of my job, as much as I liked it, the thought of returning to Canterbury excited me briefly. Still, she had mentioned a school she had her eye on for Harry, I also knew if we moved to my home town, he would miss the only grandparents he had. I felt sure she wouldn't want to move away.

I opened the front door and Harry dove into my arms. He smelled of play dough and had a runny nose again. I hugged him and kissed his cheek before putting him down.

"Where's Mummy?" I asked.

"Come here," he said towing me through to the living room. Laying on the couch with rosy, red cheeks and snoring her head off, she slept peacefully.

"Shall we go and see what's for dinner?" I asked him.

"Uncle Stuart is cooking." He said proudly.

"Mmm, shall we go and check he is okay?" Harry nodded and led me to the kitchen. "Hi honey, I'm home," I chuckled.

"Don't you honey me, you are late." Stuart retorted playfully. "How are ya, mate?" he asked.

"Not bad, you?"

"Um, yeah, I am okay. I think." He replied. Harry obviously got bored with us and left us to talk.

"You don't sound it, what's up?"

"Elliott."

"I thought things between you both were going well." I frowned.

"They are, too good. He is perfect, he is loving and caring, kind and loyal, he is everything I want in a guy except…"

"Except what?"

"Oh, I am just being an idiot. Elliott is perfect for me." He smiled. "So, how do you like your steak?"

"We're having steak?"

"Yes, Kelsey wanted to cook you a nice meal, but she has been sick all day. I told her to rest and within minutes she was snoring."

"I like my steak well done." I smiled. "Thank you."

The following night I sat at the bar in the Smuggler's Run on Ashley road waiting for Seb. Denise had said we could have the back room where there were pool tables and dart boards that we could use. Nothing like the extravaganza Seb was hoping for, but I couldn't risk taking him to a strip club either, I had been warned. I wanted to tell him that Jude was pregnant and that he had to stop whatever was going on behind her back, but I had promised not to tell, it wasn't my news, it was his. I just wished he would grow the fuck up and become the man I always hoped he would be. He was about to be a father for crying out loud.

A tap on my shoulder disturbed my painful reverie, I turned my head and Seb smiled cautiously.

"Sorry I'm late," he said warily.

"I am just glad you made it." I replied.

"It's the only stag party I am getting, I had to be here." He added. "Look, I can't tell you what's going on, I made a promise. Just know it's not cheating on Jude, I would never do that to her."

"Okay, I just hope you have learned from what happened to me, that secrets can get out of control and can fuck everything up." I warned.

"Well, this isn't my secret to tell, it is someone else's and they pleaded with me to keep my mouth shut, so for once, I am doing what I am asked to do."

"That's a first," I nudged him playfully.

"I know, what's wrong with me?"

"You need a pint in your hand for one thing." I smiled and nodded to the barmaid. She pulled us a couple of pints.

"Cheers, cuz."

"As long as you are ready for what marriage brings." I smiled.

"More than ready, I love her, more than I have ever loved anyone else. She gets me, but she keeps me in place. Not to mention the sex, I mean…"

"Here they are." Felix said from behind. "How are you both?"

"Great." I smiled thankful he stopped Seb bragging about his incredible sex life again.

Within an hour, everyone I had invited had arrived. Stuart came solo, apparently, Elliott had a family thing he had to go to but promised to make it to us later. We went to the bar and waited to be served.

"You okay?" Stuart asked.

"Yes." I nodded. "You?"

"Never been better, I have a hot new boyfriend and life is good." He grinned.

"I am happy for you," I smiled. "I was worried about you last night."

"Well, I just need to stop thinking and worrying about what if's. Besides, I am all about monogamy now." He grinned. "Mind you, what I would give to have half a chance with Sebastian, he is one beautiful looking specimen."

I grinned, remembering our conversation once when he told me I was not his type. "So, I am not your type, but Sebastian is?"

"And then some. I don't know why, but he has something," he grinned. I rolled my eyes, "Oh come on, Jez, you are too pretty for me, always have been and always will be. I like them a little rough around the edges."

"And Elliott?" I queried, I mean, he was so pretty, he could have been a girl.

"Ah, well, he's different, he is like my lighthouse, a shining beam in the darkest of nights. Elliott keeps me grounded and is my home, he is who I'll make a life with, he makes me smile and he loves me, but Sebastian, he is what I call dirty, stinking sex on legs."

"Bloody hell, mate, how many pints have you had?" I chuckled.

"A guy can dream," he winked his eye and lifted his glass to his lips, draining it.

"Well, if you don't slow down, I'll be carrying you home." I warned playfully.

"Jeremy, I said…."

"I know, I'm too pretty for you," I nodded and sipped my pint.

"You got it," he grinned with a chuckle. "Now then, it's my round, Jez, what are ya having?"

"Thanks, but I have two pints here, Stuart. I'll have one later."

"You could have a shot or two?"

"No thank you, the last time I had shots was at Felix's stag and ended up in all sorts of trouble." I explained.

"Oh yeah, I did hear, the stripper." He nodded.

"Mmm, the stripper." I frowned.

I tried to forget the night that I drank myself into a coma because Kelsey was in Majorca and I didn't know what was going on or if she was with someone else. One of the worst periods of my life, I was in a dark place and couldn't see any way out of it. No woman had ever got so deep under my skin that I couldn't bear the thought of life without her. She was going to be a bridesmaid and I was best man. I don't know how I made it through the day.

She looked sensational as she walked down the aisle and all I kept thinking about was how I wished it was our wedding. That night was the start of us again, her ex felt my fist after Jude told us that Kelsey was pregnant. I had no idea that she was carrying Harry and heard that she was heading to the States, so chased her to the airport, where I asked her to marry me. So, no, I would not be drinking shots again for a while.

Five

Kelsey

It looked like something out of a sit-com, walking down the high street in three-inch heels and being six months pregnant was not my best idea. I had promised a small get-together at my house after my idea of seeing a show was voted out, and, we're talking about Jude here, let's face it, her last official night as a single-woman was never going to be small. So, Bournemouth town centre it was, dressed up to the nines and feeling like a giant bloater fish. I was looking forward to seeing the girls though, and I certainly needed some time out.

    I hurried down towards one of the new bars in town where I was to meet Nicol and Becky, her cousin. Jude was meeting us there, though, with three out of four of us knocked up, it was not going to be an alcohol infused night. My feet and back hurt and I needed the loo desperately.

    "You're late," Jude grinned from beside a tall doorman.

    "Well, this is what you get for making me cancel the show," I retorted. I pulled a white veil out of my bag. "Turn around," I told her. I pushed the comb into her hair and smiled. "Okay," I said. She turned to face me.

"I have invited a couple of girls from work, but I didn't think, I have a line of shots on the bar and I can't touch one."

"Maybe it's time to tell them," I suggested.

"Nah, I'll give them to Nicki."

"Jude, she can't drink either." I explained.

"You are fucking joking," she gasped. "Shit, three brides, three bloody pregnancies."

"I know, it is almost spring though," I chuckled.

We found the others inside and I hurried to the ladies. When I returned to the table they were all gushing over Jude's and Nicki's scan pictures. Sworn to secrecy, they had to know the truth, neither of us could touch a drop.

"So," Nicki nudged me lightly at the bar. "Three of us all expecting at the same time, how weird is that?"

"I know." I agreed.

"Just think, we'll be able to do play dates and picnics in the park…"

"I want to move away," I blurted out. She stared at me, stunned. "I'm sorry, I know I said we would look locally, but I can't forget about what happened. She was in my house, Nicki, my bloody house and the more I think about it, the angrier I get. I can't let it go."

"What has Jez said?"

"He doesn't want to leave Dorset, but I think that a complete break will be the only way I can shake this anger I have for her." I explained.

"Have you thought that maybe you two might need a little help."

"Help?"

"Counselling." I must have frowned. "don't look like that, you and Jez have been through so much, it wouldn't hurt to get it all out in the open."

"It's bad enough it went to court and was in the papers, Jez would not go for that." I shrugged.

"Kelsey, he would if he knew how much you needed it."

I thought briefly, she could have been right, maybe I did need to air it all. "I'll speak to him." I promised. "We'd better get back."

"I've never been on a hen do where more than half of us are sober." She grinned.

"It's my second." I chuckled.

When I got home, Jez had fallen asleep on the sofa. It was never the plan to have both the hen and stag on the same night, but it meant that they would both be out of the way and as I kicked off my shoes, relief flooded my body.

Kneeling on the floor, I gently placed my lips to his as he slept, tasting alcohol as I did so. He stirred slightly and then opened his eyes.

"Hello, wife." He grinned.

"Hello, husband," I smiled. "How long have you been home?"

He looked at his watch, "About half an hour. Did you have fun?"

I nodded. "I texted mum on the way home, Harrison is snuggled up in bed, snoring his head off."

"Stuart is at a club with Seb and the others, I wasn't up to it, so came home." He explained.

"So, we're home alone?" I grinned.

"I suppose we are," he agreed as his eyes filled with excitement. Pushing his hand into my hair, he pulled me closer to him. Our lips touched, pushing his tongue into my mouth, I murmured a groan. "You taste like pineapple," he said as he kissed me.

"You taste like Jack Daniels," I replied as he moved his fingers to the strap on my shoulder and pushed it down.

Already warming by his touch, he then scattered butterfly kisses over my shoulder and around my ear. His hands moved down my body as his sweet kisses warmed my core. Lifting my dress slightly, he hooked his fingers under the leg of my underwear.

"I am wearing my very big and frumpy looking Bridget Jones knickers." I said as he smoothed his fingers along the top of my leg. "They're not remotely sexy in any way."

"Baby, I swear, you could look sexy in absolutely anything. I love your big knickers." He grinned gazing into my eyes.

"Do you know what's sexier?" I asked standing from the floor. "No knickers at all."

"Now you are talking." He agreed as I pushed them down my legs and kicking them to the side. He sat up and swung his legs over the front of the sofa. I began to un-button his flies, he wiggled pushing his jeans down his incredible legs. I smiled at his bulge resting in his lap. Taking one finger, I pulled his boxers down enough for him to pop out and stand to attention. Climbing astride him, I lowered on to him and allowed him to fill me. "Wow, Kelsey, you are horny." He said and kissed me deeply. I began to move over him, rocking my pelvis as he kissed my shoulder and neck. Pulling the front of my dress down, exposing one of my breasts, he took it into his mouth, he began to suck lightly at my nipple. I moved back out of his reach.

"I don't think you should do that," I grinned. "You could get a mouthful of milk and then be doubled up in agony all night."

"I forgot. God, you are driving me crazy, Kelsey. I fucking love you."

"Less of the talk and get on with the fucking," I ordered.

"You have a dirty mouth," he frowned.

"And you are procrastinating."

I began moving again and he groaned resting his head back, rolling his eyes up into his head. Rubbing his hands over my breasts as the burning ache in my core began to throb, making me push against him, He moved his hands to my hips, holding me down on him as we moved together.

The ache intensified, but I wasn't ready for it to end yet, as much as I wanted to let it go and ride that wave as I had almost every time we made love. I just wanted to make it last as long as I could. But try as I might, Jeremy was close and though I may have been able to hold back, I knew he couldn't for much longer.

"Oh, God," he groaned and leaned towards me to kiss me.

"I love you," I gasped breathlessly.

"I love you too," he groaned, and I knew he was seconds away. I allowed my orgasm to rock through my body like a lightning bolt, electrifying every nerve. Jeremy hooked his hands under my arms and pressed down on my shoulders groaning as he also let go inside of me. Finally relaxing back, with a sheen of sweat across his face, he smiled and licked his dry lips as he panted. "You are incredible, Kelsey Buxton." He said finally.

I grinned, but the baby moved inside of me and pressed against my bladder. "I need to pee," I said and climbed from his lap. "Meet you upstairs?"

"Okay," he smiled warmly.

After switching off all of the lights and checking the doors were locked, with my old, faithful, comfy pants in my hand, I hurried up the stairs. Jeremy was sound asleep and although my need for him was somewhat satisfied, I'd be lying if I said I wasn't disappointed. I was ready for him again.

I slipped on my nightdress and climbed in beside him. Just as I closed my eyes, my phone buzzed on the bedside cabinet beside me. I lifted it, frowning at the bright light, Jude was calling me.

"Hello?" I whispered loud enough for her to hear and hoping I didn't disturb my husband.

"Seb is cheating on me." She was crying.

"I don't think he is," I frowned.

"Yeah, well, he calls her Ms Jay in his texts and you should see the messages." I sat up and climbed from my bed. I then hurried to Harrison's room.

"You have his phone?"

"He left it here by accident."

"What does she say in them?" I asked.

"I don't know, I can only see what he has sent her because his in box is empty but is sent box is chocka. I swear, Kelsey, I am going to kill him."

"Listen, I jumped to conclusions, where did that get me? You need to speak to him and ask him. Is he home yet?"

"No, Stuart texted me to say they were in a club, didn't Jez go as well?"

"No, he is snoring his head off."

"How many weeks do I have until I can't get a termination?" she asked.

"Jude, you are talking crazy because you are scared and not thinking straight. I am sure he is not cheating on you." I explained.

"Listen to this then. 'Hey Miss Jay, how are you, my sexy lady?' Or how about, 'I can't wait to see you either. Could use a giggle. Same time and place???' Three question marks, Kelsey, three of the buggers. I will rip her fucking throat out, whoever she is." I frowned because maybe she was right, it certainly sounded like it. "I don't know what I am going to do, our wedding is in two fucking weeks, what would you do?"

"I'd confront him."

"Then he'll accuse me of being a paranoid psycho just like last time. He says I don't trust him…"

"Can he blame you? Look how he is. He was a man-slut not two years ago. I admit, he told Jeremy you are the one but… no he would not cheat on you." I insisted.

"Can I come and see you tomorrow?"

"You don't have to ask." I sighed. "I am picking Harrison up at eleven, come around before then."

"Okay," she sniffed. "Thanks, Kelsey, you are my best friend, I love you. Don't forget that."

Pain shot through me, "Jude, promise me you won't do anything stupid."

"If I lose him…"

"You are not losing him, it's probably a friend and you know how much he flirts, even with me. It should be his middle name."

"Okay," she said. "I'll let you get some sleep." She ended the call and I stared at the phone for the longest time. If Sebastian was cheating on her, why would he buy her a house as a wedding present? It didn't make sense.

It took me a while to fall asleep, I would get comfy and the baby would start moving around and then it got hiccups. It was past two when I finally closed my eyes again, I didn't even hear Stuart come home.

I left Jeremy sleeping and took a long bath. My back was aching, and I needed to remember, I was having a baby and seducing my husband on the sofa was probably not the best idea, no matter how much I enjoyed it. I smiled at the memories as I lifted the sponge from the water. We certainly still had that zing, he hit the spot every time and I can honestly say, I couldn't picture anyone else as my lover.

When I returned to our bedroom, he was reading a text on his phone, his eyebrows were furrowed together, but he still flashed his incredible eyes at me.

"Good morning," I chimed.
"Morning," he smiled. "Did you sleep okay?"
"Eventually." I answered as I opened the wardrobe.

"You are not getting dressed yet," he said. I turned to him as he pulled the quilt from his body. "Not before this is taken care of."

"Not until you at least take a shower and shave. I am not walking around with a red face all day."

"Oh, Kelsey," he whined, "please come back to bed and allow me to make love to you."

"Sorry, love, I need a cup of tea."

He scoffed, "Since when is a cup of tea better than amazing sex with your husband?"

"Since the tea doesn't mean that I will need another bath, it doesn't smell like the carpet in a closed pub and it doesn't prickle and scratch my face making me look like I have been snogging sand paper." I retorted and pulled on some underwear.

"So, what am I supposed to do with this?" he demanded pointing to his erection.

I smiled and tightened the belt on my bath robe. "I hear a cold shower works wonders." I then blew him a kiss and left him in bed.

I made tea while toasting some bread and waited for him to come down. He eventually did, with wet hair a cut on his cheek and a pouting lip. I poured him some tea and placed it in front of him as he sat at the table.

"Thanks." He grunted.

"Do you want some toast?"

"No. Thank you." He frowned.

"Jeremy?" I sighed. "You're not sulking, are you?" He shrugged his shoulders. "Brilliant." I sighed. "Well, I am going to get dressed. Jude is coming over this morning."

"Why?" he asked.

"She thinks Seb is cheating on her. She found his phone last night. Sounds pretty damming to me to be honest."

"What?" he snapped his head up.

"Do you know anything?"

"No," he swallowed and pulled his eyes from mine. He was lying.

"Well, she has his phone and there are messages. If he is, he may not have balls left." I warned and left him in the kitchen.

I pulled on some leggings and my new maternity top. Tied up my hair, allowing it to be curly and loose for a change, dabbed on a little make-up and as I stepped off the bottom stair, the doorbell rang.

I pulled it open, Jude looked terrible, her face was so pale, and her eyes looked sore. I said nothing as I pulled her against me and held her.

"Two weeks today, I am meant to be saying *I do* to him, Kelse, what am I going to do?"

"I don't know, hun, I really don't." I sighed pulling back from her. "Let's have a cuppa, I bet you have had nothing to eat or anything yet."

"I can't, fucking morning sickness is doing my head in." She groaned.

"I have Ginger Nuts, they work wonders." I linked my arm with hers and led her to the kitchen.

"Bloody hell," she said as Jeremy looked up at her. "Hanging?"

"Just a bit," he grumbled.

"What club did they go to?"

"I don't know, Stuart and Felix were with him, so I knew he'd be alright."

"Yeah, *alright*, but would he be faithful?"

"He is not cheating on you, Jude." Jeremy stood. "I would know if he was."

"Look at these then," she snapped handing him Seb's phone. Jeremy glanced at the screen. He looked at me, that, *I think you're right* look in his eyes.

"Could just be some harmless fun, you know he is a tart, he always has been, but I have never known him to cheat on someone he loves." He lifted his tea and left the kitchen.

"See." I tried to smile. "Jeremy would know." I added, not sure she was buying it, because I knew I bloody wasn't. Something was going on and after all I had been through with Jeremy, I was going to get to the bottom of it before the wedding.

She had a cup of tea and a couple of biscuits to help settle her tummy. We left Jeremy at home and drove to my Mum's to collect Harrison. Mum wasn't feeling well, so Dave stayed with Jude while I popped up to her room to see her.

Knocking gently on the door, I pushed it open. "Mum?" I said quietly. "Are you awake?"

"Yes, love, come on in." she answered. I walked around her bed, she looked so sick, her skin was almost grey. "Think I had a dodgy takeaway the other night. Been bad all night with it." She explained.

"You should have said, I would have come and picked Harrison up."

"Dave loved having him here, they watched some football and a western movie then they cleaned the car. He has had a whale of a time." She smiled. "Could you get me some water, please?"

"Sure." I nodded and hurried down to the kitchen.

"Dave was just explaining," Jude started, "Your mum has something on the day of the wedding, but they will come for a few hours later in the evening and then take Harrison home for you." I filled a glass and turned to them.

"Okay, well, if she's no better by Monday, get her to the doctors, Dave."

"You know how stubborn she is, love," Dave sighed. "I will try though."

"Mummy," Harrison announced and ran towards me.

"I'll take that up to her." Dave said taking the glass from my hand, so I could make a much-needed fuss of my son.

"Have you been a good boy?" I asked Harrison as I held him.

"Yes, Grandad Dave and Nanna got me some sweets and I watched a cowboy film."

"So, I hear," I smiled and kissed his cheek. "What shall we do today?"

"Um… go to the park?"

"We can, or would you prefer to go to see some animals?"

"Park." He nodded.

We said goodbye and returned home, Jeremy was cleaning his car out on the drive and Jude said she was going to see if Seb was ready to be picked up from Felix and Nicki's. I made Harrison some lunch and a sandwich for my grumpy, still sulking, husband. I took it out to him as he worked on his car.

"Do you want a drink?" I asked.

"I'll get one in a minute." He replied.

"Jeremy, what's wrong?" I asked.

"You have to ask?" he demanded and slammed the car door shut.

"Are you still sulking because I wouldn't have sex this morning?"

He looked around, "No, it's not just that." He leaned against his car. "You said about moving and I am thinking that maybe a clean break might be the best thing for us."

"You said you didn't want to leave Dorset?"

"Well, now maybe I do." He retorted and walked away.

"Okay," I called after him. He stopped walking and turned to me, "If it means that you would be happy, I would move anywhere."

His eyes glinted in the sun, "Really?"

"Yes, I am not returning to work, so we could go anywhere and have a clean break. Anywhere except Canterbury though." He frowned. "I can't live in a town where you dated and slept with half of the female population." I elaborated.

"It wasn't half," he groaned. "It's nice to know you think so highly of me." He added and walked away.

Six

Jeremy

I didn't mean to be such an arsehole to her, but every time I opened my mouth, I either snapped at her or said something that clearly upset her. Leaving her stunned on the drive I hurried in to my office and kicked the door shut. My head still banged, and I needed a drink, but my stupid, stubborn side, shadowed everything. My stomach was so painful, I had to think about the night before and if I had been given anything to trigger off my intolerance. On top of my disdain and the pain in my body, I was pissed off at Sebastian. He had promised me faithfully that he wasn't cheating two weeks away from his wedding, and yet the messages Jude had found told a different story.

I switched on my PC and loaded my emails from work. I didn't work from home ever, but I wanted an excuse to hide from my wife because if I told her I suspected him as well, she would never let it drop. After everything I had put her through recently, I knew she doubted us still, I knew it wouldn't take much to misplace her trust again. So, hiding was easier than facing her and her conspicuous glares and comments. She was one of those people who wouldn't let something drop, it would gnaw away at her until she could contain it no longer and then world war, whatever we were on now, would erupt.

After about an hour she gently knocked on my door,

"Come in," I said.

She pushed the door open and frowned. "I am taking Harrison to the park." She said quietly. "I will see you later, if you stay here or whatever."

"What's that supposed to mean?"

"You tell me," she sighed and turned around.

"Kelsey?" I called after her and stood.

"I am not fighting with you, Jeremy, not with Harrison here." She said over her shoulder and left. By the time I got out to them, she had already left.

I went back inside and decided to clean up, she was upset. I had pissed her off again and I can't even remember what started it. Yes, I was a bit disappointed that she had refused to have sex. Having the house to ourselves was a rarity, I just wanted to make the most of it. I should have realized that being pregnant, she was probably not up to it, especially since the night before she had seduced me. I didn't know if moving away was the right thing to do either, I just said it to be spiteful and I regretted the moment I let it out.

I packed Harrison's toys in to his toy chest and polished the furniture. I vacuumed and washed the floors. I had just started the washing machine when the front door opened. My heart leapt thinking she was back already, but then I heard Stuart's voice.

He came into the kitchen followed by Elliott and a very hungover Sebastian, who, evidentially wore a love-bite on his bloody neck.

"What the fuck?" I snapped pointing at him.

"It was a stupid dare." He grumbled and sat at the table.

"What?"

"Well, Felix and Aaron decided that I should play this game, I had to kiss a girl whose name corresponded with the alphabet, so A for Abigail and B for Beth… and so on. I couldn't find a girl with a name starting with a Q, so my forfeit was a love-bite."

"Who gave it to you?" I asked feeling sick with disbelief.

"Yours truly," Stuart answered humbly.

"I am a witness to this idiotic adolescent behaviour because I came in as Stuart was sucking on his neck." Elliott explained painfully.

"I said I was sorry," Stuart offered.

"Yes, you have said it, you haven't showed it, yet." Elliott snapped. "I have to go. I'll see you later."

"Elliott, wait." Stuart pleaded.

"Later," Elliott sighed and left.

"It's official, I am a total prat." Stuart groaned and chased after him.

"So," Seb sighed. "Have you any idea where my phone is?"

"Jude has it, she has gone to Felix's to pick you up."

"Bollocks, can I use your phone?"

"Sebastian, she thinks you are cheating on her, how are you going to explain this?" I pointed at his neck.

"She trusts me," he shrugged.

"Actually, I don't think she does. I have seen the messages on your phone, she found them and showed me them today. Judging by the way they look to me, you are cheating on your wife-to-be." I accused.

"For fuck sake, I am not cheating on Jude, okay?" he snapped and stood. "I can't tell you what's going on, it's not my secret to tell. I told you last night, if you don't believe me, Jez, then maybe I need to look for a new best man."

"Maybe you should," I replied angrily and watched as he walked out. "Where are you going?"

"To call a taxi, I need to go home." He roared as I followed him to the door.

"I can give you a lift."

"I'd rather walk." He barked.

"Fine, bloody walk then, you arrogant, spoiled brat. Walk all the way back to Blandford and when you are waiting for the best thing to ever happen to you, to walk down that aisle and she doesn't, I will be laughing my arse off." He spun around.

"Yeah, well, just remember who saved your marriage, you, arrogant prick." He retorted.

"Seb," I frowned, he was right. I owed him a lot. "Seb, wait." He stopped at the front door and turned to face me. "Alright, so, you are not cheating, but those messages are pretty incriminating, they are from another woman, aren't they?"

"Yes, she is a very close friend of the family and really going through something terrible, Jez. I am just trying to make her smile, that's all."

"Maybe you should tell Jude this."

"I need to lose this bloody hickey first." He sighed.

"Toothpaste always worked on me when I was in school." I suggested. "Go and put some on and I will make you a cuppa."

"I'd rather have a glass of coke, if you have any."

"We do." I nodded.

After a couple of glasses of coke and a slice of toast, I drove him back to Blandford. If only to explain to Jude about his love-bite. The toothpaste had reduced the colour, but it could still be seen. Once she knew it came from Stuart, I felt sure she would be fine.

How wrong can you be about a person? Let's put it this way, she'd had no sleep the night before, a whole day to wallow over the thought that Seb was cheating on her and when he came home with a love-bite the size of an apple on the side of his neck, she went ballistic. She wouldn't listen to me or Seb, she screamed and yelled until I couldn't take it anymore.

Pulling my phone from my pocket, I called Stuart,

"Hello?" he said after only one ring.

"You had better get your scrawny, little arse to Seb's and Jude's now," I growled.

"Why?"

"Because she is about to kill him, and I am talking meat grinder and everything."

"Elliott and I are in the middle of making up." He explained.

"I don't care, apologise to your boyfriend and get over here. This is serious." I insisted.

"We're on our way," he sighed and ended the call.

I sat in the small kitchen while Seb and Jude fought in the living room and bedroom. I remembered how Kelsey and I had made up in the flat after discovering she was pregnant with my baby. I thought about the nights I'd lay awake listening to the traffic outside the window, wondering if she were alright. The ache I felt while we were apart had left scars on my heart and I knew I did not want to live through that again.

We had been through so much together and I thought that we could face anything, but recently I felt like I was permanently trying to make it up to her, like she had the upper hand and I just smiled and abided by her rules. She got her way over everything and as much as I loved her, I knew we could not continue like this, a fractured relationship will eventually crumble.

I heard the door knocking, so went to answer it. I glanced at the living room as I passed it, Jude was sat on the arm of the chair crying. My heart did go out to her, I knew how it felt to think your true love had someone else. I had a whole weekend thinking Kelsey had gone to Majorca to find someone and when they returned, all the girls talked about leading up to Felix's wedding was Kelsey and her doctor called Martin.

Stuart had been crying and Elliott was waiting in the car. "Are you alright?" I asked.

"Do I look alright?" he snapped and barged into the flat. He ran up the stairs and was talking to Jude and Seb before I got there. "So, I am sorry, okay? Sebastian was as good as gold last night, he only did the stupid game because we made him and believe me, I wish we hadn't." He frowned at me in the door jam.

"So, you gave Seb the love-bite?"

"Yes."

"Why?" Jude asked.

"Because I fancied the arse off him once and he is gorgeous, you are a very lucky girl." He blushed.

"I see," she smiled slightly. Sebastian just stared.

"Right, now I have made myself look a plank, I need to go and finish making up with Elliott."

"Thank you, Stuart." Jude said and stood giving him a hug.

"It's alright, babes. I will just be playing suck up for the next three months." He said as they parted.

"Bye," Seb muttered as he walked out to the hall.

"I'm sorry…" I began.

"I thought we were friends." Stuart said sourly.

"You know we are."

"Really? So that's how you talk to your friends, is it, Jez?"

"I was desperate." I admitted.

"Yeah, well, I think it's time I found somewhere else to live."

"Stu…"

"I'll see you later." He sighed and left. Shit! I was already in Kelsey's bad books, she would kill me for this.

I left Seb with Jude talking. I didn't know what was happening or if there was going to be a wedding, frankly, I didn't care. All I wanted to do was go home and see my wife. I needed to tell her what had happened with Stuart and I needed to apologise to both him and Elliott. Of course, making up with your boyfriend was more important than an argument between two of your friends, but in a way, I felt responsible, had I been there, there is no way I would have allowed Stuart to leave a mark on Seb like that, especially after hearing he fancied him.

Stuart and I had always been friends and the truth is, I didn't have many to speak of. Maybe he was right, maybe it was because of me and the way I had spoken to them in the past. Regardless, I had to speak to my wife before he did. With her frame of mind and hormonal body, she was likely to take a swing at me and I deserved it.

Her car was on the drive when I got back. My heart sunk a little because once again, I was apologising for being a prat. I opened the door and was hit with the smell of curry. I still hadn't eaten anything that day and could certainly use a meal, especially when it smelled so good. Harry greeted me in the hall,

"Daddy!" He yelled and ran towards me. I lifted him from the floor and almost collapsed with the pain, it felt like I had pulled a muscle in my side and smiled thinking that maybe, we had over done our love making the night before.

"Hello, mate, did you have fun at the park?"

"Yes, I made a friend." He replied.

"That's brilliant." I smiled, hugged him briefly and set him down. He wandered off into the lounge and I heaved a brave breath before going to the kitchen.

Leaning against the door jam, I gazed wondrously at my beautiful wife as she moved around the kitchen. Either oblivious to her audience, or ignoring me on purpose, it took her a good few moments before she acknowledged me.

"Where have you been?" she asked frostily and returned to the cooker.

"I gave Seb a lift back to Blandford." I replied. "Something smells good." I added.

"Well, I thought as you haven't eaten today…"

"Thank you," I smiled slightly as she looked at me. "About earlier…"

"Forget it, its fine." She cut me off.

"Kelsey…?"

"I said its fine." I heaved a sigh and she turned to face me. "Stuart sent me a text and said he was moving out."

"So, he says, but we've heard that before." I said dismissively.

"Well, he said to ask you, that you knew why?"

"I bet he did," I muttered.

"Jeremy, what is going on?" she asked.

"He gave Seb a hickey last night while they were out, as Jude is already suspicious of him, she let rip, seriously, I thought she was going to draw blood. I made Stuart come over to theirs and explain. I sort of *demanded* he come and he didn't like it."

"Hmm," she frowned. "So, is Jude okay?"

"I left them talking," I replied. "Did Stuart say when he was moving out?"

"No," she turned back to the stove and stirred the curry. "Dinner won't be long." So that was my cue to leave her alone. Our conversation was over, and I was in the only place I knew well these days, the dog house.

After an incredible meal, one, I might add, I struggled to eat, not just because of the atmosphere, but also because my stomach was bothering me so much. Still she had cooked for me and the least I could do was eat it. I bathed Harry and put him to bed leaving her to watch her favourite Saturday shows.

When I finally joined her, she sat on one end of the couch and I sat the other. She normally stretched her legs out and rested them on my lap, but not that night. She stayed curled up and staring at the TV. We hardly spoke, she certainly had me where she wanted me again and it pissed me off even more. I needed something to settle my stomach, so went to the kitchen to search the medicine cabinet.

"What are you looking for?" she asked.

"Something for my stomach, it's killing me." I moaned.

"I have some Rennie in my bag, will they help?"

"They might," I frowned and turned around from the cabinet. I should have known that my stress levels would upset my stomach. "You didn't put any cream in the curry, did you?"

"I'm not bloody stupid." She snapped slamming the box of Rennie down on the counter.

"I know." I frowned as pain shot through my side knocking the wind out of me. "Shit!" I cursed.

"Jeremy?" she rested her hand on my arm.

"I need to go and lay down." I said uneasily and took the Rennie up to our room.

My stomach was killing me. I pushed off my jeans and lay on the bed hoping it would help ease the pain. I had been lucky for months, not so much as a twinge and now I was rolling around on the bed in agony. My body covered in a layer of sweat and the pain radiated down my legs feeling like bad cramps.

"How are you…?" Kelsey began. "Oh my God, Jeremy?" she frowned rushing over to me.

"Ca…Can you get your mum here?" I groaned as the pain seared through me once more. "I think I need to go to the hospital."

"Mum is sick in bed, I'll phone Dave." She explained and hurried out of the room. She was back in no time at all. "Dave is on his way." She clarified and pulled her boots onto her feet. She opened my draw and pulled out some of my joggers and handed them to me. Slowly, I sat up.

"I am sorry about this," I explained shakily.

"It's okay, love." She assured.

Dave arrived and as we headed out to her car, Stuart pulled up.

"What's going on?"

"I am taking Jeremy to the hospital." Kelsey explained.

"You haven't drunk any milk, have you?"

"No." I frowned as my legs almost gave way with the pain. He grabbed hold of me under my arm. "Sorry."

"It's alright, mate, I got you." Stuart said sympathetically.

"Can you stay with Harrison?" Kelsey asked him. "My mum isn't well, and Dave really needs to be with her."

"Sure, Kelse, don't worry, okay?" He promised as I climbed into her car.

We arrived at Poole Hospital, Accident and Emergency Department. I could barely make it up the steps to get in. As Kelsey booked me in, it felt as though the air had been sucked out of the room, my eyes blurred, and everything turned white…

***

I felt a warm hand rest on my arm, I snapped my eyes open and Kelsey lifted her head.

"Jeremy," she smiled, she looked so tired.

"What happened?" I asked croakily.

"Your appendix burst, you are actually lucky to be alive." She explained.

"I thought it was the usual, you know." I frowned.

"No, if we hadn't have acted so quickly, you would have been poisoned with peritonitis. Seriously, love, I could have lost you." Her eyes welled with tears.

"Hey, I am still here."

"They were operating on you for two hours, then they had to give you a huge dose of antibiotics. I have been sat here for two days waiting for you to wake up." She sniffed.

"Two days?" I was stunned. I had lost two days of my life and had no clue about it. "Are you alright?" I asked her.

"Aside from a back ache and a numb bum, I am fine." She tried to smile. "Sorry, I hate this place, then they had trouble waking you after the anaesthetic. I was so scared."

"I know, I never come around right away, never have. I am so sorry, sweetheart." I took her hand in mine and although the cannula in my hand hurt, I didn't care.

"You have nothing to be sorry about. I got up on my high horse again and I suppose I am a bit hormonal right now."

"What is the time?"

She looked at her phone, "Almost seven a.m. I need to phone Mark for you. I promised I would let him know when you woke up."

"Is there any water?" I asked and rubbed my neck. My throat felt so dry.

"I'll go and get you some." She said and stood from the chair. "I won't be long."

She left the room and I stared at the ceiling. Two days, gone, just like that. I remembered being moved onto a bed, I think. I had no idea, it scared me to think I could have died and left this mess in our relationship.

The door opened, and a nurse entered. "So, our sleeping prince is finally awake." She smiled. "How are you feeling, honey?"

"Thirsty," I replied.

"Your wife is getting some water, could you manage something to eat?"

"Not right now." I frowned. "I feel sick, to be honest."

"That's probably all the drugs we have pumped into you. The antibiotics are really strong and on an empty stomach, they could upset you. That's why I wanted to try you on something light."

"I'll try some toast then." I agreed. "No butter though, I can't have dairy."

"We have dairy free." She smiled, "I'll be back soon." I nodded, and she left.

Kelsey returned and explained that Mark was worried about me, sending his regards and all that. Apparently, Sebastian and Jude were waiting in the hall to see me and I agreed they could come in. Seb had been there since Kelsey phoned and told him how bad I was. She reluctantly left to go and get changed and try and sleep for a couple of hours. Shortly after, the door opened again,

"Jez," Seb sighed, he had tears in his eyes.

"Hey, none of that, I am alright now."

"I know, but you nearly died and all I could think about was what an arse I had been to you recently." He explained.

"It's okay, we're family before anything else."

"If we had known…" Jude started.

"Look, I didn't even know. I had a bad stomach, but that is nothing new for me. I thought it was the same as always." I insisted. "I am alright, you two. Honestly."

"About me finding a new best man, I didn't mean that. I couldn't get married without you beside me, Jez." Seb stated.

"So, the wedding is still on?"

"Of course," Jude smiled. "He's a twat sometimes, but I love him." She took his hand and kissed his cheek.

They left so that Sebastian could go to work. They promised to come in again and although I had slept for two days, I was exhausted. My eyes closed, and I drifted away.

I jumped awake, the room was lit by the sun and I pulled my side as I tried to move, it was agony.

"Sorry, son." My weary looking dad said sitting forward in the chair next to me. "Did I wake you?"

"No." I answered. "When did you get here?"

"About an hour ago." He replied. "I was flying back for the wedding anyway, Elle called, and I came straight here."

"Thank you, but you didn't have to."

"Yes, I did." He smiled slightly. "So, how is it?"

I grimaced with the pain writhing in my side, "I think the anaesthetic has worn off."

He looked suddenly concerned. "Are you in pain?" I nodded. "I'll go and find the nurse." He left and quickly returned with my nurse, "He's in agony." He explained.

"It's not that bad." I protested as she lifted my gown and frowned at my wound.

"We have no room for heroes here, Mr Buxton." She then smiled warmly. "The doctor is on his way anyway. It looks okay to me, but we'll get him to take a look." I nodded my head. "Are you ready for that toast now?"

"I will be once the pain eases off." I replied.

I must admit, seeing my dad there shocked me, I hadn't heard from him in months, Elle and Hermione both thought he had a girlfriend now and was keeping his distance from us in case we found out. To be honest, my mother's spirit died a long time before her body died and I wouldn't blame him for seeking comfort from another.

He told me of Julian and his new adventures, how Elle and Hermione were still running the small boutique in town and then he frowned,

"I have something to tell you, but I fear it will delay your recovery."

"Tell me." I insisted.

"Margaret is retiring, she has to care for her husband now, he has been diagnosed with cancer and its terminal." I adored our house keeper and cook, Margaret. She was my mother's governess when she was growing up and when we returned to the UK, she came to see us. Mum hired her immediately and she became a part of the family. I knew I would miss her whenever I would get the chance to go back to Canterbury.

"I'll miss her," I admitted bitterly.

"As will we all." He agreed. "I have something else to tell you."

"You've met someone." I muttered.

He looked shocked and nodded. "Yes. She's a divorcee and has two grown children. Her name is Suzanna and we get on quite well."

"That's good, Dad."

"You don't mind?"

"Why would I mind? No one expects you to be alone the rest of your life. You stuck by Mum and now it's your turn to live again."

"Thank you, Jeremy, that means a lot to me. I only wish your sisters felt the same." He sighed.

"They'll come around." I smiled. "Has Suzanna come with you?"

"No, she felt it would be wrong."

"Dad, it's been almost four years, Mum would understand."

"Unfortunately, Elle and Hermione have both made it very clear that they will never accept my moving on." He explained. "Suzanna is back in Austria for now."

"Is she British?"

"She is Swedish, actually. She was born in Stockholm." He replied. "You have no idea of how relieved I am. I have picked up the phone so many times to tell you…"

"I am happy for you, Dad." I swallowed, I only wish I felt as happy myself.

In truth, I feared that things between Kelsey and I were never going to be the same. I screwed up over Natasha and I was going to lose everything because of it. It just didn't seem fair that I didn't have an affair but felt like I was making up for the fact that I did.

He stayed with me and when Kelsey arrived, he jumped up and hugged her. Saying how beautiful she looked and that she was glowing. They talked about what had happened and I sat silently watching them. Losing her would kill me, I knew that, but I couldn't let go of the feeling that she was already slipping through my fingers. I loved her, God knows, I loved her with every breath I took. Still, I knew we couldn't continue to live like this. I had a right to voice an opinion, I shouldn't be feeling like I couldn't object to something. I had to stop allowing her to have her own way.

I never wanted to be my old self again, arrogant, cocky, confident. She took that from me when we met, she stripped me back to my core. The years I had spent building a wall that nothing could get through and the moment we met, it vanished. Kelsey smashed through me and I didn't think I could imagine a future without her. Now though, I wondered how my life would have been had we never met.

Then she turned and smiled at me and it melted my heart. What was wrong with me? Here, I had this incredible woman and we had already fought so hard to be together, she stayed with me no matter what, the mother of my children, carrying our baby and I was thinking about leaving her? Had I lost my mind?

"Are you okay?" she asked.

"Tired," I lied. Guilt hit me hard and I could barely look at her. I didn't understand what was going on and it petrified me.

Seven

Kelsey

I can honestly say I have never been so scared before in my life, watching the colour drain from Jeremy's face and then seeing the pain he was in. Everything went, my anger and frustration all disappeared. When he collapsed beside me at the reception desk, my heart skipped a beat. Within minutes they lifted him from the floor and onto a trolley.

If watching my husband not regain consciousness wasn't bad enough, he had to have emergency surgery because an infection was slowly poisoning his body. I Called and told Stuart and then I called Sebastian. He was there within an hour and he and Jude stayed with me all night and the following day.

Jeremy still hadn't woken, I sat with him all night and the following Sunday I just waited. Waited for him to open his eyes and tell me everything was alright. I couldn't picture life without him, he was the other half of me and I wasn't ready to let him go.

He finally opened his eyes early Monday morning and my heart flooded with relief. I hadn't slept, and I hadn't been home since

Saturday night. I had never worn the same clothes for so long before in my life.

Jude suggested I go home and get some rest, so after I was satisfied Jeremy would be alright, I headed home. Dave had taken Harrison to nursery and left a note to say he was heading home. I took a long bath and crawled into bed. I didn't think I would sleep without Jeremy there, but I think I was asleep before my head hit the pillow.

When I returned to the hospital, Jeremy looked so much better, sat up in his bed and talking with his dad. I was stunned to see him there and he made a huge fuss of me. When he left to head out to Buxton Manor to see his brother, Jeremy and I were finally alone.

He seemed quiet, a little offish, if I am honest. But I guessed he had been through a lot and felt a little overwhelmed by all the attention he was receiving. The doctor popped in and said Jeremy's blood was clean of infection and he would be allowed home in a day or so. The good old NHS had saved his life, I was not about to fight them over it.

I went to the toilet and to call my mum, she and Dave were collecting Harrison and I wanted to make sure that he was okay. When I came back, Jeremy was sleeping again. I sat and stared at this amazing man whom I loved so completely. I wondered what was going through his head, because he certainly wasn't himself and hadn't been for months. We used to tell each other everything, but now he seemed to clam up and I felt sure that he was hiding something from me. Not necessarily a bad thing, but we were a week away from our anniversary and I selfishly hoped the 'plans' he had made were still doable given his near-death experience.

He woke shortly after twelve when the nurse arrived with a salad for him. It was all he wanted from the menu, when it came to care, the hospital was A-class, but food wise, my God, I wouldn't serve it to an animal. He pushed the limp looking lettuce around the plate with his fork.

"Shall I go and get you something else?" I asked.

"No, its fine, I just don't seem to have much of an appetite." He said placing his fork down on the tray. "What about you, what have you eaten today?"

"I'll get something later." I shrugged.

"Kelsey," he sighed.

"I'm alright." I insisted. "Can I ask you something?"

"Yes."

"Are we um… well, I know Saturday was not a good day, but… Jeremy, is something wrong between us?"

"Why do you ask?" he swallowed, I watched his Adam's apple move in his throat.

"Well, you seem different, there's an atmosphere between us and to be honest with you, I am frightened." I admitted.

He frowned and lifted a small cup of juice from the tray pausing as he looked at it. "I am just not up to talking at the moment." He said eventually.

Pain coursed through my veins, he was lying to me, to my face. "Okay." I muttered and stood, fighting my tears, I walked to the window and gazed at Poole Park in the distance. "Actually, I am hungry. I am going to grab a cup of tea and a sandwich," I lifted my bag and walked to the door, "Do you want anything?"

"Some more juice would be nice." He replied. I nodded and left, I couldn't even look at him.

I was lying of course, I had no intention in getting a sandwich, how could I swallow bread when my husband, the man I trusted, was lying to me yet again? Didn't he realise I already doubted us, that the scars left by Natasha were still as deep and painful? Her actions had cast a shadow over our marriage and it looked as though something else was bothering him and yet again, I wasn't allowed to know.

I found the shop and bought a bottle of Hi-Juice for Jeremy. Grabbed myself a Twix and a bottle of water, then, deciding I would rather sit alone than try and make conversation with him, I found a seat and sat down. Too distracted by my painful thoughts, I didn't even notice eating the Twix, I just looked at the empty wrapper in my hand.

I rinsed my mouth with the water and pulled my phone from my bag. Jude had messaged to say that she and Sebastian had been talking, he still hadn't told her who the friend was that had sent him these messages he was replying to but promised her that he wasn't cheating, and she believed him.

When I got back to Jeremy's room, he wasn't alone.

"Hi," an attractive dark-haired girl in her early twenties, smiled. I immediately felt fat and ugly.

"Hi," I replied sheepishly.

"This is my assistant, Amanda." Jeremy explained. "Amanda, my wife, Kelsey."

"I have heard so much about you." She gushed. "You look amazing." She added.

"Thank you." I replied and placed the bottle of juice down for Jeremy.

"Amanda dropped in with this from the office." Jeremy said to break the awkward silence. He held up a *Get Well Soon* card.

"That's very nice of you," I smiled thinly. She flashed her ice-blue eyes at me and turned back to my husband.

"I'll go then, don't worry about a thing, I have it all covered."

"What about Millard's manuscript?"

"In proofing and so is Rex Wright's, it's all in hand, boss." She smiled.

He smiled back at her, "You are an absolute star, Amanda."

"And you know it," she grinned proudly. "It was nice to meet you, Kelsey."

"And you," I said.

She walked to the door. "Get well soon, Jez." She said before leaving, "We're missing you like mad."

"I will, thank you." He nodded. She left, and I stared after her for a while. He said he had an assistant and that she had bad skin and frizzy hair. So, either, that was another lie, or she had improved on her looks and who knows, it could be to impress the boss. "That was nice of the office, eh?" he said disturbing my reverie. I turned to face him.

"I suppose." I replied eventually. I sauntered to the chair and sat down. "How long has she worked for you?"

"A few months." He replied and opened the card again. I just stared at him. "She has a boyfriend." He added.

"And?"

"And, besides the fact that she is too young for me, I am not interested. That is what you're thinking, right? That because of Natasha, any pretty girl who works with me now is either after me, or I am after her?"

"I never thought anything…"

"Yes, you did." He accused sourly.

Anger singed at my spine and I sat upright. "Buxton men are natural born flirts," I frowned. "I knew that when I met you, so I wouldn't expect anything else."

He sighed loudly, "It's nice to know you think so highly of me."

"Whose fault is that?" I snapped and stood. "I have to pick Harrison up from my mother's. If I can get someone to babysit, I'll pop back later, if not, I will see you tomorrow." I walked to the door.

"Don't I even get a kiss goodbye?" he asked.

"No." I barked as I left and slammed his door shut behind me.

I arrived at my mother's house to find Harrison had gone out with Dave to the garden centre. Mum was baking in the kitchen and as she mixed dried fruit into her cake batter, I told her about Amanda and how Jeremy seemed to be distancing himself from me again. She made us tea as I sat and complained about everything, then I stopped. Suddenly realizing that I sounded terrible.

"You have a right to be concerned." She said.

"It's not that, it's I feel I am always the last to know anything. That everyone has to protect me or something. I just want to know what is so wrong with me that no one, including my husband, trusts me?"

She placed a cup of tea in front of me and sat opposite. "I don't think it's trust with Jeremy. He would rather bear the brunt than burden you."

"That's just ridiculous." I dismissed. Why would he want to do that? Didn't he learn last time, we are in this marriage together?

Although, it felt like it was becoming one-sided again and after everything we had already been through, I couldn't shake the feeling that we were on a slippery slope and if I hadn't lost him already, I was certain I would soon.

"Listen, you are probably exhausted, and I expect that he is still feeling very poorly. You have both just been through a traumatic court case and I am sure when things settle down, you will be fine." She placed her hand on top of mine. "You have to stop thinking that you don't deserve him, because you do. He loves you and I know that you love him as much. He is a stubborn sod when he wants to be, but I truly believe that he would never deliberately hurt you."

When Harrison got back with Dave, we went home. I wanted a long bath and I needed an early night. Before going to bed at nine, I phoned the hospital and the nurse said that Jeremy was fine, he had eaten and was now sleeping. It obviously hadn't bothered him that I left there upset, but I was too tired to wallow over it. I needed my bed and as soon as my head it the pillow, I drifted away.

They released Jeremy the following day on the provision that he stayed in bed and took his antibiotics. I took Harrison with me to pick him up, but as we got to the hospital's main entrance, he was walking out with Sebastian and his father.

"I tried to call you." He said. "Dad turned up and said he'd bring me home."

"Oh, well, that's fine." I turned around to walk away.

"Kelsey?" Rupert called after me. I turned and faced them again.

"I have some errands in town, you take him home. I was just trying to help you out." He explained. Jeremy rolled his eyes and pain shot through my body.

"Actually, Harrison and I have to go out anyway. So, if you don't mind, you take him home and I will see you there." I lied.

"I want to go with Daddy." Harrison whined.

"Daddy isn't feeling well, we'll go home later." I said. He let go of my hand and ran to his father. I turned around and he was hugging Jeremy. A lump formed in my throat as I knew if we were heading down this road, Harrison was going to get hurt.

"I'll go with Kelsey, Dad." Jeremy said. "Seb, if you take my dad to Burtons, you can show him the suits."

"Sure, no problem, mate." Seb smiled. Rupert handed me Jeremy's bag.

"If you don't mind, I'd like to buy my grandson something too, is there something he likes?" Rupert asked.

"Cars," Jeremy and I said together. He looked at me and smiled.

"Well, that's easy enough." Rupert smiled and left with Seb after saying goodbye and promising to come and see us before returning to Buxton Manor.

I led Jeremy to the car, my legs shaking as I walked. It felt like he was a stranger and the pain it caused was excruciating. At my car, I put his bag of medication on the back seat and slowly, he climbed into the passenger seat. I locked Harrison into his car seat and drove us home. He talked to Harrison and asked if I was okay. I wanted to yell at him and tell him I wasn't, but I didn't want to be that whiny wreck who lost him before. I had to be strong and in control, so I lied and said I was alright.

I got his bag out of the car while he and Harrison waited at the front door. He moved out of my way, so I could let them inside and then he waited while Harrison ran ahead and into the living room.

"Would you like a drink?" I asked warily.

"Tea would be great," he muttered his reply. "I think I will go and lie down, not feeling too bright right now." He slowly climbed the stairs and I went to the kitchen to make him a cup of tea.

My back ached as I sat on the chair waiting for the kettle, wondering how we had come to drift apart again. This was not how a married couple should be, surely, everything we had was worth a fight. But it felt like I was the one fighting to hold us together, I didn't know if I had the strength and will to endure anything else. We had already been through so much, maybe it had taken its toll and Jeremy finally realized that I wasn't who he wanted after all. I shook my head, I was an emotional wreck with this baby, maybe I was just being over sensitive. He had only just had an operation to save his life after all.

Eight

Jeremy

I couldn't wait to get home. I was sick of the hospital and so relieved when they said I could go after I begged them to let me. I tried to call Kelsey, either she was still upset with me or she hadn't noticed my call. My dad arrived with Sebastian and they offered to take me home.

It had been a long night led there worrying about her, wondering if she was okay. She was so angry when she left, I didn't even know if she had made it home safely or not. I wanted to call her, but decided it was better to let her cool down. I knew one thing, we could not continue like this, she didn't trust me and that hurt, hurt like nothing I had ever felt before. My wife thought I was a flirt and she didn't trust me. It made me feel sick to know that. She had stuck by me through the Natasha drama and still she doubted me.

I was surprised they allowed me home, because every time the nurse came in to check on me, I was awake. I was told I could get out of bed and if I could walk, they would allow me to leave. As much as it hurt to stand, the prospect that I could go home made the pain worth it. Sebastian helped me to dress while my dad went to the pharmacy and got my prescription.

Meeting Kelsey on the way out of the hospital warmed my heart, but she wouldn't make eye contact with me and I guessed she was still upset. I said I would go back with her if anything but to show her that she had nothing to worry about. I mean, yes, I knew we had issues, but didn't every married couple? I was not interested in Amanda and had never even considered her anything more than a colleague.

Once we got home all I wanted was my bed, I felt so drained and the pain was crippling. Kelsey was making me a drink as I struggled up the stairs and to our room. I eased myself down onto the bed and lifted my legs. My stitches pulled as I shuffled on the bed until I was finally comfortable.

"Here's your tea," Kelsey said sheepishly.

"Thanks," I said and tried to sit up. It was agony and her eyes bulged when she saw me struggling.

"Here, let me help you." She said hooking her hand under my arm. "Sit forward a bit," she told me and pulled a pillow up behind my back. "Alright?" I nodded.

"Thank you."

"Are you hungry?"

"No, I am fine." I muttered. "I have a bag of antibiotics I need to take in my bag and some pain killers." I explained.

"I'll find them out for you," she said and walked to the door.

"Kelsey, thank you."

"Sure." She said and left.

She returned a good few minutes later with a glass of water and a hand full of pills, instructing me to take them. I did as I was told, washing them down with the water.

"Are we okay?" I asked her.

"Why wouldn't we be?"

"Well, last night, when you left, you were so angry."

"I think we need to see a counsellor." She said and turned to face me. "We need help, Jeremy. I don't think I trust you anymore and I don't know what to do about it." So, I was right, and I knew that we could not carry on like this. Without trust in a relationship, you have nothing to build on. "Say something." She demanded.

"If that's what you want." I muttered.

"Well, can't you see where I am coming from?"

"I suppose I do. I just had no idea that this was how you felt, that you don't trust me anymore. I didn't cheat on you, Kelsey. I would never cheat on you, yet I'm being treated like I have, and I don't think that is fair." She stared at me. "If you think a counsellor will help then fine, we'll go, but if not, what then?"

"I don't know." She admitted.

"There can only be one outcome and as much as I love you, I would not want to stay in this marriage if there is no trust." There, I said it, I felt like an arsehole, but it had to be said.

"You mean, you would want a divorce?" she asked.

"Yes." I swallowed, that hurt more than I cared to admit.

"I see." She frowned, tears filled her eyes as the colour drained from her face. "So, uh… well, I had better see if Harrison is all right." She said and quickly left.

I don't know if I wanted a divorce, I couldn't think straight, but I did know that trust was a huge issue for us. Fear began to radiate through my body like a shock wave. If we were coming to the end of our road, what then? Do I return to Canterbury or London, do I leave her completely? What about my children? Could I leave them too? I began to feel sick, I couldn't leave it like this, I had to let her know that I didn't want this, that I couldn't live with her or the children in my life.

As I pushed off the covers, I heard the front door close and talking. I guessed Stuart was home and waited for him to come up and give me an ear bashing for upsetting my heavily pregnant wife. Kelsey was so stubborn, and I suppose I thought that if I shocked her, she would snap out of this slump she seemed to be in. Then I realized that this is what ended us before and how miserable I was without her. She was my wife; my best friend and I knew that the concept of living without her was unimaginable.

A gentle knock rattled on the door and it opened, Stuart poked his head through the opening and smiled sheepishly,

"Are you up to having a visitor?" he asked.

"As long as you are not here to lecture me, then yes." I replied. "Is Kelsey alright?" I asked as he entered the room.

"Truthfully?" he checked, I nodded. "No, she is sobbing her heart out down there. What's going on, mate?"

"Mate? Really?" I frowned.

"Okay, so you are still upset over Saturday."

"To tell you the truth, before I got back here, everything is a blur. But I don't think we can be mates, Stuart. Not anymore." *Shut up you idiot.*

"Well, can I ask why?"

"You are just like the rest of them, you use me to get what you want and then as soon as I need something, I am wrong. So, you, Sebastian, the bloody lot of you can go an…" Ouch! I tried to move, "Shit." I snapped. "Fuck, shit, fuck it."

"Are you sure you are meant to be home?"

"I can't stay in there any longer." I groaned as the pain eased. "I'll be alright in a sec."

"Did you mean that?" he asked after a few silent moments.

"No, you silly sod, I wanted to upset you for what you did to me Saturday." I smiled slightly.

"You are an arsehole," he chuckled. "But Kelse is a mess, mate, seriously, you told her you want a divorce?"

"Actually, I said that if the counselling she wants us to have doesn't work, then maybe we should call it quits. I didn't want to upset her, but she is accusing me of wanting every bit of skirt that I see and that's not fair, Stu, I never cheated on her."

"No, but you did lie, and you did hide it from her. It's going to take time." He pointed out. "Do you want out of your marriage?"

"Between us?" I checked. He nodded. "I don't know. I love her, but if she doesn't trust me… My head is all over the place, Stuart, I don't know what I want." I admitted painfully.

"I am not surprised with all you have been through, but maybe if you talk to her, tell her how you feel, she'll appreciate you being honest." I could only nod, at that point, I didn't think she could stand to be in the same building as me, let alone the same room. My head began to feel heavy. "I'll speak to her later, my pills are kicking in."

"I'll let you get some rest."

"Are you and Elliott okay now?" I asked before he left.

"We're getting there." He nodded. "I'll see you later." I closed my eyes and nothing…

A floor board creaked, and I snapped my eyes open. The room was dark, and I could smell her perfume. I tried to sit up in the bed, but the pain in my side caused me to hiss.

"Sorry," Kelsey muttered. "I didn't mean to wake you."

"What is the time?" I asked croakily.

"It's almost nine." She replied. I reached over to the bedside cabinet and switched on the light. Allowing my eyes to adjust, I saw the pain I had caused my wife on her face and in her eyes. "Harrison's in bed asleep. Are you hungry? I made a casserole."

"I am, as it happens." I frowned. "We need to talk."

"No, its fine, you told me how you feel and what you want. I know where I stand now." She said walking towards the door.

"Kelsey, please." I sighed. She stopped and turned to face me, her eyes were already filling with tears. "I don't want a divorce, I don't want us to split up but when you doubt us, when you doubt your trust in me, it's a slippery slope and I don't want to draw out the inevitable. I love you, you are my best friend and my soul mate, but I seem to make you unhappy and I don't know what I can do to change that."

"You don't make me unhappy." She protested. "Until yesterday, I didn't know how much the whole Natasha thing had affected me." I patted the bed and she sat beside me. "I don't want a divorce either, but I understand where you are coming from. If there is no trust, then we have a real problem and I thought if we got some help then maybe we can get through it." I gingerly reached over her lap and took hold of her cold hand. "I thought it was at least worth a try."

"It is, if it makes you happy, then that's all I want." I stated definitely. "So, about that casserole, when will it be ready?"

"It's ready now, I'll go and get you some." She stood from the bed, I still held on to her hand. "I am going to need my hand." She smiled slightly.

"Kiss me first." I smiled. She returned the smiled and leaned towards me, she pecked my lips and pulled back. "Call that a kiss."

"Have you ever heard of a tooth brush?" She grinned. Okay, so I had a sewer mouth.

"I see." I nodded feeling my face warm. "I need the bathroom anyway." I pushed off the covers and eased my legs over the side of the bed. My side pulled, but it wasn't as painful.

Kelsey headed downstairs, I went to the bathroom, used the loo and brushed my teeth. I also needed a shave but couldn't be bothered to stand there and do it to be honest. I went back to bed and climbed back under the covers.

A few moments later, Kelsey returned with a tray holding a bowl of casserole and a small baguette. She set the tray on the cabinet and smiled warmly for the first time in twenty-four hours. I was relieved, I must admit and already began to feel better.

"I brushed my teeth." I stated as she placed a napkin on my chest.

"I can smell it," she grinned. "If you sit forward, I will plump your pillows for you." I leaned towards her, taking in her perfume and as her hair brushed against my face and arm, it warmed my soul, how could I ever live without her? "Okay?" she asked. I leaned back against the soft pillows and smiled with a small nod. She placed the tray onto my lap and handed me a spoon. "Be careful, it's hot."

"It smells delicious."

"I always seem to cook better when I am upset." She admitted. "I'll let you eat in peace."

"No, stay with me." I insisted. She pulled the chair from beside the window and sat on it beside me. I sunk the spoon into the rich gravy and lifted out a piece of beef. Placing it into my mouth, the hot peppered meat melted on my tongue filling my mouth with saliva. "Wow," I exclaimed. "This is incredible." She smiled by my response.

"There is nothing in there that you can't have. I have to look after you."

"And you do." I agreed.

She sat with me until I finished the bowl and then said she would be back as soon as she washed up. I was due another set of antibiotics and pain killers, so she promised to bring them to me. With a satisfied belly and feeling so comfortably warm, I rested back against the pillow and closed my eyes.

My phone buzzed beside me, so I lifted it.

'Glad to hear you are home, boss, speak to you tomorrow.' Amanda texted.

I deleted it immediately, if Kelsey had seen it, I felt sure we would be back to square one. Amanda was a nice enough girl, but she in no way compared to Kelsey, I didn't know what had happened to make her so suddenly insecure, but I didn't want to add to her fears either.

She offered to sleep with Harry to give me more room in our bed. I insisted she stayed in with me and lay there listening to her breathing until she drifted off to sleep. I fell sleep shortly after, relaxed with my wife sleeping next to me, but still not convinced we were doing the right thing. How many more glitches could we survive?

Over the next couple of days, my body healed, the thoughts in my head appeased and my heart began to feel normal again. But deep down, as I watched her, I couldn't help but feel we had a huge battle ahead of us. An outsider would take one look and suggest a split, I just knew it. The counsellor she wanted us to talk with would be a professional and know that we had fought so hard already, we were both going to end up resenting each other if things didn't change and soon.

The day of our anniversary, my doctor removed my stitches and gave me an all clear meaning we were able to go out. I had planned on taking her away to the New Forrest for the night. I had even booked a night at a hotel in Lymington. But my doctor advised it was best to stay close to home, so we settled for a meal at a restaurant in Wimborne and after eating we sat in the beer garden talking.

      She explained how she'd still like to move and I suppose it would be a good idea, but I knew more than most, you can't outrun your problems, they tend to follow you everywhere. She thanked me as she drove us home and placed her hand on my knee. It was the first real physical contact she had made towards me in a week and it raised my hopes slightly.

We were a week away from Seb's wedding and as best man I still had so much to do. My dad came and saw us most days and it was nice to see him build a relationship with Harry. Dad had taken Harry to the park and Kelsey was at her final dress fitting with Jude. For the first time since I came out of hospital, I was alone.

      I sat at my computer with a half-written speech on the screen for the wedding when my phone rang. It was Mark and I guessed he wanted to know when I would be back to work.

      "Hello?" I said.

      "Hello yourself." He chimed. "How is my favourite manager feeling today?"

      "Much better. My doctor said I can return to work after the wedding." I explained.

      "That is good news but not why I am ringing you. I have some great news for you, Jez, great news."

      "Go on."

"Well, the senior manager at the head office has gotten herself knocked up. She is going on maternity leave at the end of the month and Brian Walker has asked if you would like to cover her position."

"In London?" I frowned.

"Yes, I know with Kelsey and the kids it's going to be hard, but the money up there is fantastic, and I think it would look great on your CV."

"Can I have some time to think about it?" I asked.

"Sure, just let me know when you come back to work."

"Thanks, Mark."

"No problem, mate. So, I guess I'll see you at the wedding then?"

"Yeah, need to finish this sodding speech." I grumbled.

"You only need two words with Seb, booze and boobs." He chuckled.

"Yeah," I smiled. "See you there." I ended the call and sighed, loudly. I was seriously struggling with this speech. I saved what I had and switched off the computer, I knew time was running out, but I also knew, you never watch a boiling kettle.

Nine
Kelsey

I walked down to the kitchen and burst into tears, how could he have been thinking that we should divorce, I thought everything was fine, I couldn't understand where this had come from. Stuart came home and found me blubbering and as soon as I told him, he went up to see Jeremy.

      I knew he was still in a lot of pain, but the scariest part was, I felt that he was right. Maybe we were beyond repair. We had been through so much, maybe this was the last thing to topple that never-ending cake that was building, me suggesting that we needed a counsellor was the thing to knock that cake over.

Stuart returned to the kitchen and said that Jeremy was sleeping. He said that Jeremy didn't want a divorce but admitted that we needed help and it petrified me to think that if we needed help, then we weren't as strong as I first thought. I fed Harrison and put him to bed after his bath, as he settled quickly, I popped in to check on Jeremy and felt an idiot when I stepped on the creaky floorboard and Jeremy jumped awake.

In the days that led up to our anniversary, things improved somewhat. We were talking, although I felt on edge, at least we could talk. I didn't want to push things, I remembered the night he accused me of suffocating him, so I wasn't about to give him more of a reason to leave.

He healed from his operation and the doctor said he could take me out for a meal, but we were not to venture off too far. So instead of going to the New Forest as planned, we went for a meal, which was nice. I felt we turned a corner, we talked for hours after and during the drive home, I rested my hand on his leg. I stupidly thought that maybe he would want to make love that night, seeing as it was a special night. So, braving the first physical show of affection I had showed him since our fight, was met with resilience. Okay, I know he had not long been under the knife, but he didn't show me any interest. I couldn't help but wonder if things were going from bad to worse. Although we had the house to ourselves, he stayed on his side of the bed and I stayed on mine.

The following morning, I had to meet Jude for a fitting and Rupert had kindly offered to take Harrison out for the day. Leaving Jeremy at home, I headed for my trusted bridal shop in Parkstone, Pascalis. This was my third use of the store and had parted with more of my money to pay for alterations to the midnight blue bridesmaid dress Jude wanted me to have. None of us thought I would be the size of a shed when it came to be wearing it.

"Come on then, out with it." Jude snapped impatiently as we walked back to my car.

"What?" I frowned.

"Tell me why your face looks like a slapped arse."

"I can't help the way I look, an ugly, fat cow whose husband doesn't love her anymore, whose husband told her he wanted a divorce last weekend and whose husband is leaving once he grows a pair and admits it." I barked.

"First and foremost, you are not nor have you ever been ugly and as for being fat, you are with child, love, you look incredible and I know Jez is not planning on going anywhere."

"Okay, so take last night, our anniversary and he didn't want me." I sulked.

"Oh, so the fact that he had his guts ripped open last week to save his life has no meaning to you?" she demanded angrily. "For fuck sake, girl. When are you going to realize that Jez loves you and you deserve to be happy and in love? I am so sick of this *woe is me* thing you have going on. It's pathetic. So, either, grow a pair yourself and demand he tells you what's going on or…"

"Or what?"

"Or leave him first." She frowned. I stopped walking, she turned around and walked back to me. "I should not have said that, but really, Kelse, all you do is push and push and push and you expect him to prove his love to you time and time again. He is only a man and they fuck up, fuck up like no one else. Jez has loved you since the first day you met. You know this, why would he hunt you down and make the most amazing proposal ever? Why would he turn down that slut, who happens to be sat in a cell right now, and choose to stay with you? Jez has fought for you, taken shit for you, he has proved himself time and time again to you, what else can he do?" I just stared at her, what she said hurt, but it was the truth, I was to blame. "Whatever happened to you to make you so bloody needy and pathetic?"

"I don't know." I muttered with emotion building in my eyes and throat.

"I have been your friend for years, is it Ben? Do you think his death did something to you?" I shook my head. "Kyle then, we both know what a retarded prick he was?"

"No, well, maybe some of it, he did try to rape me."

"Yes, but you fought him off and you won. You wanted Jez, you love him as much as he loves you, so why are you always waiting for something to go wrong?"

"Well, what about the fact that we lost our first baby, then we split up and he went back with his ex for a one-night stand, or the fact that my son was born with the same thing that killed my little brother, or my dad dying of cancer. Maybe it's because he is so bloody gorgeous that a tart, who is everything I am not, put the idea into his head that I am not worth it anymore? I have given my heart and soul to him, I love him with every heartbeat, every breath I take, but I would rather lose him completely, leave him, than to live a minute longer wondering when he will decide to leave me."

"Right, so what about your children?"

"I came from a broken home…"

"And look at the mess you are in. You don't trust anyone, you never have." She spat.

"I have to go." I frowned.

"Kelse, don't be like that."

"No, you are right, I am a pathetic, needy, fat and ugly cow, who is about to lose everything…"

"Shut up!" she snapped. "Shut the fuck up. I never said you are fat or ugly, no one thinks that. So, what that your fucking husband didn't want to have sex last night. So, what that he's a bit quiet at the moment. You are right, maybe you don't deserve to be happy, maybe you would be better off alone, God knows that man has all but walked through fire for you, but he doesn't love you, he wants to leave you. I am sick and tired of mopping up your mess, Kelsey Fucking Buxton, get off the pity train because it's about to crash into a wall and you will really lose everything, including me." She turned around and walked away. I watched her climb into Seb's car and speed away like a maniac and all I could do was watch.

Jude is probably about the only person I have ever allowed to talk to me like shit and forgive her for it. Nine times out of ten, she was right, and I feared that afternoon that she was right again. I had become so needy and pathetic, it was almost laughable. Why did I wait for the bad crap to ruin everything, why did I sit back and watch my world fall apart again?

No, I would not let this happen again. I would not let this destroy us, I loved him, and he loved me, what else did I need? Nothing, Jeremy was my air, my sun, and like a flower, without him I would wither away to nothing and die.

I tossed my dress on the back seat of the car, started the engine and raced home. I wanted to tell him that I would not allow this to be the end of us, that we were worth the fight.

Arriving home, I left my dress in the car and hurried inside. He was sat on the couch watching TV and when I entered the room, he flashed his blue eyes at me.

"Are you alright?" he asked.

"No," I frowned, "I have something to say so shut up and listen to me, alright?" he smiled slightly as he nodded. "Right, well. That night, the night it all came out about Natasha, you told me about the first time we met, how I changed your life for you, remember?" Again, he nodded. "Good, well, you need to know, you changed my life too. I was broken, Jeremy, broken and damaged, left by a poisonous arse who tried to rape me, broken by a dad who chose another woman over me. I didn't trust anyone and if you remember rightly, I told you I wasn't worth it."

"Yes, but…"

"Shh…" I frowned, "I said you had to listen."

"Okay."

"Okay. So, where was I? Oh yeah, so I told you I wasn't worth it, because I had been led to believe that good things didn't come my way, that I wouldn't get a happy ending because I didn't deserve it. I thought that this, you, us, this didn't happen in real life and then I met you and you bolted through my heart like no other. You made me feel like the most important person in the world to you, because, once upon a time, I was." I fought my tears back. "You are my first lover, the only one I want and the only one that I will want for the rest of my life. I believe in you, I believe in us and what we have. I know I have been unbearable lately and I am sorry, but I cannot sit back and let you walk away from me. I am not letting this be over. I am putting up a fight for you, Jeremy Buxton."

He stared, his eyes, glistening with tears, he stared, my heart pounded in my chest, thumping throughout my body and into my ears and he still stared. "You are wrong." He said eventually. My heart stopped, my tears spilled over, was I too late? "I still think you are the most important person in the world." He smiled, and my heart melted like butter. He stood and took my hands into his. "I am sorry if I made you feel you were losing me. I'll admit that since the court case, things have got on top of me and I have found it difficult. I have felt like I have had to make it up to you, time and time again. That I should prove to you that you can trust me, and I know that it will take time, but you need to understand that, I am not, nor will I ever be interested in anyone else. I have everything I have ever wanted, right here, you and my children are all I need." I threw my arms around him and pulled him against me. Weeping in his arms, the months I had bottled everything up, it flowed out, released through my tears as he held me. "I love you," he said and kissed the side of my head.

"I love you too." I sniffed. I pulled back from his damp shoulder and gazed into his eyes. He used his thumb to wipe away my tears and leaned in, kissing my lips, the first kiss we had shared since he came out of hospital. After a few moments, our lips parted.

"So, would you like a cup of tea?" he asked.

"No," I sniffed. "All I want is you."

"Me?"

"Yes, you." I took his hand and led him up to our room.

Making love as the early spring sun shone through our bedroom window that day reminded me of when we first got together. How we made the most of our free time and enjoyed exploring each other's bodies. Golden rays touching his skin, lighting up his eyes.

Jeremy has always been a generous lover, always putting me first and that had never changed. This wasn't about need in the way of satisfaction, this was about missing the closeness making love to Jeremy gave me. It had only been a week or so but felt like forever. This closeness made me feel safe and that is what I longed for, to feel safe.

I woke to the sound of voices, I could hear Jeremy and then realized that Rupert had returned with Harrison. I got up with an aching back and took a long shower to try and ease my muscles. By the time I got down stairs, Rupert was getting ready to leave.

"I must say, you look better now after some sleep," he mentioned.

"Yes, it's been a long and tiring week." I replied and smiled at Jeremy. "Was Harrison okay?"

"He was as good as gold, he is a very intelligent little boy, you both must be so proud."

"He's like his old man, right, Harry?" Jeremy grinned proudly.

"Right," Harrison agreed as he came into the kitchen.

Rupert smiled, "I have to go now, Harrison, I'll see you soon though."

"Okay, bye Grandad." He replied.

"Harrison, what do you say for a fun day out?" I pressed.

"Thank you."

"It was my pleasure." Rupert smiled proudly.

"I'll walk you out, Dad." Jeremy said and winked at me as he passed by. I poured myself some tea and sat at the table. The front door closed, and Jeremy returned. "Do you fancy going out tonight?" he asked.

"Out where?"

"Well, there's a pub in Broadstone that does a mean burger, Black Water Stream or something, anyway, there are some houses in Corfe Mullen I want to show you, they have just gone onto the market, we could kill two birds with one stone."

"Okay." I nodded and sipped my tea. "I'll get changed."

"You look beautiful as you are." He stated. "I'll put my shoes on and we'll go, I'll drive."

"You want to go now?"

"Yes, properties don't stay on the market long around here." He left the kitchen and I stared at my cup. I had to tell Jude that her talk had worked, but judging by the way she was with me, I decided to leave it a day or so. I hurried to my car and pulled my dress out of the back. When I returned I could hear Jeremy talking on the phone upstairs. Not wanting to listen, to prove to him that I could still trust him, because I did, I got Harrison washed and put his trainers on.

"So, you had a fun day today then?" I said as I tied his laces.

"Yep." He nodded.

"Where did you go?"

"Out with a lady, Susan, she is nice, pretty."

"Susan?" I frowned.

"Are you sure?" I checked.

"Yes, she talks funny and she took us to see the fishes and sharks." He replied. "Daddy," he yelled and jumped up. I turned to Jeremy.

"Susan?" I frowned.

"My dad has a new girlfriend, her name is Suzanna, she is Swedish." He explained.

"And your sisters are okay with that?"

"No, which is why he said she stayed in Austria." He frowned. "Unless he lied."

I stood from the floor, "I don't expect he has lied, maybe he sent for her after all." I pecked his gorgeous smelling cheek. "Thank you, by the way."

"Thank you for what?"

"This afternoon." I shrugged.

"You never have to thank me for sex." He smiled.

"Well, I am, because I have been a selfish, unbearable bitch and I want you to know how much I appreciate having you in my life."

"Yeah?" he beamed. I nodded. "Ditto." He pulled his keys from his pocket. "Ready?"

"Yes." I lifted my bag and took hold of Harrison's hand.

As we drove towards Broadstone, another part of Poole, Harrison talked about the fish he had seen that day and how Susan, as he called her, seemed to have spoiled him while he was out. I could see Jeremy wasn't happy about it, when we arrived at the pub, I asked if he was alright.

"It's not that I don't like the idea, in fact, I am the complete opposite, but I thought that he would have told me that she was now here."

"So, you don't mind him seeing someone else?"

"No, he's young, he shouldn't have to live alone for the rest of his life." He replied. "He stayed with Mum, through all the bad times, when she accused him of trying to rape her and of hitting her, he still stayed. She hit him, she scratched him, she even spat in his face once, but he never even raised his voice to her. So, if anyone deserves to have some happiness, I think he's earned it."

"I had my reservations about him, I must admit, but since we got back together and the wedding, my opinion has changed." I smiled. "He is brilliant with Harrison." I added.

"I know, he actually said how proud of me he was, proud of me. I never thought I'd hear that from him." He smiled. "I'll phone him in a bit."

"If Suzanna is really here, invite them to lunch tomorrow, it would be nice to meet her before the wedding… shit!" I remembered Jude's harsh wake up call.

"What?" he frowned.

"Jude and I had a fight and I don't even know if I am still invited to the wedding, let alone, being her maid of honour."

"You and Jude always fight," she shrugged.

"Yes, but this time, she was so angry." I sighed remembering the way she looked at me.

"Do you want me to call Sebastian and find out if she is alright?"

"No," I replied. "Well, maybe later, you know, like a casual call, don't make it too obvious." He reached across the table and took my hands.

"I love you," he smiled.

"I love you too." I replied.

Ten

Jeremy

My phone buzzed in my pocket, as I watched an episode of Hawaii Five-O I had recorded. Amanda sent a text to say she was looking forward to me coming back to work because Andrew, who had been given my job while I was off sick, was doing her head in. She called him a Ginger Knob and it made me laugh. I was just about to delete the message when my phone rang, it was Seb.

"Hello?" I said.

"Jude and Kelse have had a massive row, Jude is furious." Sebastian said into my ear.

"What over?" *Again*, I thought.

"You, apparently. Jude told her some home truths."

"Oh, great." I sighed wryly. "As if my marriage isn't in enough trouble already."

"What's going on?" I told him about our fights and how I stupidly said I would rather get a divorce than stay with her just because of the kids. "You want a divorce?"

"No," I frowned. "I don't, but I can't live with someone who doesn't trust me."

"After everything she has been through, seriously, mate, are you surprised?"

"I suppose not." I sighed again.

"Well, she is on her way home, cut her some slack, alright? You are good together, I want what you have more than anything in the world."

"Then why are you sending secret text messages to another woman?"

"If you knew the truth, you would understand."

"Tell me then."

"Let me talk to her first, if she agrees, I will tell you everything, okay?"

"Okay." I nodded. I saw Kelsey driving onto the drive. "She's back, I had better go."

"Good luck."

"Cheers." I muttered and ended the call.

I heaved a bracing breath and prepared for the fire of fury my wife was about to unleash. No one wound her up better than Jude, she seemed to know what buttons to push and how far to go. Kelsey, God love her, already had a short fuse, so with her pregnancy hormones raging the way they were, I was ready for hours of fighting and yelling and tears.

She told me to shut up and listen, so I did as I was told. She poured out her heart and reminded me of the girl I met and fell in love with almost instantly. She had a fire in her heart and it burned through her tears, when she told me she was fighting for me, that she would not let me go, I tried not to smile because that was what I missed, my strong, independent girl who put me in my place and kept me in tow.

I never imagined that we would have ended up in bed that afternoon. She took my hand and led me up to our room and we spent the next few hours making slow passionate love to each other. For a woman who was almost seven months pregnant, she certainly gave me an afternoon I won't forget in a hurry.

      She drifted off to sleep and I almost did too, but the thought that my father was due to bring Harry back, I decided to have a quick shower and get dressed. I kissed her bare shoulder and left her sleeping, crept down the stairs and put the kettle on.

Dad returned with Harry just after five, like he had promised. Kelsey was still upstairs, though I heard our floor boards creak, so knew she had woken. I made Dad a drink while he sat at the kitchen table.

      "Was he good?" I asked handing him a cup of black tea.

      "Good as gold, he is a lovely boy, Jeremy, a pleasure to be around."

      "Thanks, though, Kelsey is the one who needs the praise, she is a really good mother." I smiled.

      "And now number two is on the way."

      "Yes." I nodded and joined him. "I don't mind what we have, but a little girl would complete us."

"You are stopping after two?" he asked surprised.

"I don't know, I'd have a football team, but Kelsey has really suffered with this one, plus Harry being poorly."

"I know, but as soon as he's had his operation, I am sure he will be fine." He assured.

"I hope so." I sighed. "Harry has what Kelsey's little brother died of."

"I know, but technology has come along tremendously since her brother died."

"It has, but we are still worried." I admitted.

Kelsey came into the kitchen and smiled, her eyes were twinkling, and her cheeks were rosy, she literally glowed that afternoon and it felt good to know that I had a hand in that.

After Dad left, I suggested we go out for dinner, while trying to write a speech for the wedding I began searching for properties in the area and found two I liked the look of in a place called Corfe Mullen, it was about three miles from the centre of Wimborne and both had huge gardens.

When we talked at the pub, I almost told her about Seb's call, but then I thought that she'd probably think I didn't mean what I had said, that because she was upset, I just played into her hands. This wasn't the case, but I had learned early on that Kelsey was like a flame, and if you threw oil onto her, she would turn into a roaring fire. So, I kept my mouth closed this time.

We drove past the houses I wanted to show her, and she agreed they would be perfect, but wanted to get the wedding out of the way before looking into them. I knew by that time they would both be gone, again, I said nothing and drove us home.

I put a sleeping Harry into his bed and crept down the stairs. Kelsey was sat at the kitchen table with her laptop. I put the kettle on to boil and turned to her.

"They are both pretty good prices," she said. I frowned. "I just looked the houses up on here. Maybe we can get a viewing this week."

"I thought you wanted to wait?" I queried.

"I know, but I also think we really need to move and as these would both be perfect, maybe we should take a look and perhaps we can put an offer in." She explained.

"Okay." I agreed. "What about this place?"

"Oh, this will go quickly, Jill down the road, her house went on the market Monday and was sold by Tuesday night. We're in a very desired area." She added.

"Well, if you are sure." I turned around to prepare our cups.

Monday morning, we met Graham, the estate agent at the first house at eleven. Kelsey had emailed and arranged it, who knew some estate agents worked weekends? The house was stunning, extremely modern and didn't need a thing doing to it. Set in a quiet cul-de-sac and close to a good school for Harry. Kelsey said she loved it but wanted to view the other house before deciding.

  The second, while just as nice, was situated on a road that at rush hours, would be considerably busy. At one o'clock we submitted an offer on the first house and shortly after two that afternoon, it was accepted. We had bought a new house, Kelsey was ecstatic, and Graham arranged to have our house valued the following day so that we could get it on the market.

Kelsey's savings, the money that her dad had left her, had been untouched since our wedding. We coped without it, so left it in the bank. We were able to secure the new house with a large deposit from her savings and all we had to do now was sell the house we were in.

Wednesday evening, we had to be at Buxton Manor for six, it was the wedding rehearsal and my aunt and uncle had organized a dinner for the wedding party. I knew Kelsey was dreading it as she and Jude hadn't made up yet and although I wanted to call my dad out over Suzanna, I thought that I would give him the chance to tell me himself.

I sat at the kitchen table and waited for Kelsey to get ready. Harry was with Jane and Dave and as Stuart was going to be an usher, he and Elliott were due in, they were riding over with us. She had been quiet all day and the more I asked if she was alright, the more she lied. Jude and Kelsey always fought, but after a day or so, they'd make up and everything would go back to normal.

Jude hadn't called, and Kelsey hadn't called her either, I'll be honest, I was concerned about it, but felt sure the lack of contact was due to Jude being busy and not because she was still pissed off with Kelsey.

She came into the kitchen and sighed again,

"Phone and ask her," I stated.

"No," she huffed. "Maybe I should just stay here."

"You are maid of honour, love, you have to be there." She just stared blankly, I could see her mind ticking over.

"Alright, but if she starts, I will leave."

"Okay." I agreed.

Stuart and Elliott arrived, and we left. I drove as I could see how on edge Kelsey was, plus, if I had my car, she couldn't chicken out. I knew Jude wanted to see her, she had told me how sorry she was for yelling at her best friend but was so sick of how Kelsey had been recently. I just promised to get her there.

The marquee was already set up for the wedding and I don't mind admitting, it made my stomach flip over at the thought that the last time there was a wedding at Buxton Manor, I was the groom. I couldn't believe that despite how horrible I had been to Kelsey when I thought she was seeing Stuart, despite that I had allegedly knocked up my ex, so was having to marry her, Kelsey still came to the wedding to stop me making a mistake, she cared about me that much, that no matter how badly I had hurt her, she was still there.

Flashes of memories filled my mind, like how I demanded she told me why she had come and how she turned to leave, causing my heart to break a little more. When the whole thing unravelled, I turned to find her, but she had already left. Then, my idiot plan of drinking milk kicked in and I ended up in Poole hospital again.

As we climbed out of the car, I took her hand in mine and led her towards the marquee. Sebastian was arguing with his sister, Saskia and Jude was speaking with the registrar. My aunt and uncle, whom I hadn't seen for months, stood to greet us and my father, who had been sat with a stunningly beautiful blonde, also stood as we approached.

"Thank God!" Sebastian exclaimed racing towards us. "Saskia has dumped her boyfriend, Jack. He was meant to be my other usher." He grumbled. "I don't suppose you'd mind stepping in, Elliott?"

"What, just for tonight?"

"No, for the wedding."

"Okay," he smiled and looked at Stuart.

"Thank you, you are a life saver, mate, seriously." Seb smiled. "Kelse, love, looking gorgeous as always."

"Thanks," Kelsey muttered and looked over at Jude.

"How are you feeling, son?" Dad asked me from behind.

"Much better." I smiled and turned. Standing beside him, the blonde smiled nervously as he took her hand.

"This is Suzanna." He smiled. "Suzanna, my eldest son, Jeremy, though I believe everyone calls him Jez."

"It is very nice to meet you, Jez." She held out her hand and I shook it lightly.

"And you, Suzanna, this is my wife, Kelsey and our friends, Stuart and Elliott." They all shook her hand.

"Suzanna phoned, and your aunt insisted I invite her, so, here she is. I have to tell you, that she came out with Harry and I to lunch, I hope you don't mind" Dad explained excitedly.

"Of course, I don't mind." I assured him and tapped his arm.

It made me smile, because he was back, not the workaholic who avoided me like the plague, not the opinionated arse who once made me feel like I wasn't a member of the family. My dad, from when I was about seven, before we moved to the States, when we talked about books and racing cars. He was clearly happy and in love and it soothed my soul to see.

"Kelsey?" Jude called over, "Have you got a minute?" Kelsey looked at me, swallowed nervously and left my side.

After a few moments Kelsey and Jude were talking, they hugged, and relief flooded my body. She needed her best friend in her life as much as I needed Sebastian. We went through the ceremony and it made us laugh when Jude poked out her tongue at Seb as she walked down the aisle on her father's arm followed by Kelsey and Saskia and two of Jude's nieces.

The rehearsal was completed, finally, we had a few laughs and it eased the tension that seemed to hover over us all. My aunt and uncle invited everyone inside where they had a huge dinner waiting for us all.

While we waited for the main course, I headed to the bathroom, bumping into the groom himself. I knocked his phone out of his hand and crouched to pick it up.

"I got that, Jez." He said crouching with me. I glanced down at the screen and recognised the picture immediately.

"So, this is who you have been having secret texts with?" I asked almost not believing my eyes.

"It's not what you think," he groaned snatching the phone from my hand.

"Well, then, you had better start explaining," I growled. "Now!"

Eleven

Kelsey

There was no way in hell that I could just walk into that rehearsal as if nothing had happened. Jude hadn't even sent a text message and I'll be honest, I was concerned. So, sitting on my bed while Jeremy waited downstairs for me to get ready, I decided to step down as maid of honour and if I had anything to do with it, I would not be going to the wedding either.

Okay, her blunt talk with me did make me wake up to myself and stopped me acting like a pathetic victim. Jude knew me, better than I knew myself sometimes and I suppose because of her, Jeremy and I were getting on better than we had been in months. I had picked up my phone several times to speak to her, but I felt that she walked away, she would contact me if she wanted to.

Jeremy convinced me to go and as we had come so far forward, I didn't want to ruin it by being stubborn. We arrived at the Manor and I gazed at the huge marquees set up ready for the ceremony and receptions. Jeremy took my hand and we walked inside, Stuart tapped my shoulder and smiled reassuringly, I knew he would have my back should Jude decide she wanted to scratch my eyes out.

Jeremy introduced us to his father's new girlfriend, Suzanna and as we talked, I could see someone moving, I knew it was her, she frowned and then smiled sheepishly.

"Kelsey, have you got a minute?" Jude asked.

"Okay." I replied and walked over to her.

"I am a bitch, a first class one at that." She said. "I am so sorry about Saturday, I have been trying to pluck up the courage to phone you, but every time I did, I chickened out."

"It's alright." I muttered.

"You are my best friend and I just care about you so much, I hated seeing you so beaten down and…"

"Its fine, Jude, honestly. You were right about everything."

"How are things?" she asked. I glanced over my shoulder at Jeremy and smiled slightly.

"Much better, we talked, well, I talked, and he listened. We are ninety percent there." I smiled at her. "So, I should really thank you, you woke me up and made me realize that I am worth it, and I do deserve Jeremy."

"Halli-fucking-lujah!" she smiled and hugged me. "So, you are still going to be my maid of honour?"

"Yes, if you still want me."

"Of course, I do." She held me tightly. "You are my best friend, I wouldn't get married without you." As we parted she added. "Also, it means that Sasquatch is just a bridesmaid."

I smiled at Seb's bitch of a sister's pet name, she certainly showed me no compassion. "How are things with Seb?"

"He's still calling and texting her, but has sworn on his bollocks, he is not cheating on me and I decided that I need to trust him, there was no point to lecturing you over it and then not trusting my own man."

"I'd love to know who it is." I frowned.

"All I will say is, if it's that tart Natasha, I will kill them both." She stated. "So, my dad is here."

"What?" I queried in shock. Her dad left when she was about twelve. He moved away and hadn't been in touch. "How?"

"I found him through his sister, he lives in Norfolk now, I asked my mum if he can give me away and she said yes. So, he is here."

"I am really pleased for you," I said and looked over to Seb. "Does he suspect?"

"He said my boobs are bigger." She replied. "I just said that was wishful thinking on his part and laughed it off. Thank God I get to tell him Saturday."

A woman approached us and smiled, "Ready when you are, Jude."

"Thank you, Avril, this is my friend, Kelsey. Avril is the registrar, she'll be conducting the ceremony."

"You go and wait outside, I will get these boys in order." She smiled.

After the rehearsal, we retreated to the house where the Buxton's had organized a dinner. Jeremy sat next to me and we talked as we dined on asparagus soup and potato gratin, roast beef and crunchy vegetables followed by lemon tart and whipped cream. It was incredible, though Jeremy could only have sorbet for dessert, he managed to eat most of what was provided.

When he returned from the toilet something was wrong, I could see it in his eyes. He smiled nervously and sipped his juice, I wanted to ask, but with how things had been, I didn't want him thinking I didn't trust him, again. I left it until we got home and casually asked if everything was alright.

"Yes, I just had a bit of an upset stomach after that rich food, that's all." He then swallowed, Jeremy always swallowed after lying, so I knew he wasn't being honest, but felt if it was to do with us, he would have said, given the situation we were recovering from.

Over the next few days, we were extremely busy, we hadn't told anyone we had bought a new house, we wanted the sale of ours to go through first, just in case we were let down and had to pull our offer.

The Friday before the wedding, Jeremy, Stuart and Elliott were spending the night at Buxton Manor. Jude was getting ready at my house because her house in the village was too small, her words, not mine. Saskia and Jude's two nieces, Saffron and Ruby were getting ready at the Manor, they had the use of the summer house and would stay there until we arrived.

Sebastian arrived with Jude just before two that Friday afternoon. She had to go and collect her dress from Parkstone and although I didn't want to see Jeremy go so early, it made sense for him to leave with Seb, if anything, but to get the groom out of the way.

Jeremy had been so quiet since the rehearsal and I hoped that we weren't heading back to the way things were previous to our talk. I couldn't take it anymore, I would rather let him go than make him miserable again.

I pushed it all down though, this weekend was about Jude and by hook or by crook, she was going to have a wedding day to remember for the right reasons.

"I'll see you tomorrow then, love." Jeremy said carrying his bag in one hand and holding his suit hooked over his shoulder with the other. He crouched down and kissed a crying Harrison who didn't want Daddy to leave and then smiled gingerly at me.

"Twelve o'clock, on the dot." I smiled. He put down his bag and pulled me towards him. "I love you." I said.

"I love you too," he sighed and kissed me. It caused my heart to flutter and as he pulled away from my lips, a tear dripped from my eye. "I'll be alright, love. I'll call you later, alright?" I nodded. Seb beeped his horn, He smiled slightly and kissed me again. "We have so much to look forward to, new baby, new house, it's all going to be fine." He pecked my lips, turned around and walked to Seb's car.

    Jude lifted Harrison into her arms and hugged him, "Come on, we'll go get Auntie Jude's dress and then we can go for a MacDonald's." She promised. She turned to me. "Are you alright?"

    "I am an emotional wreck at the moment." I tried to smile as more tears fell. I brushed them away, "Come on, we need to go and get Cinderella's gown."

I drove her to Pascalli's in Parkstone to collect her wedding dress and then we went to MacDonald's where we scoffed Big Mac's and chicken nuggets. Jude treated Harrison to an ice-cream for eating all of his and then we headed back to the house.

    Jude had never been an overly feminine girl, she lived in jeans and rarely wore make-up or painted her nails, so she didn't want a manicure or a facial for the wedding, but it seemed Nicole and Shawna had different ideas. They arrived with Becky, Nicole's cousin. She was a beautician, so we spent the evening having our nails done and wearing face packs after relaxing massages.

Someone plopped down on my bed, I snapped open my eyes and frowned, my bedside light flicked on, Jude was crying.

    "What is it?" I panicked.

"I know I am not wife material, I know I am not good enough for Sebastian, so why the fuck am I marrying him?"

"You love him, right?" I checked as I sat up. She nodded her head. "And he loves you."

"I think he does."

"He does, I know he does." I assured her. "Sebastian Buxton worships the ground you walk on, he would die for you. You will be a wonderful wife and mother, I know you will because despite all you say, you want to be." She sniffed and wiped her face. "You are my best friend and I have been miserable without you this past week or so. You were there when my brother died, you talked to me about it and got me to talk about it when everyone else avoided me. You are a rock, you are my rock and I can't wait to see you marry Seb tomorrow." I smiled. "I used to want a sister, in fact, I used to wish that you were my sister and now I'll have the next best thing, a cousin-in-law. We'll be Buxtons together and we will make sure the family stays as real and as grounded as the rest of the world."

"I'm nervous." She nodded.

"You wouldn't be human if you weren't." I assured her. "Do you want to get in, it will be like it was when we were fifteen?"

She smiled and climbed in beside me. "I can't believe I am getting into a bed where you have had sex with Jeremy Buxton." She chuckled.

"I haven't heard you say that when you sit on our couch." I grinned and nudged her playfully.

"Oh. My. GOD!" She gasped. "Am I safe anywhere in this house?"

"Um…" I smiled mischievously, "no. Well, in my car you are, but not his."

"Actually, Seb and I screwed in Jez's car that day we went to the beach and he took you inside."

"Jeremy said you might." I smiled. "Listen to us, at fifteen we talked about Sebastian and his toffee nose cousin from America, and how we both wanted to go out with Seb, that his cousin was weird, but he had good hair. Now, I am married to that snob and you are about to marry Seb." I smiled.

She smiled and stared, her expression became serious. "Thank you, Kelsey."

"What for?"

"For being you, for being my friend. I couldn't have got through this without you." I put my arm around her. "Um, I am not getting up to anything freaky with you. I have never wanted to know what kissing a girl would be like."

I removed my arm and smiled, "Neither have I, just stay on that side of the bed." I switched off the light.

"Is this your side or his?" she asked in the darkness.

"Mine, I miss him when he's not home, so I like to smell him on his pillow."

"I see, so, do you want me to snore and fart, you know, to help you out?"

"No, thank you, I can live without that tonight." I chuckled.

"Kelse," she said quietly after a few moments of quiet. "Maybe we should try something, you know, freaky, it is my last night as a single woman."

"Jude?"

"What?"

"Go to sleep or you will have suit cases under your eyes in the morning."

"Okay, night."

"Night." I replied and closed my eyes.

A sharp pain ripped agonizingly through my calf muscle. I sat up and tried to rub my leg but couldn't really reach it.

"Shit," I cried out. Jude sat up beside me.

"What's wrong?" she asked.

"Cramp." I groaned.

"Let me help you." She reached over and began rubbing my calf muscle. She then pushed my toes back and slowly the pain appeased. "Is it better now?" she asked.

"Much." I nodded as the muscle twitched but didn't hurt as much.

"When my sister was carrying Ruby, she used to get cramp all the time." She explained and lifted her phone. "It's almost six." She stated. "I suppose I should take a shower."

"I would, we only have five hours to get you ready, Cinders." I smiled.

"Are you sure you are going to be alright?" she checked.

"Yes, now go, your hairdresser will be here at eight." I insisted.

Harrison stayed asleep long enough for me to have a shower too. He was going to be the ring bearer, which was fine, except that I wondered if he would run through the ceremony and lose them. I bathed him and dressed him in his little trousers, but only put on a t-shirt in case he got his shirt and waist coat dirty.

Jude's hairdresser, Amber arrived and began styling her hair with coiled curls and a tone of hairspray, fixing the centre of the coils with diamantes and finally a tiara. It looked amazing. She did her make-up while I had my hair pinned up.

It was almost ten when the hairdresser finally left, we were being collected at eleven, so it was time to get dressed. I helped Jude into her dress. She had chosen an antique white gown with a full-length tulle skirt that flared out from her waist, with a key hole opening at the back and the top of the dress was covered in a flower pattern of gems and sequins. She wanted a dress that in her words, didn't need to be hitched up every five minutes.

She turned to face me and smiled, my eyes filled with tears, "You look absolutely beautiful." I snivelled. "You really do, Jude."

"Do you think Seb will like it?"

"Seb will love it." I confirmed. How could he not? She was breath taking.

I pulled on my Greek Goddess, style bridesmaid dress of deep blue with a row of diamantes under my breast, she zipped it up for me and as we came down the stairs, Harrison stopped and gazed at us.

"Doesn't Auntie Jude look beautiful?" I asked.

"Uh-huh, you both beautiful ladies." He smiled.

"You are definitely a Buxton, Harrison." Jude smiled. "You could charm the pants off anyone." I went to the drawer in the hall and pulled out a black jewellery box, inside was the jewellery I wore on my wedding day, a diamond necklace and earrings.

"You can say no, but I wondered if you wanted to wear these as your something borrowed?"

"Oh, wow, Kelse, are you sure?" I nodded and grinned. "Thank you, I would love to." She smiled. I hooked the necklace around her neck and fastened it.

"Now you look perfect." I stated.

"I just need my flowers, my sister has had them made, she will meet us there." Her expression turned serious, "If I don't get a chance to later, thank you for everything."

"Oh, you'll thank me again later, remember how hard it was for me to take a pee in my dress?"

"Bugger, yes, well, anyway, thank you again." She smiled. I could see she was nervous, but didn't ask her, I know I would have bitten anyone's head off if they had asked me.

A white, stretched VW Beetle limousine stopped outside of my house. Decorated with midnight blue ribbons to match my dress and Harrison's dickie bow tie.

"Did you order that?" I asked her.

"Bloody Sebastian." She sighed. "He wouldn't tell me what car he had booked, I joked and said he would probably book me a Barbie doll pink one, at least it's white."

"There is that." I smiled. "Okay then, Miss Mitchell, are you ready?"

Harrison held out his hand, "Come on, Auntie Jude."

Taking his hand, she nodded, "Let's do this." She said.

I lifted my bag containing a change of clothes for Harrison and flat shoes for me, locked the door and followed them out to the car. Jack and Sarah, our neighbours, had come out to see us off. I waved and smiled before helping Jude into the car.

The drive to Buxton Manor was one I had made so many times, but I can honestly say that I was actually looking forward to going this time. Yes, I had a reasonable sized bump resting in my lap and my feet were already hurting in the shoes I had picked to go with my dress, but I was so relieved to be going there for a good reason, my best friend's wedding.

We had our fights, but I felt that had kept our friendship alive. When I spent my first summer at the village, the summer Ben had died, I was dreading it. I loved my aunt and uncle and their kids, I loved going there to see them, but the thought of spending four weeks there, knowing my parents were facing such heartbreak, that almost killed me.

Jude used to hang around with a girl called Gemma and she was friends with my cousin Joanne. We met at the small park that the people of the village raised money to build. I thought she was a bit of a show off, she kept swearing and acted as hard as nails. Within an hour, we were inseparable. She treated me like a real person and when Jo told her about Ben, she just said, *'Well, that's just fucking shit, isn't it?'*

The year Kyle and I broke up, I spent my first summer there alone. Looking after the cat for Diane and Jeff. When I told her about what he had tried to do, she wanted to cut off his parts and make him eat them.

When I came to stay the year I met Jeremy, I hadn't seen her for about a year and a half. My dad dying took up all of my time, he had to come first. When I called my aunt to tell her he had died, she invited me to stay for a few weeks to get my head together. It was the best and worst summer of my life. Finding Jeremy and then losing him again, that almost finished me off.

I remembered going to his wedding, when he almost married his ex, Tara, because she was meant to be pregnant with his baby. Luckily, the truth came out and he didn't have to go through with it. The day had not been easy, one I won't forget ever. When I thought about the fact that she could have made him marry her and I would have lost him forever.

As we drove up the gravel drive, the house looked amazing in the spring sunshine. As arranged, Nicki waited for us so that she could take my bag. Jude's older sister, Marnie, was waiting for us as well with two bouquets of flowers, white lily's and blue corn flowers. The car stopped, and the driver opened our doors. I climbed out and helped Harrison, Nicki took hold of his hand and then took my bag from me.

I then helped Jude out of the car,

"Oh, my God, Jude, you look beautiful." Her sister gasped.

"I scrubbed up pretty well, right, sis?"

"He's a lucky sod, I hope he looks after you." She smiled and handed Jude her flowers.

"He will." She asserted.

Within minutes we were surrounded by Jude's parents and nieces, who both looked adorable in their off-white dresses with midnight blue sashes. The photographer greeted us and began taking pictures in front of the house taking full advantage of the amazing back drop and surrounding gardens of the Manor.

After a few more moments, Stuart approached and asked that everyone except the bridal party, go and take a seat. He looked rather dashing in his dark blue morning suit, smiled and winked at me before ushering everyone away from us and into the ceremonial marquee.

"Are you ready?" Jude's dad asked.

"Um, Kelsey?" she frowned.

"Can you give us a few minutes?" I asked. He nodded. "Harrison, stand with Mr Mitchell."

"I don't know if I can." She said, her eyes filling with tears. "Everything was going great and now this woman he's texting, I mean, Lady Di married Prince Charles knowing about Camilla, so, what if I am about to do the same thing?"

I gazed into her eyes, she was genuinely concerned, "Okay, so we'll get back in that car and go. If you are sure he would cheat on you, even after faithfully promising you he isn't, then we'll go." I said calmly.

"But, I love him."

"And he loves you." I sighed rubbing her arm. "Besides, are you really going to let Sasquatch smirk and tell everyone that she was right, commoners have no place with her family?"

"No," she said and cleared her throat. "No way, Sebastian is mine and we belong together."

"Then let's go and get you hitched." I smiled and linked my arm in hers.

I followed her to the entrance of the marquee where Saskia was waiting to join us. I have to admit that she looked lovely in the same colour dress and stood beside me with a warm smile, the first friendly smile she had ever given me.

The song 'Stay With Me', by Sam Smith began to play. Jude heaved a deep breath as everybody inside the marquee stood. Watching the back of her dress as it glided over the red carpet we walked on, I listened to Sam's words and my eyes started to fill with tears. I looked up and saw my husband standing beside a smiling Sebastian. Dressed in the same dark blue morning suit as Stuart, with white button holes, Jeremy smiled, and my heart melted. God, I had missed him.

Twelve

Jeremy

Leaving Kelsey, when she looked so upset, was hard. Harry didn't want me to leave either. It had been so long since we last spent the night apart and after all we had been through recently, it didn't surprise me that it upset her.

Sebastian was absolutely petrified. Not about commitment, he loved Jude and proved that more than once. He was petrified of screwing up the most important day of their lives together. I simply reminded him of the disastrous beginning to our wedding and it seemed to settle his nerves.

When we arrived at Buxton Manor, I was greeted by my brother and sisters. Elle and Hermione were crying, and Julian said he was leaving. Great! They must have seen our father. I led the three of them away from Sebastian, he was anxious enough, he didn't need them adding to it.

"First of all, it is nothing to do with us, if Dad feels it's time to move on, then we should support him." I stated.

"But Mum," Elle began.

"No offense, Elle, but you weren't here the whole time, you didn't see what she was like. Our mum died a long time before her body gave up. Dad stuck with her until the bitter end, loyal. He is bound to be lonely now." I reasoned.

"It's too soon." Julian grumbled.

"No, actually it isn't. So, instead of acting like seven-year olds, let's give him a chance and show that we can be adult about this. Besides, she is actually really nice."

"You've met her?" Hermione demanded.

"I have, and she is lovely, she makes him happy."

"I still feel it's wrong, she would never replace our mum." Elle sniffed, I put my arm around her.

"I don't think she wants to, but we all have our own lives, none of us are kids anymore. Julian is almost twenty-one, it's time we get on with our lives and let Dad do what he needs to do."

"I'll try." Julian nodded.

"And me." Elle agreed.

We all looked at Hermione, "And you?"

"I am loyal to our mother." She stated.

"So, who says meeting Suzanna and supporting our father is not being loyal?" I queried.

When our father arrived for dinner with Suzanna, he introduced them all to her and it seemed they could all grow to like her and accept that just because our mother had died, it didn't mean he loved her or us any less. The girls headed off to their hotel in Blandford with Dad and Suzanna, Julian stayed with us and as it had been so long since I saw him last, it was nice to be able to enjoy a pint or two together.

"I'm seeing someone." Julian smiled before draining his glass.

"And?" I grinned.

"And, I think I am in love."

"You think? You don't sound very happy." I queried.

"I am, only, well. I don't think any of you will be." He stated wryly.

"Julian, I am your big brother, I have cleaned up your mess time and time again, nothing you can tell me will make me un-happy especially if it's about your love life."

"You might take that back," he warned and licked his lips nervously. "This uh, person I am seeing, well, they are hard-working, absolutely gorgeous and they make me very happy."

"That's the main thing, Jules. What's her name?" I asked.

"Charlie." He replied.

"As in Charlotte?"

"As in, Charles." Struck dumb momentarily, I just stared at his moistened top lip. "Jez?"

"Charles." I muttered and looked over at Sebastian talking to Stuart and Elliott. "So, you're…?"

"Gay." He affirmed. "You are disappointed."

"No, of course not, shocked, but not disappointed." I chuckled nervously. I couldn't believe it and did not see that coming at all.

"So, it doesn't bother you?"

I'd be a hypocrite if it did. "Julian, see Stuart and Elliott over there," I pointed to them, "they are two of my closest friends, they are gay and some of the nicest blokes I know. I am just surprised, I didn't have a clue." I admitted.

"Well, I did try the whole girl thing, I almost slept with one, but when it came down to it, I couldn't go through with it." He explained. "So, you're not disgusted or weirded out?" he checked.

"No, never. Your happiness is all that matters." I confirmed. "Does Dad know?"

"Yes, I told him the night mum died and I think that's why he left." He sat back in his seat, his hair was longer than I remembered, and he suddenly looked a lot older than his twenty-one years. "Hermie and Elle are cool with it, said it was my business, you know. I just didn't know how I could tell you. I wanted to at your wedding, then you were sick and nearly didn't make it, so… well, now you know."

"And it doesn't change a thing, you are and always will be my little brother and I love you, no matter what." I stood. "Do you want another drink?"

"Sure, but is there any cider? Lager gives me a bad stomach if I drink too much."

"I am sure there is some here. It's like a bloody pub here." I chuckled and headed to the others standing at the conservatory bar.

"Here's the best, best-man in the world." Seb announced as I approached him.

"Oh, you know it." I grinned.

"Can't believe Julian is bloody twenty-one next month." He stated.

"Yeah," I agreed. "He asked if there's cider?"

"We have everything." Sebastian stated proudly.

I phoned home just before calling it a night, well, planned on calling it a night. Sebastian had other ideas. He wanted us to drink shots into the small hours, but neither of us was up for it. Julian went to bed just after eleven. Stuart and Elliott went to the summer house leaving Sebastian and I sat in the living room.

"You're quiet, mate, are you alright?" he asked.

"I can't stop thinking about what you told me, Seb." I admitted referring to our conversation the night of the rehearsal.

"You haven't told her, have you?"

"No, but when she finds out…"

"It's not down to us to say a word, it's not our news to tell." He stated adamantly.

My insides twisted at the thought, "She is my wife, Seb, she should know."

"Well, when it's time for her to know, she will be told, in the right way, by the right person." He insisted.

"This will break her heart, you do realize that." I moaned.

"She's lucky she has you then. If and that's a big if, it's not the news we're hoping for, then we can all be there for her, but until we know for sure, why bother upsetting everyone, especially your pregnant wife?"

"I still can't get my head around the fact that she confided in you."

"I suppose I was in the right place at the right time." He shrugged. "Well, I guess it's time I got some sleep, I am sure my new wife will not be letting me get some tomorrow night." He stood from his chair.

"Are you nervous?"

"Not about getting married to Jude, I have never been more certain of anything, but I am worried about fucking it up."

"Seb, I believe in you and more importantly, she believes in you too. I am sure you will make a fine husband and don't forget, she still has that meat grinder." I added smartly.

He laughed. "Ha, ha, yes she does."

I stood also, glancing at the clock, I smiled, "Seb, it's your wedding day, look." I pointed at the clock showing it was five minutes past midnight. "Congratulations, cousin."

"Thanks." He smiled.

It took me a while to fall asleep, I hated the fact that I knew something that could possibly devastate my wife and couldn't breathe a word to her. I understood why, but I knew she would probably be more upset at being the last to know, again. I also worried about Julian, not because he was gay, that didn't bother me as much as it would have a few years back, but because of the struggle the LGBT community had to face daily. In the UK, I suppose it wasn't as bad, I was grateful it was here and not in the States or any of the other countries we had lived in for that matter.

      Being friends with Stuart certainly changed my opinion and the man who had stolen my brother's heart, all I wanted now, was to meet him, to show him that I supported my little brother. In fact, I was proud of him and the way he handled it. It made a lot of things fall into place like his troublesome years, why he had acted up so much, it seemed he was dealing with a lot more than a need to get drunk and high.

The morning flew by, we had a huge breakfast followed by a stampede to the showers in the many bathrooms in the house. Elle and Hermione arrived with our father and Suzanna. Elle had promised to help do the bridesmaid's hair and make-up. Hermione helped our Aunt with organizing the staff that were there for the day.

The guests began to arrive, so I suggested that we get into our suits. Stuart and Elliott dressed in the summer house where they had spent the night before and I went up with Sebastian. We dressed in his room, matching suits, ties and shoes, it cost me a fortune, but he was worth it. As he tried to fasten his tie, his hands were shaking.

"I thought you said you weren't nervous." I queried.

"I didn't think I was, but then it's just hit me, from twelve o'clock today I will have a wife and a mortgage to worry about." I wanted to add a baby, again, this wasn't my news and I suppose it was the same as his secret friend who had spent the last few weeks texting him at all hours for support.

"Yes, but, you are also gaining someone to share everything with, you don't have to face it alone. Jude is a great girl and she will be an amazing wife for you."

"That she will," he agreed with a proud smile. "So, how do I look?" I looked him up and down, his dark blue morning suit made his eyes seem lighter than ever. His white shirt against his skin gave him a healthy tan and his blond curls in his hair were already beginning to lighten.

"I think the term for you is a bloody catwalk model, seriously, mate, you look like you should be on a magazine cover." I grinned.

"So, do you, I mean, yes, you have gained a few pounds and the odd grey hair but…"

"What?" I frowned and rushed over to his mirror. I flicked my head from side to side checking my hair, then I caught him laughing. "Arse."

"Sorry, but you should have seen your face. You look as young as you did four years ago when we met our wives."

"I am thirty next January." I groaned.

"Age is just a number, I am only six months behind you and I haven't even had any kids yet."

"Yet." I smirked. Someone knocked his door.

"Are you decent?" Sebastian's father asked.

"We are." Seb smiled.

The door opened, and he walked in. "I have your buttonholes here," he said and handed me a white rose surrounded by small, dark blue flowers. He fixed Sebastian's to his dark blue suit and turned to me and fastened mine to my lapel.

"I must say," he grinned, "we Buxtons certainly scrub up well."

"We do," I agreed.

"It's eleven-fifty, lads, time to go to the marquee."

"Okay, Dad." Seb smiled and anxiously licked his lips.

"Let's get the ceremony out of the way, boys, then you can enjoy yourselves." He said and led us out of the room.

We left the house through the conservatory doors and walked towards the music coming from the marquee. I caught a glimpse of Saskia with the two younger bridesmaids as they waited for the car to arrive bringing Jude, Kelsey and Harry. I honestly couldn't wait to see them, I had missed them both so much, but in the back of my mind, I knew a shit storm was about to erupt and the fall out was going to be as devastating as the reason behind it.

I licked my dry lips wishing I had lifted the bottle of water on Seb's dresser and took a drink of it before we left his room. The sweet scent of the flowers decorating the marquee was drowned in two hundred different types of aftershave and perfume.

    Seb, impatiently and nervously, began jigging his right leg as he sat beside me. Avril, the registrar walked over to us and smiled.

    "She's here and she is waiting." She said and nodded over our shoulders. Sam Smith's song 'Stay With Me' began to play and we stood. Panic hit as I frantically checked my pocket for the rings, luckily remembering that Harrison was carrying them in on a pillow, I only hoped he didn't drop them. I clutched my hands in front of me and looked over my shoulder.

Jude looked so beautiful, I almost didn't recognise her, her off white dress flowed down her body in a sea of diamantes glistening in the fairy lights edging the marquee. Her eyes were fixed on Seb and I know he'd deny it, but he had tears in his eyes.

    "Daddy," Harry announced and raced towards me, he looked so cute in his little waist coat and dickie-bow tie. He almost dropped the cushion carrying the rings as he hugged me.

    "Sorry," I smiled slightly at Seb.

"It's alright." He replied. "Hey, Harry. Would you like to stay here with your dad?"

"Yes." He nodded clasping onto my leg.

Jude appeared at Seb's side, she smiled sweetly and handed her flowers to Kelsey. She smiled at me and mouthed the words 'I love you' before taking a step back to the front row of chairs that had been left for the bridesmaids.

With Harry at my side, Sebastian and Jude made their vows. To have and to hold, from this day forward. I don't know why, but it made me quite emotional. Taking me back to the day where I gave myself to my wife forever. I felt incredibly lucky and filled with warmth as I realised that no matter how many bumps were in the road, Kelsey and I could face anything together.

Harry handed the cushion to Avril and Seb placed a platinum, diamond encrusted ring on Jude's finger. She placed a platinum band on Seb's.

"I am happy to pronounce you husband and wife." Avril smiled warmly. "Sebastian, you may kiss your bride." He took her into his arms and kissed her tenderly as the marquee erupted in applause.

Kelsey stood beside me as we signed the marriage certificate and register, they wanted us both as their witnesses and I was actually quite touched that he wanted to involve me so much in his wedding.

"Are you okay?" I asked her.

"Yes, you?"

"Yes, I missed you so much." I answered.

"And I missed you." She admitted.

"Great, so if I could have the bridal party all together." The photographer announced. He grouped us around Seb and Jude, I lifted Harry into my arms, then put my arm around Kelsey.

"You look beautiful." I told her quietly.

"Thanks, you don't look half bad yourself." She replied and pressed her body against me.

After pictures, we were allowed to leave the marquee so that more pictures could be taken. Harry posed for a few but got bored and decided it was far more fun playing tag with Uncle Julian, with my father and Suzanna laughing at them.

After the pictures, drinks and canapes were served. Luckily for me, most of them were dairy free except for the ones topped with cheese. Sipping my glass of juice and munching on tiny crackers with olives and Palma ham was my idea of heaven. It had been a long time since I had anything like the food I grew up on and it sort of made me feel like I was home.

I am not a snob, not really, but I do enjoy fine food and wine, it was how I was raised, on the best and it had been so long since I'd had anything like it, I suppose it gave me that familiar fuzzy feeling that reminded me of a time when Mum was okay, and Dad had his diplomat friends over for dinner. Where the clanging of silver-wear and the chimes of crystal glasses took me right back into our dining hall. I was doing well at Eton, the girls were home from Roedean in Brighton, Julian was still a snot nosed brat, but still, life was okay and much happier then.

"Are you alright, love?" Kelsey asked me.

"Just getting a blast of nostalgia." I smiled and finished my last canape.

"What, from stale crackers and dried out ham." She chuckled.

"Well, it's the food I grew up on." I shrugged. "It took me back home."

She frowned, "I see, well, I am sorry you have had to live on commoner's muck for food the past four years." She snapped and walked away.

"She's still as hot headed as ever, I see." An American accent said from behind. I turned around and came face to face with my Texan friend, Frazier.

"Mate," I grinned putting my plate down on a table, "how are you?"

"I'm good, Jez, really good. In fact, I have some news for you."

"Spill..." I goaded.

"I am getting hitched, found me a nice little country girl, beautiful, full on English accent, she is everything I have ever wanted in a girl."

"That's great, do I know her?" I asked.

"Define knowing."

Fear and dread shot through my body, "She's not an ex of mine, is she?"

He grinned, revealing his perfect, white teeth, "Now, have I ever settled for your sloppy seconds, Buxton?"

"No." I swallowed. "So, who is she?"

"Promise you won't get mad?" he checked.

"Yes, I promise."

"Elle." He said. My mouth just dropped open.

"My sister?"

"Yes, your stunningly, beautiful little sister. We bumped into each other just after the Holidays and have been talking to each other every day since." He elucidated.

"My Elle?" I queried, was I hearing this right?

"Is there another Elle in your life?" he grinned proudly. "Elle, darlin', come on over here." He called over to her. She blushed as she approached wearing a light pink dress with beaded straps and scooped back. He put his arm around her and she smiled. "I was just telling your brother of how you stole my heart."

"I thought we were going to wait until after the wedding." She frowned.

"Why wait, your already knocked up…?"

"She's what?" I snapped, I felt the colour draining from my face.

Elle burst into hysterics, "You should see your face." She laughed.

"My face," I frowned. "I was about to break Frazier's."

"Buddy, I am having you on. Although, I am getting hitched, I met a girl in Houston, we just have to set the date." He chuckled. "Sorry, but you have always been an easy target."

"It's lucky you confessed, mate, I was about to pound seven tonnes of shit out of you." I admitted feeling my colour return.

"Seven tonnes of shit in me, I don't think so." He scoffed.

"Well, they seem to stack shit your height." I smirked as Elle left us. He began to laugh, and I have to admit, for moment there, I honestly thought he was telling the truth.

"You'll come though, right?"

"It does depend on the when the wedding is," I replied and looked over to see Kelsey chatting with my sisters. "Kelsey has about five weeks until the baby is due, and I know she would never leave the children behind."

"Well, when we have a date set, I'll send a 'save the date' and then you can see if you'd like to come. It would be amazing if you both could, but I understand if you decide not to." I nodded and looked over at my wife, she stared and then she turned her back on me.

I pursed my lips wondering how long I was in the shit for this time, "I need a drink, mate, what about you?"

"Let's find the bar." He grinned.

Thirteen

Kelsey

I watched Jeremy leave the marquee with Frazier, my stomach was in knots and I knew I had over reacted again, I just couldn't seem to help it. It had been a tense few days at home and I couldn't help but wonder what I had done so wrong this time.

Hermione and Elle made a huge fuss of Harrison and me, it was lovely to see them both again. Elle looked stunning in a candy floss pink dress with gems on the spaghetti straps over her tanned shoulders. Hermione wore a black and white dress with huge blocks of colour and matching hat.

Previous to his departure, Elle was called over to Jeremy as he spoke with Frazier, they all began to laugh, but I could see Jeremy was more relieved than happy. Elle returned and grinned,

"Frazier is such a wind up," she chuckled.

"Why?" I asked.

"He just told Jez that we are getting married, I thought Jez was going to punch him." She added.

"He looks so angry," Hermione peered over at them. "I need a refill, you up… oh, yes, sorry, Kelsey. Would you like some more fruit juice?"

"No, thanks, I need to find Harrison and take him to the loo before we sit down to eat." I looked over at Jeremy stood at the bar with Frazier, our eyes met briefly, but I turned away, I needed to find my son.

I left them, found Harrison and took him inside to the bathroom. Gretchen, Lady Buxton, smiled as we passed,

"Oh, Kelsey, we are just about to eat."

"I just need to take Harrison to the loo and we'll be right there."

"You are all on the top table, I sat you beside Jeremy and Harrison beside you."

"Thank you." I smiled and hurried to the downstairs bathroom.

As we arrived back at the marquee, Jeremy was sat at the top table alone, I walked towards him and he sighed loudly, lifting his glass to his lips. I sat Harrison in the middle of us, thinking Jeremy could share some of the responsibility of keeping Harrison in his seat and sitting nicely while we had some lunch.

"Are you in a better mood?" he asked me.

"I didn't think I needed to be in a better mood." I responded.

"Well, you snapped at me, again and walked away from me, again…"

"Because sometimes you can be a right bloody snob." I frowned.

"I am sorry then, I am sorry I had a privileged up-bringing, I am sorry that the canapes brought back some happy memories. I thought you would have been happy for me, but I was wrong again." He lifted his glass to his lips, knocking back the contents and breathing out a Jack Daniels scented breath.

"How many of those have you had?" I asked thinly.

"One, and I am just about to get another." He retorted and stood from the table.

Lord and Lady Buxton joined us as everyone began to sit down. I searched the room for my mum and Dave, they had been invited, though said they couldn't stay for the whole thing. They were going to take Harrison home early so that Jeremy and I could stay, not that I wanted to now.

Jeremy returned, and our starters arrived, melon balls, in early April, they were so cold they gave me a brain freeze. Harrison thought they were ice-lolly lumps and began licking them. Jeremy and I barely shared a word during the meal, his demeaner was frostier than the starter. At least the main course was roasted meat with vegetables and warmed me up a lot.

After dessert the speeches began, Jeremy stood beside me and cleared his throat,

"Can I have your attention please?" he asked. As everyone turned to face the head table, I noticed my mum then with Dave, looking incredible from across the marquee in a lilac suit. She smiled when she saw me, and it caused a lump in my throat, I just wanted to leave. "Thank you. For those of you who don't know me, I am Jeremy, Sebastian's cousin and only friend. So, I sort of had to be best man, he didn't have anyone else he could ask." He smiled.

"Cheeky bugger." Sebastian scoffed.

"You know it's true." Jeremy chuckled. "Anyway, almost four years ago, I moved here from London and Sebastian let me move in with him. That weekend we met a couple of cracking girls, they were best friends and had come to a party here at the Manor. Sorry, Auntie Gretchen, nothing was broken, promise. I remember Sebastian bringing this fiery red-haired knock-out over and introduced her to me, "This is Jude." He said proudly and then introduced me to my amazing uh, wife, Kelsey." I smiled awkwardly as all eyes seemed to look at me. "I didn't know how things would turn out and had no idea that these girls would even give us a chance, let alone agree to marrying us, we Buxtons have a reputation, luckily they looked beyond that and here we are. The road isn't easy, there are more bumps than one cares to admit, but the journey is enriched and so much more worthwhile with an incredible girl riding that road with you."

"I'll be honest with you, I had no idea of what sort of speech to do, I mean, this is my second time at being a best man, but for two completely different people, one is debonair, charismatic, charming and the other one is well, Sebastian." Laughter echoed out. "I decided to look up best man speeches on the internet. It's amazing how much is on there, two hours later I realized I should be looking up some tips for the speech. It's not all a waste of time though, I did come away with two Russian marriage proposals, a gadget that makes all vegetables into spaghetti and a booked appointment for Sebastian, it's tomorrow night with a beautiful girl called Donna Makes Tricks, weird name, but I am not one to judge. I am sure she will be lovely, you know, especially if Jude decides to finally use that meat grinder on you." More laughter. It's lucky I knew he was joking.

"I am actually quite nervous today, I mean, the last time I had to stand up in front of people and speak, I was found guilty." If only everyone laughing knew how not funny that was. Jeremy could have been the one on trial only a few weeks ago. "So, what can I say about my cousin? He is charming, good looking, rich, (yeah, right) uh… sorry, Seb, I can't read your writing here, is that hung like a donkey, or has an eye that is wonky?" That made me laugh, it settled my tightening stomach. "So, I could talk about our school days at Eton, but between suspensions for drinking, constant detentions and trying to date Miss Falmer, our drama teacher, we didn't really have much time left. I could also talk about the teenage years, where Seb had so many spots, that had he been charged per head to get into a night club, he would have blown his month's allowance on getting in. Or about his job, where he is called God, no one ever sees him and if he actually does any work, it's a bloody miracle." He laughed. A few whoops came from the back.

"Joking aside though, Sebastian and Jude make a wonderful couple and if I could give you some advice, it would be to lie, steal and cheat. Lie in the arms of the one you love, steal every moment of happiness that life has to offer and cheat every adversity. Never go to sleep on an argument, stay up all night fighting, the make up after is amazing. One thing I have learned from my marriage, know when to be wrong, even though you might be right, in her eyes, you will always be wrong." A lot of the men clapped and cheered. I just glared up at my husband barely recognising him at all. "Jude love, you look absolutely beautiful, Seb is a lucky man, the bridesmaids, I am sure you'll agree, they look stunning. But as I am married to the maid of honour, I suppose I could be biased. Thank you, that's it except, don't forget, my name is Jeremy, what are you drinking? If you see me at the bar later. Please raise your glasses and join me in wishing Jude and Sebastian a lifetime of love, laughter and happiness." We raised our glasses, "To the bride and groom."

He sat down beside me to an applause and drank down his glass of Jack and coke, blowing out a relieved sigh.

"Was that okay?" he asked.

"Yes." I muttered.

Sebastian stood and pulled a piece of paper from his pocket,

"Thank you, dear cousin, I am docking fifty quid from your payment for that." He smiled. "Right, well, I am a man of few words, so I just want to thank you all for coming today, it means the world to us both that you could be here. Jeremy, as you are all in the wedding party, Jude and I wanted to do something for you as a family to thank you for everything you and Kelsey have done for us, so, we have booked you a week away in Jersey, where you can take the new baby when it arrives and have a much-needed holiday." He handed Jeremy an envelope and winked at me, I hugged Jude quickly and pecked her cheek with watery eyes. "I think you will all agree they are an amazing family and support, we are all lucky to have them in our lives." Applause rattled around us as I wiped my eyes quickly. "Stuart and Elliott, our ushers, this is for you." He held up gift bags for them, "Elliott stepped in on Wednesday, so thank you both. To my sister, Saskia, we also booked you a weekend away with Jack, but… well, you can take a friend instead." She came to the table and took her envelope.

"Mum Buxton and Mum Mitchell, Jude lifted two huge bouquets of flowers with gift bags and gave it them as they stood. Dad Buxton and Dad Mitchell, these are for you, we just want to thank you all, Jude's sister, Marnie, not only allowed her daughters to be our flower girls, but she also made the beautiful flowers, so we have also booked you a family week away at Butlins in the half term at the end of the month." Red faced and grinning, she came to the table, Sebastian handed her an enveloped and she kissed his cheek, then embraced Jude before leaving. "There is just one more thing I have to say, to my beautiful wife, Jude, you left me speechless today, I didn't think I could ever love you more than I did already, but you proved me wrong. You have changed me, tamed me and you have made me a better man. Thank you for accepting my proposal, for putting up with me and most of all, thank you for making me the happiest man alive today." He pulled another envelope from his pocket. "I know things have been a bit tense recently, so, here's part of the reason why. This is the deeds to a brand-new house, newly built in Blandford, it will be ready in two weeks when we get back off our honeymoon."

"What?"

"I bought us a house," he smiled.

"Seriously?"

"Yes." He nodded. She stood and threw her arms around him, as they parted she whispered something to him. "Really?" she nodded. He kissed her deeply and brushed a tear out of his eye, "Uh, Jude has just informed me that she is expecting, we're having a baby." He announced, the marquee erupted in applause once more.

I brushed away my own tears. The day had already been a whirlwind and now with everyone around me getting all they want, it made me realise just how much trouble Jeremy's and my marriage was in. they were only just beginning, were we coming to the end?

While the marquee was set up for the evening reception, I went to see if I could find my mother, I needed to know if she was leaving early, I wanted a lift. I was not going to watch Jeremy drink himself senseless and then try and get him home, I had already spent a night without him, I was sure I could survive another.

"Sit down, love." Mum said as I found them sat on some garden furniture. "Jeremy is getting us some drinks." She smiled as I sat at the table with them. Harrison was sat on Dave's knee and I could see he was exhausted.

"I wonder if they'll mind if I find somewhere for Harrison to take a nap." I said.

"We're going soon," Dave said. "He can come home with us and sleep at ours tonight. I am sure Jeremy will be a bit hung-over tomorrow."

"The way he is knocking back Jack, I am afraid you're right." I sighed and slipped my feet out of my shoes. "My feet are killing me."

"Here you go, Jane, one Pimm's no ice and a shandy for Dave." He placed two glasses on the table.

"Thanks, son." Dave smiled.

"That was a really good speech, Jeremy." Mum praised. "Where did you find the jokes?"

"A best man website, it was nerve wracking, more so because I know most of the people here. At Felix and Nicki's wedding, I hardly knew anyone. It was much easier."

"Well, you wouldn't have known, sweetheart, would you, Kelsey? It was a good speech."

"Yes, it was." I agreed and pulled my dress up. My feet had swollen. "I need my flat shoes," I frowned. "I'll go and find Nicki, she has my bag."

"I'll go and get the bag, love," Jeremy said as he stood. "You rest those feet."

"You have a wonderful husband there, Kelsey." Mum grinned proudly. "And how kind are Sebastian and Jude, a week's holiday in Jersey, that's fantastic." I could only nod, yeah, a holiday, but what if we do split up, what then?

Harrison fell asleep on Dave's lap, which was so cute. I had put my feet up on a spare chair and sipped the milky cup of tea Jeremy had got for me. I could see he was trying, but his eyes held something that petrified me, it felt as though he were slipping through my fingers, all I could do was watch as he walked around speaking to the guests, kissing and hugging women I could only assume he knew, laughing with Seb and his brother, who had barely spoken to me as well.

Mum excused herself for the ladies and said, as she stood, that it was time to go. Harrison still slept soundly and although Jeremy popped back a few times, he didn't seem bothered if we were there or not.

"I'm going to come back with you." I told Dave and stood to find Jude. I caught a glimpse of her, she beckoned me over.

"Look." She said holding Seb's phone out in her hand, "She's here, J is here. *'Darling, you look gorgeous, so glad to be a part of your day. Have something to tell you, meet me inside in ten minutes, J.'* She is bloody here, and I want to find out what's going on." She grabbed hold of my hand and towed me with her.

We stormed through the house, I could hear voices, and as we rounded the corner into the living room, Sebastian was hugging my mother.

"Mum?" I frowned.

"Hiya, love." She smiled and brushed away some tears. "What's up?"

"You tell me." I stated as she stepped back from Seb.

"I found your phone, Sebastian." Jude growled angrily. "Where is she?"

"What?" he frowned.

"The tart you have been texting with, where is she? I know she's here."

"Jude, what on earth are you…?" Seb frowned.

"I read your messages, she is here, and I want to know what is going on?" she demanded. Seb's parents arrived with Jeremy. I just stared at my mum, why was she crying? Was there something going on between her and Seb?

"Okay," Seb stepped further away from my mum, "I'll explain later."

"No, I want to know now, I want to know if I need to get this marriage annulled."

"Oh, for Christ sake." He snapped. "I am not and nor have I ever been cheating on you, Jude."

"Jude, sweetheart, I think I need to explain something." My mum said quietly. "I have been the one texting Sebastian, it was me, it's nothing sordid, it's just that…" she looked at am. "I found some lumps in my breast, I had a mammogram and they wanted to take biopsies to check for cancer. I had just been given this news and wandered into Poole. I bumped into Sebastian and burst into tears." She explained. I heard everything, but all I could think about was that my mum has cancer. First my dad and now my mum. "Sebastian has been texting me to check that I am alright and trying to cheer me up with pictures of fancy and funny wigs in case I had to have chemo. I didn't want to say anything until I knew for sure, so he and Dave are the only ones to know." She looked at Jeremy, I followed her line of sight and his eyes lowered, he knew too. "I got the 'all clear' yesterday and happy to announce that I don't have cancer after all."

"So, I haven't been cheating, Jude, just looking out for Kelsey's mum."

"Kelsey?" Mum frowned at me. That's when I felt the wetness of my cheeks. "I am alright, love."

"You thought you had cancer and you didn't tell me. I made you look after Harrison, I made you have him more than normal and you have been through surgery and everything. I am glad you are okay, I am, but I am bloody furious with you, Mum."

"Hey, Kelsey," Jeremy said and appeared at my side. "She was worried because of you getting stressed with the baby and everything." I turned to him.

"So, you knew." I frowned.

"I found out Wednesday." He admitted. My eyes filled with tears, that's when he changed towards me. "I wanted to tell you, but it wasn't my news to tell you."

"You knew that my mum could possibly have cancer and you kept it to yourself." I accused. "Do you hate me that much?"

"No, not at all." He replied. I turned around and looked at my mum, at Jude and then Sebastian.

"I'm leaving." I said.

"Kelsey," Jude came towards me, "please don't leave."

"I'm sorry, but I can't be here with liars, with people who keep things from me, who try to protect me. I thought that had ended last year when my husband was practically forced into having an affair."

"Kelsey, I didn't…" Jeremy began. I raised my hand.

"I am going." I said again.

Mum stepped forward, "Come on, love, if you want to blame anyone, blame me."

"Oh, Mum, believe me, I do blame you, in fact. Fuck you all. I am done with this life, with lies and secrets with bloody excuses, but most of all, I am done with the Buxtons, you are a breed like no other." I walked towards the door. Jeremy turned as I passed him. "Do not follow me and do not come home tonight. I don't want to hear, see or speak to any of you right now. If you follow me, I will leave, and you will never see me or your children again." I snarled.

"That's not fair," Jude called out.

"I know, it's just how I feel." I replied and hurried outside.

I found Nicki and pulled her away from Felix.

"Kelsey, what is it?"

"I need to leave," I cried, "can you give me a lift?"

"What's happened?"

"I'll tell you on the way home."

"Okay, I'll tell Felix, you get your things." I nodded and walked towards Dave.

"Kelsey, love, are you alright?"

"I'm going, can you give me Harrison's car seat please?" Elle came running up to me.

"Jeremy has just smashed his fist into the living room wall, what has happened?"

"Ask him?" I frowned.

"I have, and he said to stop you leaving, that you need to sort this out."

"If I stay, I will ask him for a divorce. I need time to think, tell him to respect my wishes and to stay away from me."

"I don't know what he has done…" she began to cry, "he is so upset in there."

"I just need to go home, Elle." I hugged her quickly and left. Nicki carried Harrison who was still sleeping to her car. Dave hurried over with the seat and I strapped him in.

"Thank you, Dave, look after my mum, okay?"

"Oh, Kelsey," he sighed. I hugged him goodbye and climbed into Nicki's car.

I explained everything to her as we drove home, she said she understood how I felt, but thought that I was punishing Jeremy when I was really angry at my mother. I can't say that I was angry, I was more upset than anything, upset and disappointed. Everyone, all through my life, had treated me with kid gloves. I was not a delicate flower, I nursed my father to his death for God sake. I did not need protecting from the truth, all I ever wanted was the truth.

The times over the weeks where I had dumped Harrison off on my mother, not knowing that she was sick and had lumps cut out of her breasts. I felt terrible that she had gone through this alone, well, not alone, but without me. She would have expected me to be honest with her if it was me.

When we got back to the house, Nicki came in to make sure I was okay. I thanked her for bringing us home and hugged her goodbye. I put Harrison to bed, fully clothed and then went to my room. I undressed and went to the bathroom, staring at my reflection, I gazed at my eyes, edged in red where I had cried so much, angry at myself for not being stronger, for running away again and for leaving Jude on her important day. But I knew she'd be alright, she had her sisters and her husband now.

I showered and put on my night gown before going into my room, staring at the bed, the bed where Jeremy and I had slept so many nights together, I knew there was no way I could sleep in there for a while.

I went down stairs and made sure everything was locked up. Pulled the curtains closed and sat on the couch. In my head, I was right to do what I did, in my mind I thought I would be fine, my heart had other ideas.

Jeremy and I had more heartache than most, we have been through so much, but he had let me down again and I knew I couldn't carry on in a relationship where one half found it so easy to lie to me. Was I that stupid, that dense? Everyone treated me like a flower, with delicate petals, weak and pathetic.

I switched on the TV and stared at the screen, it was almost eight o'clock and no one had dared to try and contact me, it had been an hour since I left them, and they had done as I asked, they had left me alone, for now.

Fourteen

Jeremy

Her perfume lingered long after she had walked away. Jane burst into tears, apologising to everyone as anger and humiliation filtered through my veins, Kelsey had threatened me with my children and that was not acceptable. Hermione and Elle came in, asking for the happy couple to come and start their first dance.

Jane sat down, my aunt asked my uncle to make her a cup of tea and I just stood there.

"Jez," Seb frowned.

"It's fine," I insisted. "I'm fine."

"She'll calm down, you'll be talking by ten." He said as he tapped my shoulder. I nodded as he passed towing his bride behind him.

"Jez, perhaps you should go out and try to find her." My uncle suggested as he handed a cup to Jane.

"Did you not hear the part where she threatened to disappear taking my kids with her if I did?" I demanded angrily. "I am so sick of living like this, of always being wrong, of never being allowed to make a decision."

"Jez?" Elle tried to reason.

"I have had enough." I snarled. I wanted to hit something, "No one knows what she has put me through, none of you." Hermione reached her hand towards me, "Don't Hermie, just, leave me alone." I growled. "I can't do anything right, no matter what I do… I give up."

"She'll calm down, Jeremy." My uncle offered.

"You don't know her," I roared. I turned around, saw the wall. "Threatening me, how dare she?" Wham, my fist made contact with the living room wall, blood exploded from my knuckles and I gazed at them while the ache throbbed, and my knuckles came back to life. Hermione wrapped a handkerchief around my hand as Elle left the room. "I'm sorry." I muttered. "I am so sorry."

"Jeremy," my father said from behind. Elle was crying, and my father put his arm around me. "Come on, son, let's go and get some ice for that hand."

I sat at the kitchen counter while my dad hunted the freezer. From the marquee, I could hear an applause and music began to play. Ed Shearing's song, 'Thinking out Loud' echoed out around the house. Jude and Seb were having their first dance and their best man was sat in the kitchen with ice on his knuckles.

"What happened?" Dad asked. I told him everything and how I had been feeling for the past few weeks. "I thought things were tense when I arrived, but I had no idea that it had gotten so bad for you, son."

"It's not all her fault, I realise that, but I suppose you can only say you are sorry so many times. I mean, am I supposed to spend the rest of our lives together apologising for everything day in and day out? That's not a marriage, Dad, it's not even a relationship."

"So, what do you want to do?"

"I don't know. Mark has offered me a promotion to work in London for a year, maybe I should take it."

"It won't be easy, son." He warned.

"I know, but if I am not here, then I can't miss them as much."

"You will miss them no matter what. I do know one thing, you are going to have to talk to her, you need to tell her what you are feeling and what you are thinking of doing. She has a right to know, Jeremy." I nodded and sighed. "Do you want to go to her now, I could drive you?"

"No, I'll stay here tonight, just as she ordered me to." I affirmed.

"Okay, so come and get a stiff drink, everything will look brighter and better in the morning."

"I truly hope so." I admitted.

I sat at the bar for the rest of the evening, Stuart and Elliott hovered around me and tried to reassure me that everything would be alright, but I knew that nothing would ever be alright again.

The happy couple's taxi arrived just after ten to take them to the airport. They were going to spend a week at Lake Garda in Italy and I was so jealous, a week away from everything seemed extremely appealing that night. I watched them leave and turned to my family. They all looked concerned and I suppose that they had every right to be.

My life was about to change and as much as I loved my wife and children, I couldn't go on like this. My eyes filled with tears at the concept of losing them all, I turned away and hurried to the pond at the back of the house, I just wanted to be pathetic and alone.

"Come on, Jez." Hermione said putting her arm around me. "Kelsey will cool down and then…"

"Until something else triggers her off. I can't do this anymore, I can't, I would rather be on my own than live with a ticking time bomb."

"She loves you, Jez, that is obvious." She tried to assure me.

"Okay, and where does it say that you can treat the one you love like this? I didn't tell her, I try to protect her from everything because knowing something I said hurts her, that all but cripples me."

"So, you're contemplating leaving her then, you'd walk away from Kelsey and the children because she doesn't want you to protect her from the truth?"

"Being on my own has to be better than living like this."

"Yeah, you should try it sometime, then you'll really know how horrible it is. You left Tara and met Kelsey then you left Kelsey and went back with Tara, you have never been single for more than a few weeks."

"I have, I have been so alone and felt like nothing and guess who made me feel like that last time, Kelsey." I snapped and moved away from her. I turned to face her. "All I have ever done is try to keep her happy, well, not anymore." I began to walk away.

"Where are you going?" she chased me.

"To speak to my boss, he is here somewhere." I affirmed, marching towards the marquee. I saw Mark dancing with Steven, walked over to him and tapped him on the shoulder.

"Jeremy, are you cutting in?" he asked.

"No," I blushed slightly, "sorry, but can I have a word?"

"I'll get us some drinks." Steven said and left us. Mark and I walked off the dancefloor, my families' eyes were boring into my back.

"About that promotion."

"Yes."

"When can I start?"

"Are you sure, is Kelsey okay with it?" he asked.

"It's not up to her, it's my life and I am saying yes." I stated.

"I could probably get you up there by Wednesday next week."

"Great, I'll be in Monday, so, we'll sort it all out then." I tapped his shoulder with my throbbing hand, "Thanks, Mark."

"Sure, Jeremy. No problem."

I then went to the bar, got a bottle of Jack Daniels and a glass. Julian came over to me,

"Want to share that?" he asked.

"Not particularly," I said lifting it, "but okay, get yourself a glass and meet me in the conservatory." I told him and left the marquee.

After three glasses, the pain of the previous few hours began to dissipate, as was the growing angst against my wife. I knew I was, what I call, silly drunk, because I texted her.

'Hope u r okay'

A few moments later, she replied.

'I can't sleep, but I am fine'

'Me neither' I replied.

"Jez," Julian frowned. "Leave her alone."

"I am." I sighed. "So, how did you meet Charlie?"

"He works at a bar in the city, I was there with a few friends and we got talking."

"So, he's a barman?"

"No, he is a law student, but works in the bar at night."

"And was it 'love at first sight'?" I asked.

"Um, well, I fancied him, if that's what you mean." He smiled. "We talked for hours and met up a few times before anything remotely romantic happened."

"I am happy for you," I smiled. "Just remember me in this state though, love was something I thought, worth fighting for, but when the fighting takes up more space than love in a relationship, it leaves you this empty shell. I feel hollow."

"It's just a bump in the road, Jez. Everything will work out, you'll see."

"Not this time, buddy." I sighed wryly.

I woke early, which surprised me, after drinking almost a bottle of Jack with my little brother, I thought I would have at least slept till ten. I remembered Kelsey's face as she discovered that those she loved and trusted had all let her down and then I remembered her threat. Anger began to rear its ugly head again and it wasn't until I sat up, that my head began to thump.

Julian slept soundly on the couch in my room. I have no idea why he decided to share my room he had his own, but I was glad to see him. Had he not been there, I feared I probably would have just gone home.

I pulled my jeans over my boxers and a clean t-shirt over my head before standing, slowly, from my bed. My mouth felt like I have been licking the pavement and my eyes were so sore, I had no idea of why, but when I got down to the kitchen, my uncle greeted me and explained how upset I was when they had put me to bed at one in the morning. So, not only had my wife humiliated me by scorning and threatening me like a child, I evidentially bawled my sodding eyes out and became a snivelling mess who had to be assisted to bed by a bloody Lord. Add the fact that my knuckles were still sore with black scabs over them, I looked a sight.

After a black coffee and some hot toast with jam, I took some paracetamol and decided that it was time to go home. My aunt informed me that my father had arranged for us all to go out to lunch before everyone was to leave to return to their lives and a huge part of me wished I could go with them.

Just after eleven, Julian emerged from his bed. Elliott's brother came to collect him, and Stuart and I asked if I could get a lift with them. Julian insisted on coming with us, so that I didn't make an arse of myself with Kelsey.

"I had no idea this was going on." Stuart muttered beside me in the back of the car.

"Well, it's all blown up in our faces." I sighed.

"She'll welcome you in with open arms," he nudged me. "She loves you."

"You should have seen the way she looked at me." I frowned.

"Yes, but we all know with Kelsey, she blows up and then regrets it."

"She'll regret it this time, that's for sure." I muttered.

"Why, what's going on?"

"You'll see."

I gave Elliott's brother, Tim, ten pounds for giving us a lift and climbed out. Stuart said he would come home later, after things had calmed down. Julian took a nervous gulp just before I put my keys into the lock.

"Maybe I should take a walk down to the shop, I could use a can of coke."

"You don't have to."

"I think you both need to talk." He insisted and walked back up the drive.

The TV was on in the living room as I passed it, I could smell strong disinfectant and Fabreeze, Kelsey's new way of dealing with stress seemed to be by doing housework, well, when she wasn't screaming at me.

She was wiping over the counters when I entered the kitchen, she stopped immediately when she saw me standing there.

"I didn't hear you come in." She said.

"I had my keys." I replied.

"So, did it all go off alright?"

I shrugged my shoulders, "I suppose."

"Where is all of your stuff?" she enquired glancing over my shoulder.

"At the Manor."

"Aren't you staying then?" she then asked wiping the table over with the cloth in her hand.

"After what I have to say, I doubt you'll want me to stay." I frowned.

She stopped wiping the table and looked up. "I see." She said and pulled off her Marigolds.

"You might want to sit down." I said pulling out a chair and sitting at the table.

"Aren't you even going to ask where Harrison is?" she asked frostily.

"No, I assume he is either upstairs or out with your parents."

"Actually, he is out with your sisters, they came here last night so that I wasn't alone." She explained as she sat opposite.

"That's nice of them." I grumbled.

"Okay, say what you have to say."

"I'm moving to London for a year."

"What?"

"I was offered a promotion and I accepted it last night." I elucidated.

"Without talking to me about it?"

"I was planning on speaking to you first and then, well, you know what happened."

Her eyes filled with tears and pain shot through my heart, it hurt so much to say this to her, it almost crippled me.

"So, um, you just decided to leave us."

"You know how bad things have been, even after all the promises of changes, it means nothing if it's not followed through. I can't take much more, Kelsey, as much as I love you, I would rather walk away now than watch you grow to hate me more and more each day. I can't do it and I won't."

"We have just bought a new house, we are expecting another baby and Harrison, he will be devastated."

"I know, but I can't help how I feel. I'm sorry…"

"You're sorry," she sniffed. "Well, that's makes everything all right then."

"Kelsey," I began. "You need to listen to me. I am not allowing you to call the shots anymore, you are not having that power over me. I have done it before and I will do it again if I have to. I am taking back control of my life, these past four years you have been chipping away at me and piece by piece, I am falling apart. I am losing the will to go on and that is not right."

"So, you get to go away and abandon us, doing whatever you want, and I have to raise your children?" she snarled.

"It's either I go away now with the intention of returning when the contract ends, or I stay and do nothing as I watch the love I feel for you change and wither until it turns to contempt and eventually hate. I love you, I love you with everything that I am, but I am only a man, a man who has made mistakes and been a bit gullible, regardless of that, I still deserve respect. You don't respect me, you have treated me like a child and I feel I have no say in anything. You have called all of the shots, you ended our relationship before, you would have gone through life allowing me to believe that Harry was the result of a one-night stand and when all of this shit blew up over Natasha Mason, it was you who decided that we would get through it. The time apart will…"

"Destroy us." She frowned, her voice cracking under the strain of emotion.

"It won't be easy, I'll miss you and Harry, but I can't stay." I glared at the table, if I had looked into her eyes, I probably would have crumbled.

"So, when are you leaving?" she asked, I looked up at her, her eyes were full of tears, but she wouldn't let them drop as the end of her nose turned pink.

I felt the tingle in my own eyes, and adjusted in my seat as I replied, "Wednesday."

"This week?"

"Yes."

"Right, well, are you going to be staying here before you go or…?"

"I don't think that will be a good idea, do you?"

"I suppose not. What about the move? Will you come back for that?"

"If I can, I will be there for when the baby comes too."

"No, you will not." She stood. "You want to go and search for your soul, then fine, but as for moving, I will withdraw the offer and decline the sale of this place. Where this baby is concerned, you will not be a part of its birth. If you are abandoning us, then that's up to you. You don't get to pick and choose when you will be and won't be a part of this family."

"I'll go and pack some clothes." I stood abruptly, the chair screeched on the floor.

I hurried upstairs and into our room. On the floor, by the chest of drawers, lay our wedding album. Picking it up from the floor, I sat on the edge of the bed, I opened the first page and stared at her, how beautiful she looked that day, remembering how all I wanted was make her happy, spend my life making her life better and all I seemed to do was make it worse.

I snapped it shut, not wanting to be reminded of that incredible day, not wanting to face the cold hard fact that I was breaking her heart again. I felt suddenly sick, my hands were shaking, and my head thumped. I hurried to the bathroom and threw up my breakfast down the toilet. The more I thought about actually walking out of that door, possibly forever, my insides twisted and heaved.

I rinsed my mouth and brushed my teeth, to help my mouth feel better, but that was all, nothing I did was right. I learned a long time ago that reverse psychology never worked on Kelsey, she would rather take the pain than admit she was wrong. Technically she wasn't, the thing that upset and angered me the most was how she turned on me, her mother hadn't told her something and it was all my fault.

I found my cases and began to pack my clothes into them, my heart shredding as I did so. This was not the way I planned it, I was hurt and angry, but I hoped she would agree that a break would do us both the world of good. In my head, it had worked out perfectly, but I should have known by now, Kelsey would never admit that I was right about anything.

I could have quite easily gone down to her and admitted I was wrong and screwing up again, but I knew that in a few weeks, I would regret it. As much as this hurt us, as much as the thought of losing her forever almost killed me, I knew I had to go through with this. I had to show her that I was done taking threats and orders.

After packing as much as I could, I carried my cases down the stairs. As I got closer to the kitchen, I could hear her crying, sobbing, in fact. Maybe all was not lost, maybe there was a little hope for us. I stood and waited until her sobs slowed, my heart felt as though it were being crushed knowing this was because of me. I placed my cases on the floor and stepped into the kitchen. She saw me and turned away, wiping her eyes with a soggy tissue.

"Have you seen my car keys?" I asked.

"On the table by the door." She replied without turning to me.

"Thanks." I frowned and turned to leave.

"I didn't know," she said. I turned back to her, she was still facing the wall, but glanced over her shoulder, "I didn't know that I made you feel like I didn't respect you, I can only apologise for that."

"Thank you," I muttered. She turned to face me. The agony I was causing her, already left scars on her face, she was devastated.

"I didn't mean any of it, I never do, not really. It's just easier for me to throw out spiteful words, than to believe that you might be right. If you want to leave, I can't stop you, but know that I would never cut you out of the children's lives. I may be losing you, but it doesn't mean that they should suffer because of me." She sniffed. "So, good luck with your job." She walked towards me, I caught her scent as she passed me and walked towards the stairs.

"It's not the end of us, Kelsey. I wish you could understand that. I don't want to lose you and that's why I think a break will help us both."

She turned to face me again. "If you need to go a hundred miles away to try and *save our marriage*, then all hope is lost for us to ever recover from this." She snapped.

"That's not true, I'll be home every other weekend, I'll be here for when the baby comes, and I will be on the end of the phone whenever you need me." I reasoned.

Her eyes finally spilled over and tears streamed her face, it crushed my heart to see her so upset, but I had to do this. "I knew you'd leave, I knew you would break my heart again."

"I am not leaving you, and the last thing I want is to hurt you." I insisted and moved towards her. She wiped her face with a quivering hand and looked down at my cases. "Can I come and see you Tuesday night, before I go? I'd like to see Harrison, if that's okay."

"If you want." She sniffed. "I am sure he will want to see you."

"And what about you?"

"What about me? I don't count, do I? Not to you or anyone. I am just a flipping princess who is to be locked up in a tower away from the truth because it might hurt me, away from secrets in case I flip my lid. That's me, sad, pathetic, Kelsey, she can't cope with anything, she isn't woman enough to face facts. There she goes, the one who is as fragile as glass and as stupid as they come." She retorted. "Goodbye, Jeremy." She then ran up the stairs and slammed our bedroom door closed." Suddenly my plan didn't seem the right thing to do after all.

I stood there, staring up the stairs listening to my wife as she fell to pieces and why, because I broke her. My hands were already shaking, and I felt so sick again, I was about to run up to her when the doorbell rang. I pulled it open and Julian frowned at me,

"Is everything alright?" he asked. "I can hear crying from outside."

"No, um, come in." I told him.

"I am guessing she didn't take your news too well."

"I don't know what to do." I sighed, I truly didn't.

Fifteen

Kelsey

It's remarkable what goes through your head when the house is still and all you can hear is the ticking of the clock in the hall. Memories of good times and bad, of my dad's death and funeral, of the night we met. Jeremy and I had been through more in a four-year relationship than most couples see in a lifetime together.

I couldn't shake the feeling that something bad was going to happen, my insides twitched all night and I couldn't relax. I realised very quickly that nothing about this was Jeremy's fault, not really. He had this infuriating trait where he felt he had to protect me, to stop something hurting me, he would prefer I didn't know about it. I thought, after the previous year, that he would have realized that I always preferred to hear the truth, no matter how painful it was.

Shortly after the reception finished, a gentle knock rattled on my front door. Elle and Hermione both frowned as I pulled it open, secretly hoping it was Jeremy.

"We wanted to make sure you were okay." Hermione explained.

"Come in." I told them. They followed me inside. "Did you come on your own merit or did Jeremy send you?" I asked leading them into the lounge.

"He is, as we speak, drowning his sorrows in a bottle of Jack Daniels." Elle replied. "He has no idea that we were coming here."

"Is he um… is he alright?"

"No." Hermione replied bluntly.

"Is he alone?"

"Julian is with him." Elle answered.

"Please, have a seat." I said and curled my foot under me as I sat in the arm chair.

"What the hell happened today?"

I pursed my lips and rolled my eyes before telling them everything that had been going on between us. How we came to be at a wedding and fighting. I felt bad for talking about our relationship to his sisters, but at the same time, it was nice to off load onto them. Jude had been too busy and my mum, well, she was sick. I'd had no one, not even Stuart.

"You two need help." Hermione grumbled.

"I know, but when I suggested it, he told me that he would want a divorce if a counsellor told us how bad things really are."

"Are things really that bad?" Elle asked.

"I'm angry, all of the time and I don't know why." I admitted. "I don't know if it was what happened with Natasha or if it goes back further. I do know that I love him with all of my heart and

I do know there would never be another, but I honestly don't know if us being together is right for us."

"Of course, it's right. Look at what you have built together, Harrison is yummy, and you have another one on the way." Elle insisted. "If any couple belongs together more, it's you and Jez."

"If that's true, why do we keep doing this to each other?" I asked.

"That's love." She smiled. "Come on, no relationship is plain sailing and you two have been through so much. Jez was practically raped by that hussy and then he was rushed in to surgery, which, I might add, saved his life. It's been one thing after another, but somehow, you always seem to find a way to get through it." She made sense and I suppose she was right, no, actually she was right. We were stronger together. We would sort this out because that is what we did.

"That, which doesn't kill us, makes us stronger." Hermione added.

"Look at me, my manners. Would either of you like a drink?" I asked feeling slightly better.

"I'd love a cup of coffee," Hermione smiled.

"Tea for me, if you don't mind." Elle added.

"Of course, I don't mind."

They decided to stay the night to keep me company and went up to sleep in my bed, I was going to stay on the sofa, but promised if it got too uncomfortable, I'd use Stuart's bed. A text message buzzed on my phone from Jeremy, asking if I was okay. I suppose I was but admitted I couldn't sleep. He replied bluntly that he was having trouble too and I'd be lying if I said it didn't ease my insides a bit. But sleep didn't find me, so, I spent the night cleaning, emptying the fridge, scrubbing the floors of the kitchen and utility room.

    Around four in the morning, I pushed open the door to Jeremy's office. The strong odour of his aftershave mixed with coffee and cedar wood furniture polish filled my lungs. Bringing him home and standing him right in front of me. I wanted him there, needing his arms to fold around me as I begged him for forgiveness.

    I knew that I should never have threatened him like that, it took me all night to realize that, but I only hoped after a good night's sleep, he would come home, and we would do the one thing we did well, make up.

I must have dozed off on the couch, though it was daylight when my eyes finally closed. I felt a warm hand on my shoulder and opened my eyes, Elle handed me a cup of tea and said that she and Hermione wanted to take Harrison out for a few hours. I agreed if only to have an empty house for when Jeremy came home so that I could grovel in private.

I didn't hear Jeremy come home, lost in a world of dirty counters, well, they were in my eyes. I wiped over them vigorously.

Everything had to smell and look clean, it had become a way of coping with stressful times.

     I felt my face harden as he told me what he was doing, he had finally grown a pair of balls and decided to leave me. That's all I heard, truth be told, working away in London, not being here with me, growing to hate me, leaving me. I retaliated in the only way I knew how, I bit back and felt terrible as soon as he left the kitchen to pack.

     What would I do, how would I cope without him there? He was my everything and I had finally done it, I had pushed so hard that he couldn't take it anymore. I wondered where he would live in London, how I would manage the bills, not to mention the fact that we had sold our house and bought another. I couldn't go through that alone, not without his support.

Washing the sink out of disinfectant, that's when it hit me, the one thing I had feared, the one thing that petrified me was losing him and I had. I had lost the love of my life because I was mean and stubborn, I was selfish and angry. I fought against my tears, fought hard, but I couldn't stop the wale leaving my body as reality chipped at my walls. Jeremy was leaving me, and I didn't know what I was going to do.

After he had packed two cases and come back to the kitchen, I apologised to him, allowing my wall to build again, I told him to go, to do what he had to do. It crushed me on the inside, so much so, that I couldn't watch him leave, but I couldn't make him stay and I certainly wouldn't beg. He had made up his mind, he had decided this was what he needed to do, to make him stay now would be wrong.

My heart exploded in my chest as I said the mortal words, "Goodbye, Jeremy." And ran up to our room. Where the emptiness I felt all those summers ago when he had to leave me to wed Tara, smothered me like a blanket. Crawling over my head and pulling me down.

My legs collapsed under me and I fell to the floor, where I sobbed and sobbed. Every part of my body hurt, writhing in a physical pain for the emotional agony my heart was in. Why did I do this to myself? Why did I have to push him? I loved him, Oh, God, I loved him, but I wouldn't beg him to stay, I wouldn't blackmail him in to not going. He had to go now, he had to do what he needed to do and though he promised to stay in touch, I felt that the war we had been fighting for so long, was finally lost. Each battle we had faced together had taken its toll on us and now there was nothing left.

Besides the pain, my body felt so empty, empty and hollow as if everything I was had been ripped out. I glanced at his side of the wardrobe, empty hangers, swinging slightly, where his clothes once fit next to mine. I wiped my eyes with a tissue and blew my nose. Harrison could not see me in this state. I had to get my shit together, if not for me, then for my kids. I was going to be the only parent they would have, I had to be stronger than this.

Someone knocked gently on my door, I was surprised to see him standing there, Jeremy. His face was unshaven, his blue eyes had fogged over, his eyebrows furrowed together and his fists, jammed into the pockets of his jeans.

"I thought you were leaving." I frowned.

"I was worried about you." He said softly. "I couldn't leave you in that state."

"Well, as you can see…" I began and stopped myself. "I'm sure I'll be okay, eventually." I insisted.

"About what you said, that you didn't count. Of course, you count, Kelsey. You are and always will be my one true love. That hasn't changed, and it never will."

"And yet, you have taken a job for a year in London. I didn't know you could hate someone so much and still claim to love them at the same time." I sighed.

"Sweetheart, I don't hate you. I am just afraid that if we carry on like this, then I will grow to resent you and you will grow to resent me, if you don't already."

"I don't." I affirmed. "Is there anything I can say to make you change your mind?"

"The way you spoke to me last night, if felt like a knife into my heart, as if you had reached in and crushed it. To do that to someone you are supposed to be in love with tells me that we are in a lot of trouble. I truly believe that some time apart, just for work purposes, will help us." He reached out and took my hand. "We're not splitting up or even separating, the job was offered to me last week and before last night, I was still considering it. The money, for one thing, is amazing and it will help with the move and new baby furniture. It's not ideal, but I think it can work."

"And I think that as soon as you are away from me, then that ring will come off and no one will even know you're married." I accused sourly.

"So, again, you don't trust me. I don't know what I am meant to do." He moaned. "I am not interested in anyone else, I mean, no offense love, but keeping you happy is a full-time job as it is. I couldn't do that and keep a bit on the side happy too." He smiled slightly. "I don't need anyone else, I have a wife and I love her."

"A wife you claim to love and yet you are still leaving."

"To save us."

"Usually, people don't separate to save a marriage, they work harder at it, together." I snapped. "I'm sorry. Okay. I am sorry for doing this to us, for pushing you away. I am sorry for everything, my trust issues, my temper, my stubbornness, my anger, my insecurities, but that is me, they all make me who I am and if you can't handle that, if it's too much, then maybe you leaving is the right thing to do, because I can't change the things that make me who I am, no more than you can." He just stared at me. I felt I had truly lost him, he kept saying I hadn't, but no one can tell you how to feel. Feelings are rarely wrong. "I'm alright now, so if you need to go, you had better go before Harrison comes back and sees you."

"Are you going to be alright?"

"Yes." I lied.

"Can I have a hug?" he asked hopeful. I stared at him, as much as I wanted those long arms around my body, I couldn't let him hug me, I would never have let him go.

"No." I replied coldly. "No hugs, no kisses goodbye. I am not going to make this easy for you and believe me when I say this. I will never be able to forgive you for this."

"Kelsey…"

"Please, just go, Jeremy." I frowned and turned away from him.

"I'll phone you later." He muttered and then he left.

I watched him place the cases into the boot, Julian hunched over, trying to look anywhere but up at me. Jeremy glanced up at the bedroom window before climbing into his car. I watched as they drove up the road and then I allowed the last of my tears to fall.

Hermione, Elle and Harrison arrived back almost as soon as Jeremy's car was out of sight. I washed my face and blew my nose. Though my eyes were red and sore from my salty tears and the tip of my nose looked red, I tried desperately to show that I was alright.

Inside I crumbled like a decaying cliff face, dropping into a boundless ocean of pain and darkness, on the outside, I had to show that I was alright.

I opened the door wearing my bravest smile, but as soon as I saw the image of Jeremy running towards me, I broke, I broke in places I didn't know that I could break. Maybe I was glass, I had been chipped and cracked, scratched and now I had been shattered into a million pieces. I fell to my knees with my arms open and allowed Harrison to run into them.

    I kissed the side of his head and fought hard against my tears with a stunned Hermione and Elle standing and watching as the impact of Jeremy leaving hit me like a bullet to my heart.

    "Mummy," Harrison complained trying to pull from my grasp, "Mummy, let me go." I opened my arms and allowed him to leave my body.

    "Kelsey," Elle frowned, "what's going on?"

    I heaved a shaky breath and shook my head, I couldn't bring myself to say it, to actually utter the words, he has left me, my heart screamed in agony and I couldn't reel it back in, I couldn't gain control and that petrified me.

    "Harrison, let's go and make Mummy a cup of tea." Elle said, touching my shoulder with her hand as she passed me. I stood from the floor. Hermione, whose own eyes had spilled over, swallowed, fear across her face.

"What's happened?" she asked.

"I can't… I can't say it." I sobbed.

"You are scaring the shit out of me, Kelsey, what's happened?" she demanded.

I stumbled into the living room and curled up on the couch, sobbing into a pillow. She knelt on the floor in front of me and stroked my arm as I cried. The more I tried to control it, the worse it became.

I heard the front door close, the letter box rattled as always, and I stupidly thought it was him, that he had changed his mind and come home, saying that he was just trying to shock me, to make me realize that we were good together and to get over this stupid phase we were stuck in.

Stuart, humbly stepped into the lounge wearing a grin that lit up his face. He was literally glowing. I stopped crying, well, tried to stop crying. I sat up and pulled a tissue from the box on the end table.

"Guess what." He said. I couldn't answer, clearly, he could see I was up-set or maybe he couldn't. "I have asked Elliott to marry me and he said yes." He added proudly.

"Congrats," Hermione smiled.

"What do you think, Kelsey?" I looked up at him and his smile changed to a frown.

"What do I think?" I snapped. "I think marriage is a waste of time, I think love is an infliction not a gift. All it does is cause pain and heartbreak. When you love someone, you can actually destroy them. Who wants that? I think you are a fool if you think you can get a happy ever after, because you won't, all you will get is jealousy and anger, fights and pain, you will hurt them, and they will hurt you. Love is evil and if you had any sense you would run a mile."

"Have I missed something?" he frowned.

"I think it is something to do with Jeremy," Hermione explained. "He's been here, because his car is gone."

"Elliott's brother dropped him and Julian off about an hour ago, I thought he was going to sort things out." Stuart explained.

"Oh, he has." I stood. "He has sorted his life out, only it doesn't include me anymore. He is moving to London for a promotion and leaving us here."

"No," he frowned, "He would never do that."

"If you don't believe me, call him and ask him yourself. Jeremy and I are over… I can't do this, I have to get out of here. Can you watch Harrison for me?" I asked.

"Where will you go?" Hermione asked.

"Away from here, I just need an hour or so." I replied, lifted my handbag, slipped my feet into my flats and hurried out to my car.

I didn't know where I was going, I only knew I wanted away from everything, if only for an hour or two. I couldn't face life alone, I know I had Harrison and the new baby on its way, but the thought of going it alone petrified me. I just needed some time out.

Sixteen

Jeremy

"I never knew you could be such a heartless, selfish bastard." Julian growled as we drove back to Buxton Manor.

"I beg your pardon?"

"You heard me, she is a lovely girl, Jez, she has a few hang ups, I get that, but to leave her, four weeks before your baby is due, that's unacceptable."

"I can't back down now, it will mean that she wins again."

"Who says that you are in competition with your wife? There are only losers when a marriage breaks up. I thought marriage was a partnership, for better or worse, through good times and bad. You are not the man I thought you were, not by a long shot."

"You have been in a relationship five minutes and you think you can lecture me." I barked.

"Did you not hear her back there? Did you not feel anything as she sobbed her heart out because I did, and it tore me to pieces? Yes, you may have problems, but to turn your back on your wife and children in some feeble attempt to teach her a lesson is just wrong." He retorted. "Yes, I have only been with Charlie a short while, but I would never treat him the way you have treated Kelsey. If she ever forgives you, it will be a miracle."

"I can't tell my boss I changed my mind." I sighed.

"You could if you talked to him today." He shrugged.

"I have messed Mark around so much that he would probably sack me if I tried." I explained.

"Huh, so you'll be jobless, but at least you will still have a wife and family. Do you not see how lucky you are? I know men who would give their right arm to have what you have." He grumbled.

"Julian, you aren't even twenty-one, don't tell me you are ready to settle down."

"Why not?"

"Because you haven't lived, because you need to experience some more of what life has to offer, that's why."

"Well, maybe I just want to get married to Charlie, adopt a couple of kids and just spend the rest of our lives happy."

"Jules, look at me, I am a mess. I didn't want this to happen. Getting married is great and then the real work begins. I actually told Kelsey once that I consider our marriage the hardest job I had ever worked at. It's about mortgages and bills, work and life on balance with each other, sharing everything you have and everything you are. You aren't you anymore because the old guy who liked to sleep in till twelve on the weekend, who would go down the pub and piss a hundred quid up the wall in one night. The one who would order a take away and still be eating it two days later because he couldn't be arsed to cook anything or even order anything fresh, is gone forever." I explained. "I miss the old me. But at the same time, I hate him too. I love that girl so much," tears pierced my eyes. "Still, I'm afraid of losing her, of what we have. We just seem to be on a road we can't find an ending to but can see in the distance that huge word divorce flashing in neon lights." I pulled off the road and put on my hazard lights as I stopped the car. "I was so convinced that I had done the right thing, but now, I am not so sure."

"Where does Mark live?"

"Blandford, his house is on Salisbury Road, why?"

"We need to go and talk to him."

"What, now?"

"Yes, now. The longer we leave it, the less chance you'll have making it up to Kelsey."

"Why do I have to admit I am wrong?" I frowned.

"Because real men will admit when they are wrong even when they know they are not, to keep their wives happy and contented. Look at it from her point of view, if she had come home from work and said she had decided, without even letting you know, to move away to London for a year, how would you take it?"

"Okay, that is a good point, but…"

"I respect you, Jez, you are my big brother, and when you stood up to Tara that time, I was so proud of you. When you let Kelsey leave that New Year's Eve, not so much. You are who I look up to and right now, I am having a hard time being in the same car with you. Now, let's go to your boss and tell him you can't leave your wife this late in her pregnancy and then we can go to your house and beg her to forgive your sorry arse."

I hadn't realized just how much Julian had grown, not just in years but in mind. He spoke a lot of sense and I knew then that the guilt I was feeling inside, could only be one thing, I had made another mistake. Why did I think I could leave her and she would be okay with it? Why did I allow my pride to ruin everything time and time again? I wanted to spend the rest of my life making Kelsey happy, that's what I promised to do on our wedding day, and somehow, I had forgotten how happy we were when we looked into each other's eyes and said, 'I do'.

We arrived at Mark's house and I climbed out of the car. Before I could knock, Steven, Mark's blond-haired husband, opened the door and smiled.

"Hi, Jeremy, how are you?"

"Not so good, Steven, is Mark about, I need a word?"

"He's cooking in the kitchen, come on in."

"Thank you, this is my little brother, Julian."

"Hello, Julian." He smiled warmly. Julian blushed slightly, I suppose Steven was a good-looking man, light, dusty blond hair and light blue eyes, a square shaped jaw and perfect teeth.

"Hello," he replied shyly. I am not sure if I liked seeing my brother go gaga over my boss' husband.

"Jeremy!" Mark announced wiping his hands on a tea-towel. "This is a nice surprise."

"I am sorry to disturb you at home, but we need to talk."

"Is this about the promotion?" he asked.

"Yes."

"You have come to say that you have changed you mind." He frowned.

"I was drunk and angry and…" he raised his hand.

"It's fine, I haven't even spoken to Brian yet."

"Are you sure? It's just Kelsey and she's…"

"I wasn't going to tell Brian until I spoke with you tomorrow anyway." He explained. "You looked pretty upset last night, and I was worried that you made a decision out of anger rather than objectively."

"So, you are not annoyed?" I queried.

"No, at least I don't have to look for someone to replace you now. So, go home and sort it out with your wife. She needs you." He tapped my shoulder.

"Thank you," I muttered.

We left, and I headed back to Branskome, hoping and praying that Kelsey would accept my apology. She didn't appear to be as upset when we left, but the threat that she wouldn't be able to forgive me lingered at the back of my mind.

Arriving back at the house, Elle's red, Mini, Clubman sat where my car usually parked and Kelsey's Nissan, Juke was nowhere to be seen. I wondered if she had gone to see her mother, but when I was greeted by a frantic and crying Hermione, I discovered Kelsey had taken off and no one knew where she was.

Pulling my phone from my pocket, I dialled her number. It didn't even ring, going straight to voicemail.

"Hi, this is Kelsey, leave a message and I will get back to you."

"Kelsey, love, it's me, call me as soon as you get this." I said and ended the call. "So, she didn't say where she was going?"

"No," Hermione sniffed. Harry was in the living room watching Paw Patrol and hadn't even noticed I was there.

"Shall we go and drive around, we might see her?" Elle suggested.

"She could be anywhere." I sighed and rubbed an anxious hand over my face. "I'll start with her work mates, Stuart, you call your cousin and Elle, get the phone book in the hall, Kelsey has an aunt and uncle in Winterbourne Kingston, she loves it there, phone them, Di and Jeff their names are. See if she is there."

"Okay."

"Can I take your car?" Julian asked.

"Not on your life," I frowned and looked at Stuart as he returned to us.

"We can go in mine if you want, Julian?"

"Thanks, Stuart." I said.

"She's not with Shawna or Lou, they haven't seen her since Jude's hen night." He explained as he lifted his keys. "Come on, Julian, let's take a drive around the town centre." They left, and I phoned Nicki and Felix to see if they had heard anything while Elle tried Di and Jeff's. No one had heard from her and all we achieved was to spread the worry around.

Hermione sat with Harry on the floor while I tried Kelsey's phone again. Again, it just went to voicemail,

"I'm at home, Kelsey. We need to talk, please, baby, come home." I fought hard to keep my tears from falling. I was petrified, for the first time in my life, I was absolutely petrified. I had no idea of where to look or if she even had her phone with her.

I stood in the window, gazing up and down the street to see if I could see her coming. Inside, my shredded heart thudded in my chest. Choosing to leave her was not easy, but in comparison to how it felt not knowing where she was and if she was safe, I don't think I ever felt so helpless.

"For God's sake, Jeremy, sit down." Hermione snapped.

"I can't sit down," I frowned.

"What on earth happened here today? I left with Harrison and she was humming in the kitchen, she hadn't slept a wink and even though she was exhausted, she couldn't wait to see you. What did you say to her to destroy her like that? I don't think I have ever seen anything so tragic before in my life."

"After her outburst at the wedding, I allowed my pride and anger to overshadow me and I did something in retaliation to hurt her and I think she is beyond repair."

"So, what did you do?" she pressed.

I turned to face her and leaned against the windowsill. "I accepted a job offer in London. I told her I was leaving."

She covered Harrison's ears, "Oh, my God, Jez, you fucking-arsehole." She growled.

"Thanks, sis," I sighed.

"Well," she sighed taking her hands away from Harrison's ears. "When she gave a lecture to Stuart about how love is an infliction, that it destroys you and not to bother marrying Elliott…"

"Stuart is marrying Elliott?" I queried.

"He said yes. Apparently." She said, rolling her eyes. "Oh, Jez, seriously, no real man runs away from their problems, she is a mess and it's all your fault."

I frowned, "I know that."

"And she is out there, doing God knows what, because of you."

"I know that too." I heaved a shaky breath as my eyes twitched with tears again. "I have been to see my boss, I have told him that I have reconsidered, and he agreed. So, I am not going after all."

"But the damage has been done. If she comes back, you better get on your knees, brother and sort this out. You have a wonderful family and for some insane reason, that girl worships you."

"And I worship her, look, I will sort this out, I will beg her for forgiveness and if she wants me to go after," -the house phone began to ring-, "then I only have myself to blame." I left her to answer the phone, "Hello?"

"Jeremy, it's Di, is Kelsey back yet?"

"Hello, Di, no, she's not. I am worried sick."

"It's a long shot, but there is somewhere else she could be."

"Where?" I frowned.

"Christchurch, it's where they scattered her father's ashes, over by the nature reserve out there."

"Okay, thank you."

"Will you let us know that she is back safely?"

"Of course." I promised and ended the call. "I need to go out." I told Hermione as I returned to the living room.

"Where?"

"That was her aunt, she suggested where they scattered her father's ashes in Christchurch at Hengistbury Head, there is a nature reserve there." I explained. "She told me they scattered her father's ashes in the water over there."

"What if she comes back?"

"Well, I can't just do nothing."

"No, we'll call Stuart and get him to drive out to Christchurch."

As I tried to call Stuart and Hermione called Elle to see if she had any news, someone knocked on the door, I pulled it open and Jane smiled cautiously. Dave looked concerned and followed her in.

"Nannie." Harrison yelled and ran towards her.

"Is she back yet?" Jane asked.

I was stunned as I hadn't thought to call her, "No."

"My sister phoned me. I understand why no one called me, I am probably the last person she would come to see right now." She let go of Harrison and he returned to watching TV. I had never wanted the TV to babysit my children, but today I didn't care. "I never meant for any of this to happen."

"I know, neither did I. Maybe it's time we treated her with some integrity, she is a lot stronger than we think."

"With all she has been through, then losing a baby, I didn't want to be the reason to cause her distress that harms this baby and look, I have anyway." She sighed and sat on the arm of the couch.

"Jane, I accepted a promotion which meant that I should move to London. I think we both will be eating a huge bite of that humble pie. I thought it would help us, I suppose I am as stubborn as she is, and this is the result of it."

"So, are you going?" she asked.

"No, I can't leave her. Jane. I love her, and I need her. If she forgives me for this, I would be surprised, but right now I just want her to walk through that door, to be home safe and sound."

"What time did she leave?" Dave asked.

"Almost two hours ago now." Hermione replied. "Look, why don't I make us a cup of tea and hopefully, she'll be back soon. She promised she wouldn't be long and maybe we are just blowing this all out of proportion."

"Good idea, love." Dave smiled. "I'll help you." They left the living room and I sat on the couch beside Jane.

"I don't think I have ever seen her so angry." She muttered, "I never thought that I'd hear her threaten you like that. I am so sorry, Jeremy. I truly am."

"It wasn't just last night," I admitted. "Things have been off since we went to court. She can't seem to trust me, and I don't do anything to help her. She is jealous of my assistant, of our clients, if I have to meet any of them, she gets quite upset. We needed to do something, and I thought that by taking the year's promotion, I'd give her some space. Of course, Julian pointed a few things out to me and it made me realize what an idiot I am. I have everything I have ever wanted here with Kelsey and I don't want that to change. I don't need time and space, I just need my wife." My eyes filled with tears because it hit just how vulnerable she had become and why, because of me, she didn't trust me because of what happened and even after promising her I would never leave her, the minute things get tense, I do the one thing she feared, I tell her I am leaving, what a prat?

"Don't do this to yourself, Jeremy," Jane said and tapped my leg. "She has always been headstrong, but always felt she didn't deserve to be loved. For some reason, she didn't believe in love, only the pain it caused, and I suppose that's down to me and her father." She explained. "She watched us as we fought and argued, then when he moved in with a supposed friend, it damaged her. I don't think she'll ever forgive her father for what he did to us when we needed him the most."

"I don't know what's wrong with me," I frowned. "I have the most incredible, beautiful wife in the world and she has given me so much, why isn't it enough to just do everything she wants and keep her happy. Why have I got to fight her on it?"

"A marriage is about sharing, sweetheart. You should not feel like you have to give her everything she wants and agree with every decision. You should be able to sit and talk about it and if you don't agree, well, that's okay too. I am not saying that she is to blame for anything, but by you making a decision about something without her, maybe it's given her a shock." Dave and Hermione returned with cups of tea.

Jane's words gave me little comfort, though she was right, we should share a lot more and decide things together, that afternoon, all I wanted was for her to walk through that door, so that I could take her into my arms and hold her. But as the time ticked on and she was nowhere to be seen, I would have settled just to know she was safe somewhere.

Seventeen

Kelsey

I drove across town and sat on top of the east cliff in Bournemouth watching the sea gulls dance on the wind. Tears fell silently as I tried to wrap my head around the fact that Jeremy left me, and I had let him go. Why, after everything I said to him, didn't I just tell him that I wanted him to stay? I asked if there was anything I could say, but what I should have said is I didn't want him to go, end of story.

    I felt dishevelled, washed out. I felt like my left arm had been removed and he hadn't really gone yet. Like a fractured piece of glass, just waiting to break while still being filled with water. Jeremy and I had our problems, but did I really expect him to go? No, because he promised to love me forever, he convinced me to have faith in us and I did, he had pulled the rug from under my feet and I didn't like the way it made me feel.

    I lifted my phone to call him and saw my battery was dead, so I couldn't phone anyone. I wanted to beg him to stay, I wanted to plead with him to come back but most of all I wanted to apologise. I was fed up with accepting that these things were out of my control, I shouldn't just sit back and allow this to happen. At the same time though, I was afraid. Afraid of letting him see how much I needed him in my life, not just as a husband, he was the other half of me and I didn't know how I could face life without him around.

After an hour or so, I started my engine and began to drive home, but the thought of going back there and facing that house alone, I just couldn't do it. So, instead I headed out of town and drove to see someone I had wanted to visit in a long time and never seemed to find the time.

I knocked on the door, a few moments later, it opened.

"Kelsey." My Uncle Ian smiled warmly, his light blue eyes sparkled with delight.

"Hello," I smiled slightly. "Time for a chat?"

"Of course, love, come on in." He opened the door. "This is a nice surprise." He said leading me through the house.

"I'd be lying if I told you this was a planned visit. I am in a bit of a mess." I admitted.

"Well, you know tears and laughter are always welcome here."

"That's good." I tried to smile, but my face felt tight and it wouldn't move.

He made a hot drink as I sat at the table in the kitchen and told him everything that had happened at the wedding and leading up to it. How Jeremy had accepted a job offer just to be away from me.

"So, he will be coming back each week, just working away?"

"Yes, but…"

"And the money is good?"

"I believe so." I answered as he placed a cup of tea in front of me. "I just feel like it's the end."

"I can't imagine it is. Jeremy is a solid man, Kelsey, he loves you and little Harrison, with another on the way, maybe, after your fight, he felt he was forced into making a rash decision, that perhaps it would shock you both into realising how fragile your relationship is at the moment."

"Okay, so, what if I don't want him to go?"

"Have you told him this?"

"Not yet, I won't beg him to stay." I stiffened.

"Sweetheart, maybe that's what he needs to hear from you." He tapped the top of my hand. "We men can't read signals or signs, we need to be told outright. It's not enough to hint or talk around what you want, you need to tell us straight." He elucidated. "Where is he right now?"

"He is at Buxton Manor, near my Aunt Di's." I replied and sipped my tea.

"Maybe you should go and see him." He suggested.

I shook my head, "No, he is coming over Tuesday night, before he is meant to leave on Wednesday."

"You can't leave it, Kelsey. You need to talk to him."

"What if I fail? How will I cope without him?" I demanded.

"And what if you don't even try? Could you live with that?"

I felt sick inside. "I suppose not." I admitted.

"Why don't you phone him?" he asked.

"My phone is dead." I replied. "I'll go home soon and put it on charge, I'll call him tonight." I promised feeling slightly optimistic. "Do you think he will listen? I have always had a problem admitting that I needed anyone, I have always supported myself and now, well, I have learned to rely on having him in my life. I honestly don't think I can face life without him now."

"Then that's what you need to tell him, no threats, no arguments, just cold, hard truth." He smiled. "I have been trying my hand at baking and have made some cakes, would you like to try some?"

Realizing how hungry I was as I hadn't eaten a thing since the meal at the wedding, I nodded and smiled, "Yes please."

After a slice of his lemon drizzle cake, which was incredible, I actually said I thought he should go on Bake Off, it was that good, we had another cup of tea and I decided that I should make my way home. I thanked him as I hugged him and left with a promise to let him know what happens.

I had left his house at around three and was still on the road an hour later. There had been an accident on the ring road to Bournemouth and I sat in traffic, crawling along at snail speed. I listened to the radio as Lady Antebellum song, "Need you Now,' began to play. The song that Jeremy and I danced to at our wedding and hearing it on possibly the worst day we had lived through, felt extremely significant to me. Especially as I had only been looking through our wedding photo album that morning.

As my fingers drummed on the steering wheel, I glanced at my rings, all three of them, glistening in the setting sun. I remembered what he had said to me when he gave me the eternity ring at the reception, the reason he was late to our wedding, how I made him a better man and he was going to spend his life loving and protecting me, true to his word, this is what caused this mess. Secrets and lies, hidden from me to protect me from the pain they might cause. That's when I realized, he loved me that much, he would rather live with the pain than inflict it on to me.

The traffic moved tediously slow and all I wanted to do was to go home so that I could phone my husband and beg him to come home. I turned off at the airport and took the busy back roads home, cutting through the roads by the University and heading to Branskome that way.

As I drove towards my house, I saw Stuart's and Elle's cars, my mother's car, and there, on the drive, was Jeremy's white Evoque. My heart lifted and filled with both nerves and excitement. Maybe he had changed his mind, maybe he had a change of heart. I didn't care, he was there, and I only wanted him.

I unlocked the door, they were in the living room discussing me. Stuart said he had been all over the town looking and Elle said she had done the same. My mother said that she would call my uncle Ian as I approached the door. I stood there for a few moments, as they talked.

"Mummy!" Harrison yelled and came running towards me. I opened my arms and welcomed his hug.

"Kelsey?" Jeremy stood from the couch and came in to view. "Where in God's name have you been?"

My heart sunk a little as I realized that I could have been wrong, "Out, what's going on?"

"We have been worried about you," my mum explained. "No one knew where you had gone and in your state of mind, we were beginning to think the worst."

"What?" I frowned.

"Well, you were really upset, Kelsey." Hermione interrupted, "You have been gone for four hours."

"I drove around for a bit and then went to see my uncle, I didn't know I was being timed." I snapped and then I closed my eyes, I was doing it again. "I'm sorry, I'm sorry." I repeated. "I um, I'll be back." I left them all standing and went out to the kitchen. Feeling sick, all of a sudden, I clutched the back of the chair as a sharp pain raced through my side.

"Are you all right?" Jeremy asked.

"Just a funny turn," I lied. "Did they get you back here?" I asked.

"No, I came on my own merit. We need to talk."

"I know…" I nodded as the pain writhed again.

"Are you sure you are all right, you have lost all of your colour?" he queried.

"Um, I don't, I don't feel well." As I said that, warm fluid gushed from inside of me soaking my leggings and splashing over the kitchen floor.

"Oh, my God, can someone help me?" Jeremy called out as the room lit up white and I fell into his arms.

I opened my eyes, I was laying on the kitchen floor and Jeremy and my mum were holding my hands, Jeremy was talking on his phone and mum looked so scared.

"Mum?" I frowned.

"It's okay, sweetheart. Jeremy, she's come-to."

"She's woken up," he said into his phone. "It's more of a watery blood, no not like when the waters went last time, this isn't right." He gazed down at me and letting go of my hand, he pressed his fingers to my forehead. "Yes, she is very hot. Um… about four weeks to go. Okay… thank you." He looked at me and smiled slightly, "They're sending an ambulance."

"Why?" I asked.

"Because the baby may be in trouble, they need to get you in to take a look." He replied and pressed his lips to my forehead. "It's all right, I am going with you." The pain began to writhe again, and I wish I could say it felt like I was in labour, this was a different pain, it was nothing like I had with Harrison.

I heard Stuart talking and two women dressed in green overalls entered the kitchen and smiled.

"Hello, Kelsey," one of them smiled, "I'm Gina and that is Zoe, what's happened?"

"I felt sick and then this pain, I think my waters have gone."

"Looks like it to me." Zoe smiled. "Are you feeling contractions?"

"They're not just labour pains, this is something else." I explained.

"Can I have a feel of your tummy?" Gina asked kneeling beside me. Mum moved out of the way. She lifted my jumper and placed her cool hands on my tummy, "Feels like it is contracting, looks like your baby is coming."

"No, I am too early."

"You can have that baby when its good and ready to come," Zoe smiled. "It's coming today, whether its early or not." She stood. "I am going to get a stretcher. Dad?" Jeremy nodded. "Can you get your partner's…"

"She's my wife."

"Okay, well, I am assuming the bag is packed?" she looked at me, I nodded.

"Bottom of the wardrobe, ouch!" I yelled out, "I think I need to push."

"I doubt it, honey." Gina said. "Can you get the bag, we need to get Kelsey to the hospital now."

"I really need to push," I insisted as the contraction and building pressure bore deep into my pelvis.

"Kelsey, you may have a prolapsed cord, or the placenta could have detached which is very dangerous for the baby. We need to get you to hospital now, okay?"

"Okay." I agreed. Collectively, I was lifted onto a stretcher and taken out to a waiting ambulance. Within minutes Jeremy was at my side, bag in hand and a concerned expression across his pale and tired looking face.

"We're here with Harrison," Elle assured.

"Thanks." Jeremy smiled slightly.

"Dave and I will meet you there." Mum promised, I could only nod as the pain began to writhe again. I grabbed hold of Jeremy's hand and squeezed.

"It's all right, love. I am not going anywhere." He promised and pecked my forehead.

The engine started, and I lay my head back on the pillow trying to breathe through the pain. Trying to focus on that ball I used in my head when in labour with Harrison. Thinking about pushing it up that hill as the pain increased and then down the other side once the pain began to settle. Only this time there was no relief, the pain level would rise and dip, but never easing up completely.

My head began to thump, and my mouth felt so dry. I felt like I couldn't breathe properly as the pain shot through me once more. I cried out in agony.

"Not long now, Kelsey." Gina assured me. A few more painful moments passed as the ambulance screeched to a stop. The back doors opened, and I was pulled forward, lifted out and pushed into the hospital.

We were taken into a room and I was surrounded by midwives and doctors. They put a monitor on my tummy to keep an eye on the baby and then an Indian looking doctor, with dark brown eyes and jet-black hair said he was going to do a scan before examining me.

I watched his face as he scanned me, frowning at the screen, the baby's heart seemed to be thumping away, but I didn't know if that was good or bad. He decided to try an examine me and by that point I was so scared, I just laid back and gazed at Jeremy.

"We have a class two placental abruption," he said quickly.

"Baby's heart rate just dipped," a midwife said.

"Okay, Kelsey, I am Dr Kumar. This is what's going to happen, you are having your baby tonight. Now, I would normally recommend a vaginal birth, but because of the pain you are in and the fact that the baby is showing signs of distress, I feel it would be safer for both of you if we perform a caesarean section."

"Will I be able to come in too?" Jeremy asked.

"Of course." He nodded.

"Theatre has been prepped so, if you could follow the nurse, sir, she will take you to get into some scrubs. We'll get Kelsey ready and then you can join us, okay?"

"Okay," he nodded. Before he left he kissed me, stared into my eyes and I watched as they filled with tears, he was scared and that scared me too.

A cannula was inserted into the back of my hand after I was stripped and put into a hospital gown. I was then taken into another room where I had the unimaginable agony of an epidural, so that I could be awake while the baby was delivered, all while being monitored. To have a needle inserted into your spine, it's not something I would forget, nor want again, but at least the pain disappeared and as I lay back on the bed, aside from being petrified, I could relax at last.

Jeremy appeared at my side and pecked my lips again, taking my hand in his he smiled slightly as a green sheet was raised in front of us.

"Kelsey, can you feel this?" the doctor asked with a mask over his face.

"I can't feel anything." I replied gazing into his chocolate eyes.

"Good, then we can begin." He smiled. "Scalpel…" I tried not to listen as they passed different instruments to each other, I could feel some tugging, but no pain and within minutes I heard a high-pitched scream. "There we go," the doctor said. "Dad, do you want to see your baby?" Wait, he gets to see the baby first?

"We'll see the baby together," he told the doctor. One of the midwives came towards us, wrapped in a blood-stained blanket was our baby, crying and shaking its little hands.

"Did you know what you were having?" she asked.

"No," Jeremy smiled teary eyed.

"Well, you have a beautiful baby girl."

"Really?" Jeremy checked. The midwife nodded and handed her to me and I pecked her forehead.

"Six pounds seven ounces, so a good weight for a month early. Have you chosen a name yet?" she asked.

"Not yet," I replied and pushed the blanket away from her face, she had stopped crying and yawned in my arms. "We have a daughter." I smiled at Jeremy.

"We do." He kissed me and then kissed her forehead.

"Would you like to hold her before we take her to the baby unit?" the midwife asked Jeremy.

"Is she all right?" he asked concerned.

"She's fine, but due to her heartrate dipping and her low temperature, we want to keep an eye on her for a little while. As soon as Kelsey is ready, we'll bring you both to see her." Jeremy took the baby from me and nestled her in his arms, everything, the anger, the frustration and the fear had gone, all I wanted was him and I hoped he wanted me too.

My head felt so heavy all of a sudden and I felt so cold, "Jeremy," I frowned.

"What is it?" he asked.

"BP is dropping fast," a nurse called out.

"We have bleeding here." Another said.

"I have some here too." The doctor said.

I watched Jeremy as he handed the baby to the midwife, "Jeremy, I…" the words wouldn't come, I tried so hard to force them out, but my lips felt funny, everything felt… wrong, "Love…you…" I could fight my heavy eyes no longer, falling deep into a pit of black, feeling icy cold and so alone…

Eighteen
Jeremy

"Kelsey?" I panicked, she passed out as monitors began beeping around us, lights flashed, and the baby began to cry again.

"I think she's haemorrhaging."

"Take the baby to SCBU," the doctor ordered, "where are those units of blood?"

"What's happening?" I asked, almost too afraid to.

"Uh, we are not sure, Mr Buxton, why don't you wait outside and as soon as we know something, we'll fill you in?" The midwife explained ushering me towards the door.

I stood there, numb, from top to toe. I couldn't move an inch, not even when they came out with the baby and raced her up to the special care baby unit. My life, my world, had crashed down before me in that theatre, one minute we were overjoyed then the next, Kelsey passed out.

Fear radiated through my body, touching every nerve as it filtered through me. A physical pain that made me want to scream. I stood there, still hearing that alarm, that beeping drilling into my brain telling me that my wife, my beautiful wife was in there fighting for her life.

"Jeremy?" Jane said from behind, I turned to face her. "What's happened? We were sent to the wrong place. Where is Kelsey?"

"She's in there." I muttered.

"And the baby?"

"We have a daughter." I said staring at the door.

"Oh, thank God, a beautiful baby girl." She exclaimed.

"Yeah," I tore my eyes away from the door. "The placenta had detached so they had to do a C-section." I explained. "The baby is fine, she really is the most beautiful thing I have ever seen."

"Oh, that's wonderful." She smiled. "So, is Kelsey okay?"

"I don't know, she was, she held the baby and everything and then, and then…"

"Jeremy?"

"…she passed out. These alarms started going off, they said she was haemorrhaging. That's when they pushed me out of the theatre, I don't know what's happening…" A tear dripped from my eye. This was because of me, what I had done to her, she was dying because of me. "It's my fault, Jane, she could die and it's all my fault."

"She is in good hands, sweetheart."

"I know." I nodded. The door to the theatre opened and Dr Kumar removed his hat. His scrubs were covered with my wife's blood and it wretched at my heart to see.

"Mr Buxton." He said. "Kelsey's haemorrhaging has stopped, she is stable, but I have to ask, has she ever had a bad reaction to anaesthetics before?"

"Yes," I nodded. "She had an ectopic a few years back, she was quite poorly after."

"Mmm, well, she isn't waking up, even though there is no reason why she shouldn't. We're going to transfer her to a ward and we'll monitor her during the night."

"But she is okay?" I checked.

"Yes, it's not uncommon to haemorrhage after a detached placenta, we have stabilized her blood pressure and raised her temperature. I am sure that as soon as she decides to wake up, you'll be able to enjoy your daughter."

"Can I see her?" I asked.

"You can, she might wake for you."

"Thank you." I tried to smile, but until I saw her, I would not be relieved.

"Thank you," Jane added as he led me towards the door.

"I won't be long." I promised her and followed the doctor back in to where Kelsey was.

She was no longer in surgery, they had moved her into a recovery bay. She looked so peaceful, aside from the heart monitor beeping beside her and a drip in her hand, you would have just thought she was asleep. It broke my heart to think she was in this mess because of my actions and the stress I had caused her.

I took her hand in mine and kissed her forehead, "I am so sorry, my love, so, so sorry." I said with my lips pressed against her skin. "Time to wake up now, sweetheart." I added as I sat on the chair beside her. She didn't move, her eyelids stayed firmly closed and it frightened me, what if I lost her, what if she never recovered from this? I would be left with two children and a gaping hole where she was once in my life.

"Mr Buxton?" a nurse muttered. I looked over to her, "We are going to move Kelsey to a ward now. If you wait out in the corridor, we'll let you know what ward in a little while, okay?" I nodded and kissed her again before I left the room and returned to my mother-in-law.

I told Jane and Dave that I needed the toilet, but I just wanted to be alone. I left them waiting outside of the recovery room. I needed to be alone so that I could kick my arse and call me all the senseless idiots known to man.

Wondering down the corridor my phone buzzed in my pocket. Elle had texted, I pressed to call her as I walked.

"Any news, Jez?"

"Kelsey had to have a C-section, we have a baby girl." I replied.

"That's fantastic, Jez, and are mum and baby doing well?"

"Baby is in special care as the placenta had detached, but seems to be okay, Kelsey um… Kelsey haemorrhaged and lost consciousness, she still hasn't woken up."

"But, she's okay?"

"She's stable." I muttered, "Look, I'll call you back as soon as I know more, okay?"

"Okay, Harrison had pasta for supper and we put him to bed after a bath." She explained.

"Thanks, Elle," I blinked, and a tear fell. "Thank you for being here."

"It's our pleasure, give Kelsey our love."

"I will." I sniffed and wiped my eyes. I ended the call and looked up. I was standing outside of the chapel and gazed at the cross on the wall.

I gingerly walked in with my eyes fixed on the cross. I have to be honest, though a Catholic, I hadn't stepped inside of a church since my mother's funeral. I instantly felt that good ol' Catholic guilt, when you know you should have gone to Mass a million times over and hadn't been once. We were going to get Harrison baptise and then he was so sick, we delayed it. Before long, Natasha and her hailstorm smashed through us and Kelsey found out she was pregnant again. I had wanted to go, especially when I felt I couldn't turn to anyone else, still, I hadn't been to Mass for such a long time and now, I suppose, God could see it that I only seemed to use him when I needed to. I sat on a chair and heaved a sigh.

"I know I have no right to be here, let alone ask you for anything, but, if you could see your way fit to looking after my wife and daughter, I promise you, I will be the best husband and father they could ask for." I wiped away my falling tears. "I haven't done much today to be proud of and for some reason I keep making mistakes. I try to be everything she needs, everything a good husband should be, but I let her down and I keep letting her down. Please, I am begging you, please don't take her away from me." I began to sob as the thought of life alone, without her by my side was my worst nightmare and today, it had come so close to becoming a reality.

"Jeremy," my father said from my side. I looked up and dived into his arms. "It's going to be okay, son." He said softly patting my shoulder as I cried in his arms. "She's up on a ward, the doctor has asked to see you." I let go of him and tried to pull myself together. "Come on," he said leading me out of the chapel and towards the stairs.

He explained as we walked that Jane and Dave were in a small room with Suzanna. Hermione had called him and told him that I might need him. I suppose they could all see how serious this was. You hear of the horror stories surrounding mothers losing their lives during child birth, you never think anything could happen to you or your wife. You never consider the possibility that she may not recover, and you could have no choice but to face life alone.

We were greeted at the nurse's station by Dr Kumar, he smiled as we approached, my insides were gnawing in fear. I swallowed a nervous gulp as he led me into a small room.

"I just wanted to let you know, that your baby is doing very well. I checked on her before coming up to here. She is screaming her lungs out which tells us they are working properly, she is very hungry though, was Kelsey planning on breast feeding?"

"I don't think so, she didn't with our son."

"Are you happy for us to give her a bottle of formula if she doesn't settle?" he asked.

"Yes, of course." I agreed. "Is Kelsey going to be okay?"

"That seems to be up to her. She had a huge dose of antibiotics as well as the anaesthetic."

"But you have seen this before though." I queried.

"I haven't, but there are known cases where people don't react as expected. I am sure she will be fine, you'll see." He smiled and shook my hand before leaving.

I was shown to her bed side, she was by a window that over looked Poole park. The lights of the town lit up the darkness. Kelsey's heart monitor had been removed and she slept soundly. I hadn't noticed at first, but Jane had followed me in. I sat on the chair beside the bed and lifted Kelsey's hand. If felt warm, for the first time that day, she actually felt warm. I moved my lips to her hand and pecked the back of it.

"Her father was like this, he could never go under without having problems when it came to waking-up again."

"She did this last time, when we lost the baby, remember?"

"Yes," she smiled sadly. "All the stress I caused you both in the last twenty-four hours, you have to know, I was only thinking of Kelsey. She is all I have left."

"I didn't help, it's no wonder her placenta detached. I am a despicable man, I don't deserve her." I frowned.

"Yes, but I should have known that by keeping something like this away from her, she'd take it badly, see it as some sort of betrayal."

"And after everything that we went through last year, I promised I would never keep secrets from her ever again, not even six months later and I broke another promise."

"Oh, for crying-out-loud, will you two please shut-up?" Kelsey asked. I looked at her, her eyes were wide open, and she looked totally pissed off. "Seriously, I am in too much pain to even think about what's happened in the last twenty-four minutes, let alone hours. I'm okay, all right?" she insisted.

"Oh, thank God." I exclaimed and kissed her. "I am so sorry, my love."

"So am I." she sighed. "To you both. Mum, I understand why you did what you did and so relieved you are okay and Jeremy, if I ever turn into that nasty, evil witch again, kick my arse, because I know I have been unbearable these past few weeks. Now, we're all sorry, we've made up and everything is wonderful, more importantly, we have a daughter." She smiled. "Have you seen her yet, Mum?"

"No, love, I wanted to make sure you are okay first." Jane replied.

"Well, I am fine, bloody starving, but fine." I began to laugh and kissed her head.

"I'll go and find you something to eat if you want."

"No, stay." Kelsey said as she reached out to my hand. I took hold of her hand again and smiled.

"I'll find a nurse." Jane said and left us to it.

I moved closer and kissed her tenderly on her dry lips, "So," she said. "What happened?"

"You haemorrhaged." I replied.

"I feel so sore across my tummy and a little bit groggy." She grumbled, "Still, at least the baby is okay."

"Dr Kumar has been to see her, she is demanding a feed already."

"Can we go and see her?" she asked.

"We'll ask when the nurse comes." I promised. "We need to think of a name too."

"I have a few I like." She smiled slightly.

"Such as?"

"Aria, Lily, Leah, Daisy, Thea, Isla, Freya and Willow." She replied. I smiled at the names, she really had thought about a girl's name. "It will have to go with Pricilla though."

"What?"

"Your mum's name."

"My mum hated her name." I frowned. "She'd go mad if we named our daughter after her. It's a lovely thought though."

"Okay, so what do you think?" she asked.

"I think I really like Willow and Isla, but for me, I think Freya is perfect." I replied.

"Freyer Buxton." She smiled. "Okay, Freyer…"

"Jane, after your mum, Freyer Jane."

"Are you sure?"

"Yes, a beautiful name for a beautiful little girl." I stated proudly. "Kelsey, I want you to know something, okay?" she nodded. "I went to see Mark after leaving today, I have told him to let Brian know that I won't be taking the promotion. So, I am not moving from your side. The next time I act like an imbecilic moron, you can kick my arse too."

"I was coming home to put my phone on charge to call you and beg you not to go." She admitted. "I realized that we can't let this beat us, we are stronger together. Look what we can do when we are."

"I love you, Mrs Buxton. Thank you for loving me, for putting up with me and above all else, thank you for giving me the most beautiful family."

The curtain pulled back and a nurse smiled at us. She informed us that she was getting a wheelchair so that we could go and see Freyer. Another nurse arrived with a cheese sandwich and a cup of tea insisting that Kelsey get something inside of her, before we went down to see the baby.

After eating and drinking, the nurse returned, and I walked beside her, down the corridor. My father and Suzanna were now sitting on chairs with Dave and Jane. As we approached they all stood.

"Are you coming with us?" Kelsey asked.

"Where?" Jane frowned.

"To meet your grand-daughter, Freyer Jane Buxton."

"Freyer Jane?" Jane smiled.

"Yes," Kelsey grinned proudly, "Do you like it?"

"I love it." Jane pecked her forehead. "Come on then, Mr B. let's go and meet Freyer."

I wanted to ask Kelsey if she was sure she could forget about everything that had happened, but grateful for small mercies, she seemed contented for now, though I was certain all we had been through would come up again. But that evening, all I cared about was that my wife still wanted me, and we had a beautiful little girl, Freyer Jane Buxton.

We were allowed in a few at a time, I went in with Kelsey first and gazed around at these tiny babies fighting to live. Freyer was next to a tiny baby boy called Joseph. His parents were sat, loyally beside his incubator.

"She has a healthy pair of lungs on her." The dad smiled.

"Sorry, bit of a traumatic entrance to the world." I explained.

"Don't apologize, we'd love to hear our little man cry like that." He took hold of his partner's hand. "I'm Matt and this is Louise, by the way."

"Jeremy and this is Kelsey." I said.

"She is beautiful, so much hair." Louise gushed.

"Thank you, at least I know why I suffered with indigestion so much." Kelsey smiled. "Joseph is gorgeous."

"Thank you, it's been a long three months."

I gasped shocked, "Joseph is already three months old?"

Louise nodded and smiled, "Afraid so, he was three months early, weighed two and a half pounds at birth, he's almost seven pounds now. Still forgets to breathe while he sleeps, and he hasn't cried yet, well, not the screaming a new born is supposed to make anyway."

"How much longer do you think he will be in here?" I asked.

"We don't know." Matt sighed. "Still, at least he is kept an eye on and until he remembers to breathe when he sleeps, we'd be happier with him here. They are fantastic." He smiled.

I gazed at Freyer, her tiny chest moved as she breathed, sleeping soundly. I could only imagine what Matt and Louise were going through. I placed my hand on Kelsey's shoulder and she held it in hers. I could sense her anguish, of course she wanted to hold her baby, we both did.

I went out so that Jane and my father could go in and see her. Dave and Suzanna waited patiently and after about half an hour, Jane came out in tears,

"She is so beautiful." She sniffed. "Dave, you go on in, make sure to use the hand gel by the door."

"Are you sure?" Dave asked.

"Of course, mate, go on in and meet your grand-daughter." He smiled and went in as I sat beside Suzanna.

"I bet you didn't expect this sort of drama when my father invited you over." I remarked.

"You have a wonderful family, Jeremy. Yes, there is a little drama, but how boring is a family without its ups and downs?" she smiled warmly. "I have had an amazing visit and I am thrilled that you have a baby girl."

I grinned and nodded, "I really wanted a daughter too, a pigeon pair as they say."

"She is so beautiful, Jeremy, you and Kelsey make gorgeous babies. Then again, I suppose I am biased." Jane gushed.

"Would you like to see her, Suzanna?" I asked.

"I would love to, but I think your brother and sisters need to see her before I do. Thank you for asking." She smiled as the door opened and my father smiled through the tears streaming his face.

"You did good there, son." He said and used a handkerchief to wipe his face. "How to turn a man in to a snivelling mess, introduce him to his grand-daughter."

Nineteen

Kelsey

"Hello, sweetheart." A voice I hadn't heard in such a long time spoke from the blinding white surrounding me.

"Dad?" I frowned.

"How is my little girl?" he smiled as he appeared on my bed.

"Not so good, Dad." I sighed. He looked amazing, glowing almost, his blue eyes brighter than ever.

"I can see that." He said. "That husband of yours is as stubborn as you are."

"I know," I smiled warmly. "He's my soulmate though, I couldn't cope without him."

"You are a strong girl, Kelsey, always have been, I know you would cope better than most." He placed his hand on top of mine. I gazed at his gold signet ring, pressing against the skin of his little finger. "You have beautiful children, sweetheart."

"I am very lucky. Married life, though, it's much harder than I thought it would be, we've been through so much already, I keep wondering if the next thing will cause us to tumble and fall completely."

"But you have many hands holding you up, friends, family, even your uncle, all supporting you, all there for when you fall. I have always admired you, Kelsey, your strength, your capacity to keep going, to keep fighting against the odds. You never truly lose hope, hope is the one thing you hang on to, even when things seem their worst, you find hope in there somewhere and it gets you through. Don't give up on anything, it's when you shine the most." He grinned.

"I miss you," I admitted.

"I miss you too, angel." He replied. "You need to wake up now, you need to be a stronger wife and mother, you need to accept that you are worthy of being loved. That man worships you, worships the ground you walk on. As a father, that is all I could hope for, that he loves you and looks after you, but you have to ease up on him, love. Let him be the man of the house and let him decide for himself, men need that, we need to feel we are in control."

"I don't mean to be this way."

"I know, he knows that too. He will never leave you on his own accord, but you have to stop pushing him away." He stated. "Do you understand?" I nodded my head. "Now, come on, time to wake up, your husband and children need you."

I could hear Jeremy's voice, he was talking, "Dad, wait…" I frowned as he stood from the bed. "I love you."

"I will always love you, I am with you, every day…" he said and disappeared.

I could hear Jeremy's voice again, though it wasn't clear a first, I could hear him, and I felt his hand in mine. His voice vibrating through his fingers as I listened to him blaming himself for whatever had happened. I heard my mother's voice then, the pair of them, riddled with guilt and all I wanted was to open my eyes and tell them to stop.

Damn eyes, bloody open!

The room was dimly lit, I gazed around, I saw Jeremy sat beside me, he was talking to my mother, she was claiming to have caused me so much stress… This had to stop. They both jumped when I spoke, no longer feeling groggy or tired, I was more excited and hungry, my God, I was bloody starving.

We finally got to meet our daughter properly, after a discussion over names and agreeing on Freyer Jane, a nurse arrived with a wheelchair. We were led to Freyer's incubator, she had been placed beside a tiny little boy called Joseph. His parents spoke with us when we arrived which was nice, but I kind of wanted to hold my daughter and it was frustrating seeing her, like looking at sweets in a shop window, they are almost there, but unreachable.

I gazed into her incubator, with the constant beeping around us, it was soul crushing to see so many miracles, clutching on to life with wires and respirators. Thankful that Freyer was healthy and the only reason she was there was because of her traumatic delivery, I felt bad for feeling so frustrated at the fact I couldn't hold her yet. Joseph's parents had been there for months.

Rupert came in after mum. He had always come across as a proud and stern man, he rarely showed emotion, though, he had changed. I could see that with how taken by Harrison he was, he literally crumbled when he saw Freyer for the first time.

"She is so beautiful." He smiled teary eyed.

"It's those strong Buxton genes." I agreed.

"Well, I can only see her beautiful mother in her." He gushed. I blushed at his kind words. "How are you feeling?"

"Like I have been cut in half by a magician and then sewn back together again." I admitted.

"Both Elle and Julian were caesarean babies."

"I didn't know that."

"Yes, Jeremy, forty-seven hours labour." I felt my mouth drop open with shock. "Hermione, she was here in just under three. Elle had a few problems, so Pricilla had to have a C-section, she was in a unit in America like this. Julian was fine though, nine pounds, seven, fifty-six centimetres long and cried for three days. They didn't want to risk a natural birth after Elle, so he too was a C-Section." He explained.

"And it's just you and Jeremy who can't have dairy products?" I queried.

"Yes, though, he is far worse than me. I was surprised to hear Harrison didn't have it too."

"Well, looks like this little lady has escaped it as well, she's already had a bottle of milk and kept it down, so that's a good sign. Seeing Jeremy so sick with his allergy at times, it really upsets me."

"He's used to it, nothing like buying ice-cream for the house and he is stuck with an ice-lolly." He sighed. "Still, at least he'll never have to fight the bulge. "One thing this allergy has done for me, its kept that belly fat to a minimum, for now, anyway." He smiled. "I can't tell you how relieved I am that you are both sorting things out. I worked away from them for many years and for some reason, it's now I feel the guilt for it, I truly believe that our lives would have been so different if I wasn't the ever-absent father, especially where Julian is concerned."

"Julian has grown so much these last couple of years." I smiled.

"Since he came out as gay, I don't know, it's as if the tension between us has lifted so much. Can you imagine feeling that everything you are, and feel is wrong? Poor boy."

"I hadn't been told Julian was gay, it makes a lot of sense now." I was surprised, but not really when I thought about it. "As for Jeremy, I am glad he chose to stay, but I wasn't going to give up the fight." I clarified.

"You are a good woman, Kelsey, I may have underestimated you at first and for that I can only apologise. You are a wonderful wife, an excellent mother, and I am proud to have you in our family."

"Thank you," I smiled. "That really means a lot."

"Sorry, love," Dave interrupted, "your mum said to come in."

"Don't be sorry, it's fine, meet your grand-daughter, Freyer." I smiled proudly.

"I do like her name." Rupert grinned. "A beautiful baby girl with a beautiful name."

"I can only agree." Dave gushed.

A nurse arrived a few moments later and asked if I wanted to feed Freyer, of course I did. She returned with a small bottle and Rupert said he would get Jeremy to come back in so that he could see Freyer feeding for the first time, I knew it wasn't her first feed, but it would still be our first time.

Jeremy returned and pecked my cheek as the nurse handed me a small bottle of milk. She showed me where my hands would go into the unit, using one to hold her up slightly and the other with the bottle, as soon as the teat touched her tiny lips, her mouth opened, and she began to drink. I rubbed my thumb over the back of her hair, feeling how soft it was and how warm she felt now.

A tear formed in my eye, I daren't blink, knowing it would fall, it just seemed such a special time and all I wanted to do was hold her and kiss her. When Matt returned with Louise, they smiled, and I reeled it back in, at least Freyer would be home soon and Jeremy and I would get to enjoy as many cuddles as possible.

I reluctantly left her so that we could go back to my ward, I would have stayed there all day and night, but as Freyer was sleeping, I felt silly just sitting there and not doing something. So, we returned to the ward and to my bed. Jeremy pushed me, and Rupert held open the many doors, showing the secret picture of Freyer, he took on his phone to Suzanna.

As Jeremy pulled back my curtain surrounding my bed, Elle and Stuart stood. Guilt flooded my body because of all I said to Stuart when he announced his engagement to Elliott. Elle hugged me and handed me a bunch of pink roses,

"This is all they had at the garage." She explained.

"They are lovely," I smiled. "Thank you." I said as Jeremy helped me onto the bed, I was still numb across my middle, but at least the feeling in my legs had returned.

"We're going to head off, love." Mum said and kissed my cheek. "I am so proud of you."

"Thank you, Mum, for everything." Dave pecked my cheek and they left. Rupert and Suzanna left shortly after and Jeremy walked down to the shop to find something to eat. Leaving Elle and Stuart with me.

"Harrison is sleeping soundly, and Hermione sends her love." Elle said.

"I really appreciate everything you have done today." I said. "It can't have been easy seeing as Jeremy is your brother."

"All that matters is that he saw sense, Julian really laid into him apparently. Called him selfish and accused him of running away from his responsibilities." She explained.

"Kelsey, if I had known… I am so sorry. I didn't mean to rub my news in your face after you got the worst news imaginable." Stuart sighed. "I was just so happy and the first person I wanted to tell was you."

"You have every right to be happy. I should be apologising to you. I was a complete bitch to you and I am so sorry. Elliott is a lucky chap and I am thrilled for you both, but please, do not ask me to be a bridesmaid, I cannot get pregnant again, not for a couple more years at least." I chuckled.

"I'll bear that in mind." He grinned. "We haven't talked about the wedding or anything yet, I just needed to show him how much I love him."

"Aww," Elle squealed, "that's so bloody cute, it's a shame you are gay."

"You are not the first girl to say that." He grinned proudly. "So, things between you two are…?"

"Good." I nodded. "No, better than good. Someone wise has reminded me today just how much you need to work at something, and, Stuart, when I said love was an infliction, I didn't mean it. If I lost Jeremy tomorrow, I would be devastated but one day, I know I would look back and be grateful for what we had while we had it. Love is a gift; a true gift and I am feeling one lucky girl tonight."

"Whoever this person was, they sure worked wonders on you." Elle smiled.

"They always have." I agreed. The curtain pulled back and Jeremy smiled.

"The nurse said that you needed to get some rest now, so…"

"We're off." Elle stood. "Need a lift?" she asked Jeremy.

"I was going to stay…"

"Stay where?" I frowned. "There is only this chair. Go home, sleep in our bed and be there for when Harrison gets up in the morning."

"If you are sure?" he checked.

"I am sure." I smiled. "You can take the roses home, they don't allow them here anymore."

"Okay." He agreed.

Elle and Stuart said goodbye and Jeremy said he'd meet them downstairs, "Are you sure you will be all right?" he asked.

"It's not like I can go anywhere, I still have a catheter in." I added. "I'll be fine, I am going to read my Kindle and get some sleep too."

"All right, my love." He leaned in close and kissed my lips. "In case you missed it today, I love you."

"I love you too." I smiled. "Don't forget to call everyone and text me when you get home." He kissed me again to seal his promise and left.

I was woken early the following morning, Dr Kumar had returned and wanted to examine me to ensure everything was healing as it should.

"The paediatrician has seen the baby this morning, she is doing very well and maintained her temperature. She had three more feeds during the night, I believe he is happy with her and could discharge her from the unit later today, she'll be with you then." He explained.

"How long will I have to stay here?" I asked.

"If everything is fine with the baby, and her doctor agrees, I will discharge you both tomorrow." He smiled. "I'll have the catheter removed this morning and then you can get out of this bed and move around. Obviously, you will be sore for a few days, you won't be able to drive or vacuum for approximately four weeks and we will speak with your GP and midwife so that they are aware."

"We are meant to be moving soon." I grumbled.

"Well, I hope you have lots of help, you need to take it easy, Kelsey. Everything went well, you are healing as expected and I am happy for you to go home tomorrow. The baby will be seen again later today and then we'll let you know. You must promise me though, no heavy lifting or anything that will cause an infection." I nodded, I would agree to anything if it meant we could go home and return to being, a real family again.

Two nurses came and removed the catheter as promised and it felt so good to be able to get out of bed. Though at first, my new scar pulled when I stood, as soon as I started to walk around, the pulling eased off a bit. It felt good to be walking again and not rely on someone pushing me. My stomach had gone down quite a bit and I was relieved, because the last thing I wanted was to add to my insecurity list.

Jeremy arrived just after I had managed to eat some cereal for breakfast. I say Jeremy, to be honest, all I saw was an array of pink, flowers, balloons and gift bags entered my ward, followed by my exhausted looking husband.

"Harry didn't want to go to nursery, he through a major tantrum before we left." He explained. "I suppose the last few days have really played on him. I just thought it would be best to keep him in his routine."

"Did you let his teacher know?"

"Yes," he smiled. "They all love her name, there are gift bags here from your mum, my dad, my sisters, Julian bought the balloons and the flowers are from me."

"They're beautiful, Jeremy, but they won't let me keep them here, that's why I made you take the roses home last night." I explained.

"Oh yeah, I forgot." He shrugged. "How are you feeling?"

"I have been for a little walk, I have had breakfast and all I really want now is a kiss from my husband and to go and see our daughter."

"Of course." He smiled again and kissed me. "Mark said to say hello and congratulations, he said he will come and see us when you are home."

"That reminds me, we might be coming home tomorrow, the doctors are really pleased with Freyer."

"That's fantastic news." He grinned. "The estate agent called, they want to complete on both properties next Monday, so it looks like we have a busy few weeks ahead of us."

"Bring it on." I beamed.

Twenty

Jeremy

I flopped down on the sofa and yawned. All of the boxes were finally unpacked. Kelsey was upstairs having her daily bath, a condition of her early release from hospital. Freyer slept soundly in her crib beside me and Harrison was in bed snoring his head off.

It had been the craziest of fortnights and at the same time, the best. Getting Kelsey and Freyer home was my main priority, we couldn't make good on our promises to do better until we were under the same roof again. Harry missed her like mad and I did too.

He adored his little sister, and every time she cried, he gave her a new car in the hope of stopping her. He had adapted to the new house quickly and loved his new bedroom with spaceships on the walls. Freyer only cried when she was hungry, which was great, to have her complete our family was one of the best gifts I could have had. When I held her in my arms and talked to her, she seemed to take in everything I said to her.

Sebastian and Jude returned from honeymoon expecting to see that Kelsey and I had split up, they were so surprised to find that we hadn't and that Freyer had come early. It made me realise how bad things must have looked to people around us, ones we had shared so much with, including our dirty laundry.

Jude had stopped talking to Kelsey though, she was furious at her so called best friend leaving her on her wedding day and it was an axe I didn't want to try and smooth. It was something they had to sort out together and both Sebastian and I decided to stay out of it. Of course, it upset Kelsey, but she never really admitted just how much she missed Jude in her life.

Jude, who now glowed as her bump had begun to grow seemed too angry to argue with, and given the way Kelsey's hormones raged, Seb and I decided it was best not to push it. They were eagerly awaiting a move in date for their new home so as much as it upset Kelsey, I knew they would find their way back to being friends again.

Stuart and Elliott had finally moved in together, our move spurred Stuart into looking for a flat, he couldn't afford it alone, so Elliott moved in with him and they were keenly planning their wedding.

Kelsey and I worked hard every day to make our marriage work, some days were harder than others, I won't lie and say it was all plain sailing, but it was so much better than before. She seemed to give me more of a chance, an opinion and she listened to my suggestions instead of just shaking them off. If she disagreed with something, I would watch as she would fight to hold her tongue and sometimes I just wish neither of us had to fight against who we were, but I suppose, in time, we would be back to almost perfect. Well, Kelsey and Jez perfect. I learned a hard lesson that Sunday that almost cost me my wife and daughter, I learned that if you hold a butterfly in the palm of your hand with your fingers encased around it and stopping it from flying, you only destroy it.

Kelsey had dealt with all sorts of crap her whole life, me trying to protect her from it now, was the main reason we had so many problems. I had to open up and she had to listen, that's where the work came in.

"Is she still sleeping?" Kelsey asked as she sat beside me on the sofa.

"Yes," I smiled and looked at her legs, they were red. "You are meant to be having warm baths, not scolding hot ones."

"I don't feel clean when I have a warm bath." She complained.

"You don't need to be clean, they are meant to help you heal."

"I am fine, the stitches are all out, the scar is clean, and I feel almost normal again." She explained. "Inside and out." She added.

"I am pleased to hear that, love." I said taking her warm hand in mine. "I must admit, I have been worried with having to return to work in a couple of days."

"I'll be fine, bored silly, but fine." She admitted. "Dave is driving me to the school for a couple of weeks and then it's back to normal." Freyer began to stir in her crib. "My turn." She smiled and stood from the sofa.

Two days later, I walked into the office for the first time since my appendix burst. It seemed like months since I was there last. The drive in took me at least thirty minutes less which was a huge bonus, but I have to be honest, leaving Kelsey in bed that morning pinched slightly.

I was glad to have my all-time favourite team on the radio for company during my drive in. Heart had never let me down, even when I lived in London, I listened to Heart in the mornings. Zoe and Rich were talking about the fact that Zoe's daughter would be starting school in September and I realized that Harry would be too, by that time Freyer would be five months old.

Life was flying past us and we had no control over that. Harrison was starting school and I knew damn well it meant that one minute he would be in reception, the next he would be going to high school. The concept petrified me.

I was greeted by a very excited Sebastian; he and Jude were going for a scan after lunch and then they were collecting the keys to their new house.

"How is Kelsey?" he asked.

"She's fine, almost back to normal." I replied as he led me to my small office.

"I have tried to get Jude to phone her, but you know what she's like."

"I have one of my own, remember?" I smiled. "These women, I never knew a species to hold grudges the way some of them do. They never forget it completely either. After everything that happened at your wedding, I am just waiting for it to come up again." I admitted for the first time out loud. I placed my bag on my desk and sat in my chair.

"Things are better though, mate?"

"It's better than it's been for a long time. Watching her on that operating table, I thought she had died, Seb, I really did. You have no idea how hard it was to be sat in that corridor and feel completely helpless. I put so much stress on her that day, what idiotic prat does that to his wife, tells her he is leaving her only weeks from her having their second baby, only to cause her so much stress, her placenta detaches, and she almost dies as a result? We still don't know if she can have more children." I frowned.

"But you two are all loved up and then some, Jez. Whatever happened that day, I think it shocked you both, now for fuck sake, just enjoy your lives, you have been given a second chance, make it work."

"Listen to you, you have been married five minutes and you think you know it all." I jested.

"I may have only just got married, but my wife is happy, happy and in love with me, I intend to keep her that way. Happy wife, easy life." He grinned.

"Okay, let's just see what happens when the baby arrives." I scoffed.

"Our baby will be the best-behaved baby in the world."

"My dear cousin, you are in for a huge surprise, mate." I chuckled as he left the office.

He phoned that night to say that they finally had the keys and that the baby was growing well. Jude was having a baby boy, so Harry would have a cousin to hang around with. I went up to our room to tell Kelsey, she was sorting through the laundry and putting it into piles.

"Jude's having a boy," I said excitedly.

"Great." Kelsey replied despondently and continued folding Freyer's tiny vests.

"I thought you'd be happy for them." I grumbled.

"I am, but, well, she's made her choice." She shrugged. "I don't blame her, I was at fault and I suppose if she had abandoned me on my wedding day, I would have reacted the same way." I could see she was getting upset. "Let's change the subject."

"Let's not, we need to sort this out, sweetheart," I pressed rubbing my hand up and down her arm. "You said you wanted her to be godmother to Freyer."

"I have changed my mind." She stiffened. "We'll keep the christening to family only and stick to your brother and sisters as godparents for Freyer and Stuart, Nicole and Felix as godparents to Harrison." She then stopped folding clothes and looked at me. "Unless you have someone else in mind?"

"I would have liked Seb and Jude, but if you are happy with your choices then I am too. Although, if you are keeping the christening to family only, then you might want to re-think on Harry's god parents, they are all friends. Don't forget, Seb is still my family."

"Close family and friends then. I am not changing my mind, so we need to go to the church and speak with the priest. I promised your grandmother at Seb's wedding that we would get both children baptised before, in her own words, she 'pops her clogs.'"

I smiled, "My grandmother definitely has a way with words."

"She is an amazing woman," she agreed.

"Love, we will have to sort something out with Jude though, she is Seb's wife and will naturally be invited with him." I insisted. She heaved a sigh. "Have you even tried to call her?"

"No, she sent me a text a while back, saying congrats on the baby, but she will never forgive me for leaving her at her wedding. It wasn't like I missed the ceremony and I didn't cause a scene, I left early, that's all." She stood from the bed. "It's fine, she only used me when it suited her anyway. I was never her best friend, not really."

"What about their gift to us, the holiday in Jersey?" I queried.

"They can have it back, I am not interested, and I certainly don't want anything I have to thank her for." She snapped and left the room. I was banging my head against a brick wall and should have known, Kelsey was so stubborn, she'd never back down.

All the work we had put in to making things right again, they dissipated from that night on, I felt like we were fighting a losing battle and the more I tried, the harder things got. I loved her with all of my heart, but I was beginning to dislike her, and I know that wasn't fair, still, it was how I felt. Life had dealt us so many blows, we'd had more ups and downs than any other couple I knew. Felix and Nicki were deliriously happy, as were Jude and Seb and I envied them, I envied what they had. Kelsey almost dying knocked me for six, but was I really meant to never argue with her again? Did I have to feel like this empty shell for the rest of my life? It was as if she was sucking the life out of me, the constant strain on us both was taking its toll and all I really wanted was five minutes to myself.

The weeks leading up to the children's Christening, things hit an all-time low, things were so bad at home, I didn't want to return there after work. I worked late most nights and when I got home, some nights she was already asleep in bed.

I loved our children, implicitly, I would have died for them, but I could see us destroying them and the farce that had become our marriage began to wither away. I didn't know if she was suffering with depression or what, I only knew how I felt and what I feared the most was that our marriage was truly over.

We barely talked anymore and when we did she'd make some comment about my privileged upbringing and how not all of us were lucky enough to have nannies and housekeepers.

I planned a visit home after the christening, but Kelsey said she wouldn't take Harry out of school so if I wanted to visit my sisters in Canterbury, I was to go alone. I felt that it was something that we both could do with, a break.

***

We arrived at the church at eleven, I held on to Harrison's hand and Kelsey held Freyer in her arms. Kelsey wore a dusty pink dress with flowers on it, she looked beautiful and smiled proudly as everyone complimented her on her body and how she had got her pre-baby body back in such a short time.

I wanted to tell them how much she had changed and how cold she was towards me now, but didn't want to ruin the day, I wanted at least one family gathering to be Kelsey drama free.

Jude declined her invitation and that meant Seb wouldn't be there either, he felt bad but as our wives were oblivious to the pressure they had placed on us, I can honestly say, both honeymoons were well and truly over.

The ceremony lasted for about an hour, the priest, Fr John, had talked about the oils he anointed the children with and how raising them in the Catholic religion meant that Kelsey and I had to promise to bring them to church, to raise them to know Jesus and God, how important it was for us to ensure we instilled good family values into their lives. I almost choked the words out because how could we do this to them?

We had hired a room in a pub for the gathering after, they had decorated the room and prepared an amazing Buffett for everyone and after a few pints, I was ready to go home. I sat at the bar and was promptly joined by Stuart.

"How are things?" he asked.

"Honestly? You don't want to know." I sighed and sipped at my pint.

"That bad huh?"

"You could say that."

"I thought, well, you know, after the wedding, you two were back to normal." I looked over at Kelsey feeding Freyer on her lap.

"If I tell you something, you swear to not say a word?" I checked. He nodded as I turned back to him. "I think we made a mistake. I think that when we broke up that New Year's Eve, we should have stayed broken up. I think that I have tried and tried and tried and no matter what I do, I am always fucking up and why? I'll tell you why, I am the worst husband to ever live. I have let this go on too long and now I think as a punishment, I am going to live like this for the rest of my existence."

"Come on, mate, you and Kelsey are like fish and chips, you are perfect together, yes you have had a few more bumps in the road than most but you do love each other, you have two beautiful children and are perfect for each other."

"I used to believe that too." I sighed and sipped my pint. "I am stuck now, if I leave her, I am the arsehole, so I stay and feel like an arsehole for feeling this way."

"Jeremy, I think you both need some help, someone professional to talk to. You can't leave this, it's sounds serious."

"Maybe." I nodded. "Just uh, just keep it to yourself, the last thing I need is for Kelsey to think I have been talking behind her back."

"You have my word, but you have to promise me that you will try everything you can to make this right, without you and Kelsey in my life, I don't know what I will do." I could only nod, I was petrified of losing her, but at the same time, we had travelled down this road too many times, I couldn't continue like this, no matter how much I loved her, we had to talk, the trouble is, would she listen?

Twenty-One
Kelsey

I knew it was coming, I could feel it. The distance between Jeremy and I had grown to the size of the Grand Canyon, and I was okay with it. I had two beautiful children and as much as I loved Jeremy, I felt we had gone too far down the road now. He tried, he really did, and I suppose I could have tried harder, but in truth, I didn't want to. If we couldn't work without trying so hard to make it work, then we never would.

I thought the move would help, he seemed so happy at first and I suppose I was too, but then he'd get that look in his eye, when he was meant to be watching the TV or working in his office, his mind was elsewhere and mine was too. Going over everything we had been through, fighting to survive in a relationship that seemed to have an expired shelf life.

For the first time since I had met him, I honestly felt strong, like I would cope on my own if I had to. I knew it would hurt to lose him, but I was tired of clutching on to him by threads, we were unravelling like a badly knitted jumper, we were beyond repair and I accepted that it was now just a matter of time before we would both admit our defeat.

His incessant whining about mine and Jude's friendship irritated the hell out of me. It was my choice to leave the wedding, it was my cross to bear. Not his, and he didn't have to act like ruddy Mr Maker on TV and fix us every time. Sticking tape over a huge crack was never going to be strong enough to hold us together for much longer. It was no longer a case of if, it was a case of when.

The christening kept me distracted for a while, writing invitations and searching for a christening gown for Freyer had preoccupied me for weeks. I no longer noticed when he showed me affection, a peck on the cheek here or a touch of the hand there. It never seemed to mean anything, more like empty gestures and as for sex, he hadn't been near me since Freyer was born. I honestly think he felt I was damaged.

The day of the christening, Hermione arrived with Jeremy's christening outfit for Harrison, as I held up the little white trousers tears filled my eyes.

"Kelsey?" she frowned.

"I'm okay, a little overwhelmed." I lied.

"I think I have known you long enough to know when you are lying, what's going on?"

"I am an evil woman, I am nasty and spiteful, and I don't deserve anything." I admitted and wiped my cheeks with a tissue.

"Why would you think that?" she asked.

"I can't tell you," I cried.

"Why?" she pressed.

"Because it's about Jeremy and I feel absolutely horrible about it." I sniffed and sat on the edge of the bed. "I love him, Hermione, I love him so much, but… but I don't think I am in love with him anymore, I think the spark has gone and that we would be better off alone."

"You tried that before, remember, and then you took him back, you have two children, Kelsey. Do you realise how lucky you are, to have what you have, well, do you?"

"I do, I did. The truth is though, I think if you asked him, he would admit it too. We are done, we have come to the end and as much as I love him, if we don't do something about this now, it will get ugly." I explained. "We have tried and tried, and we can't fix everything, Jeremy and I are on different paths."

"So, what are you going to do about it?"

"I am going to talk to him tonight."

"Jesus, Kelsey, you are about to promise the church that you will raise these children in a Christian family, with both parents…"

"We will always be their parents, Harrison and Freyer will always know how much we love them and I want you all to remain a big part of our lives, I just can't be with Jeremy anymore." Then I gasped, "Oh, my God, I just said it, I can't be with him, Hermione. We're too broken."

"I am so sorry." She frowned as tears filled her eyes. "I love you like a sister, Kelsey, what's going to happen now?"

"Maybe we can be amicable, maybe we can be different." I looked at my rings, sitting together on my finger where they had been since our wedding day. "It's not going to be easy, but it's time to admit defeat."

The christening was lovely, perfect. Perfect weather, perfect company, a perfect day. It was so nice to see everyone happy and smiling. My mum and Dave were planning a trip to America and part of me wanted to go with them. Jeremy's dad couldn't make it and for that I was glad. I felt a failure and he would only remind me of how he stuck by Jeremy's mum despite her illness, he never gave up on her.

After the ceremony, we headed to a pub near our home in Wimborne. They had set up the back room and placed food out on tables for everyone to eat.

I was glad to let the family see us together, it was how I wanted them to remember us. We were happy once, I am sure of it and I knew one day we could be happy again, just not together. As much as I felt I needed him, I realized I had already gone almost six weeks without him, he was like a ghost, empty and hollow and I hated that I was doing this to him.

I watched him at the bar, sat alone until Stuart joined him. Freyer drank her bottle in my arms as I allowed my hair to cover my face, I looked up and watched them talking. At one point, he turned around and looked at me and had Stuart not done the same, I could believe they weren't talking about me.

As the afternoon wound down and people began to leave, Jeremy and I collected the plates together and filled black bags with rubbish.

"That went well," he remarked.

"Yes, it did. We have so many gifts to unwrap tonight."

"Harry kept asking me if he could have some birthday cake now." He chuckled lightly.

"Bless him, at least he will sleep tonight." I smiled.

"You look lovely in that dress." He grinned.

"Thank you." I blushed slightly. "I had better check on Freyer." I said and left him at the table.

Okay, I admit it, I was afraid of what the next few hours would bring, but I didn't want to drag this out any longer. We had to talk, we had to tell the truth, no matter how painful it was, it was happening.

I hugged Hermione, Elle and Julian goodbye and climbed into the car. Freyer was stirring, so I knew she would be crying for a feed soon and Harrison was tired, he kept yawning. I watched Jeremy as he spoke with his siblings, hugging them goodbye and confirming his visit with them. A visit that couldn't have come at a better time.

Arriving back at the house, I took the children inside and started to make a bottle for a now screaming Freyer. Harrison was whining and wanting to go to bed and Freyer relentlessly screamed her lungs out while Jeremy unloaded the car and brought everything inside.

"Come on, mate," he said to Harrison, "let's get your pyjamas on." He took Harrison into the living room as I screwed the lid on Freyer's bottle. I lifted her out of her car seat and carried her into the living room. Harrison was now full on crying because Jeremy said he wasn't to open his gifts yet.

In a tantrum, Harrison lifted one of his toy cars and threw it in his father's face, catching Jeremy on the cheek, just under his eye.

"Harrison!" I snapped. "That was naughty."

"Daddy is mean." He cried.

"No, he is not, now you can wait until tomorrow to open presents, you are going right to bed, young man." I stated sternly. I could see Jeremy was angry, he stood from the sofa and lifted Harrison, who was now screaming, and took him up the stairs.

I had finished feeding Freyer by the time he got back to the living room. I had broken her wind and started changing her nappy.

"Are you alright?" I asked him. His face had a red mark under his eye and looked so sore.

"When did our son turn into a spoiled brat?" he asked angrily.

"He's not a brat." I frowned and began snapping Freyer's buttons together.

"He bloody is, look at my face."

"I know, he has never done anything like that before." I sighed. "Is he asleep?"

"Yes. Little sod."

"Jeremy, don't call him a sod." I snapped. "He's just over excited, too much sugar and he had a lot of attention today, it's not all his fault."

"My dad would have slapped my legs for that."

"Mine would have too, but we live in different times now. He'll be fine tomorrow, you'll see." I explained and lifted Freyer from her changing mat. "I am putting this one down now too." I carried her towards him, "Night, night, Daddy." I said. He smiled and kissed her head.

"Night, night, beautiful." He said sincerely.

After settling Freyer down in her cot, I checked on Harrison. He was still sobbing in his sleep and it broke my heart. I smoothed my hand over his tear-soaked hair and kissed him gently, Jeremy and I were about to change our children's lives forever and that didn't sit so well.

With shaky legs and a quivering heart, I went back downstairs to speak with my husband. I was petrified of how he would take this, after all of our promises and hopes, we were about to blow our world apart and I knew the fall-out would be just as devastating.

I stood in the doorway to the living room watching him for a while, he was still so gorgeous, he still caused my heart to flip over with his smile, but it wasn't enough to want to continue, I had to be firm and I had to be strong, this was my decision and I felt better for actually making it.

He sat watching the TV, engrossed in something, completely oblivious to me or what I was about to do. As I stepped forward, his eyes, his incredible blue eyes flashed at me,

"Is she settled?"

"Yes," I replied as I sat on the edge of the sofa. "Harrison is still sobbing in his sleep though."

He turned to look at me, the red mark from the car still prominent. "Are you alright?" he asked. I lifted the TV remote and switched it off.

"We have to talk." I said.

"Okay," he turned in his seat to face me.

"You know I love you, that I will always love you." He nodded, the colour slowly draining from his face, it was as if he knew what I was going to say. "When do you go to Canterbury?"

"Wednesday, I have a few things to do at work tomorrow, packing Tuesday and I will leave first thing Wednesday morning."

"Jeremy," I swallowed my emotion, my eyes tingled with tears, "Uh, I don't want you to come back here." I muttered eventually.

"What?"

"I think we should separate for a while, in fact, I know we should." I admitted painfully.

He stared at me, stunned by my words, maybe he didn't expect this, "You want me to leave?"

"I think it's for the best, don't you?"

"I can't… I can't think." He said and stood from the sofa. "How long have you felt like this?"

"A while."

"Is there someone else?"

"No. Never." I replied. "We can't carry on like this, I love you, but…"

"You are not in love with me." He finished. I pursed my lips and nodded. "I had no idea." He sighed. "I know things are bad, I mean, I could feel something was wrong. I didn't think you would want this, a separation. It seems so final."

"Final, but inevitable." I agreed. "You will always be the love of my life, but I can't give you anymore, you deserve more, and the sad thing is, I don't think I want to. I don't want to get twenty years down the line and not even recognise you anymore. I thought after Freyer was born things would get back to normal, but we were faking it, Jeremy. That's not a marriage, it's a farce."

"When you almost died that day, I promised God if he brought you back to me, that I would be the best husband and father in the world, but I can't even get that right. My whole life has been one fuck up after another and then I met you, you made me who I am today, but I have often wondered how much more we could do to each other and survive? It's as if we are toxic, we have spent so long fighting to get things right that we forgot the most important thing in a marriage, love, without it there is nothing left. You love me, and I love you too, love you more than I have ever loved anyone, but I get it. I understand where you are coming from. I don't think we are in love anymore. This is the last thing I want, but also, it was expected." He sat back down. "I have spent so long trying to be the man you deserve and for a little while there, things were perfect. I can't do this anymore either. I'm exhausted."

"So, you agree, and you don't mind?"

"Of course, I mind, I don't want this, I don't want to lose you, but if you feel like this, if I feel like this, there doesn't really seem to be much point in carrying on, does there?"

"No, maybe after some time, things can change." I offered.

"And if they don't?"

"There is only one thing left to do." I nodded realizing this would be painful, my heart sped up in my chest. "I'm sorry." I said as tears began to fall.

"I am sorry too." He replied, his voice cracking as he fought to hold in what he really felt and if it was anything like me, I felt like the world was collapsing and crushing my insides.

He stood and walked out of the room. I gave him a few moments, sitting there with the ticking of that clock in the hall, listening as my husband cried like a baby. I don't know if it was despair or relief, I only knew how much it hurt. I went out to find him in the kitchen, he was leaning over the kitchen sink, sobbing.

I gingerly placed my hand on his back and stroked it as his chest heaved and dropped, he turned to me and took me into his arms, pulling me against his chest. I allowed my tears to fall and cried with him. We had been through so much, it was almost tragic to realise that it was over, after all of the ups and downs, the many bumps we had endured together, we always found a way to make it back to each other, but since that day when he told me he was leaving, things changed, and I knew I was to blame for all of it.

I pushed and pushed and eventually our tower of strength had collapsed, weeks of suffering in silence over shadowed my love for him until it became too hard to just be the girl he fell for. I had lost myself, I had become so caught up in being Jeremy's wife, I forgot how to just be me. Independent and strong, ready to take on the world. I had to find that again, but I couldn't as long as I was still Jeremy's wife, the real me would remain trapped.

I wanted so desperately to make it work, to beat the odds and not become another statistic, but I see now how things changed for my parents after Ben died. My mother changed, she hardened and pushed my dad away until he found comfort with someone else. Luckily, Jeremy and I weren't there, not yet and as much as I knew it would destroy me to see him with someone else, I realised that I could never be the wife he both needed and deserved.

Eventually we stopped crying and parted, he used kitchen roll to wipe his face and sat at the table.

"What if we realize we made a mistake, would we get back together, try again?"

"How many times can we keep trying again, Jeremy? I honestly think this is the end of us. It hurts to admit that to you, still, it needs to be said. You shouldn't have to change who you are, and I know you miss your old life, your friends, your family. I am the reason you don't see them, even Sebastian, he is like your best friend and you can't see him outside of work because of me. That's not right."

"I don't want to leave and be alone, I can't handle that." He sniffed.

"You can, besides, I doubt you will be alone for long." He snapped his eyes up at me. "You are gorgeous, when they learn you are single again, they will come running." I smiled trying to lighten the atmosphere.

"So, there is nothing that can be said?" he asked.

"It's a separation for now, maybe I will miss what we have…"

"Don't give me false hope, Kelsey. You just said there is no hope of us trying again." He sighed and stood from the chair. "I need to go out for a bit, will you be alright on your own?"

"Yes." I swallowed and watched as he left.

Hearing the door close behind him made me jump. I had done it, I had ended us. I felt sick and empty as the realisation that soon he would be gone forever hit me. Jeremy and I were broken, smashed to smithereens and there was no way back for us, not now, not ever.

Twenty-Two
Jeremy

Numb!

I climbed into my car and literally felt like my soul had been removed. Kelsey and I were over, after everything we had been through, all the promises we had made to each other, we were done.

Although I had suspected things were bad, I was knocked sideways when she plainly told me not to come home. How can someone tell their husband to just not come home? It threw me, I'll admit and then as she explained, the devastation I felt ate away at the shards of my torn and threadbare heart.

I thought about the last few weeks and the toll everything must have had on us. I even considered leaving off my own back, but I made a promise not just to her, but to God, and alright, I wasn't overly religious, not like a Catholic ought to be, but I believed in the miracle that she recovered fully and both she and Freyer were okay.

I may have been stunned, but it felt right, it may have hurt, but I knew the pain would ease because I agreed with everything she had to say. Maybe not the part about us never trying to reconcile, but the rest of it, the whole, we were no longer in love with each other thing, that was true.

      The finalisation of our relationship cut like a knife, for the first time in months, I allowed my true feelings to show and I cried, I cried like no man should ever cry. I had lost the fight, she had thrown in the towel and I felt the sore loser. I had lost my wife, my best friend, I had lost the only girl I had ever truly loved.

Holding her in my arms as we cried together, it ripped me in two. Part of me wanted to scream at her, to fight for us again, but the biggest part, well, that was upstairs, packing my bags ready to leave. It felt so wrong and yet, it felt so right at the same time. We could not continue the way we were, something had to break, I wasn't expecting it to be my heart.

Leaving her alone was stupid, but I had to get out, I had to do something to stop me begging her to try again. We were done, Kelsey wanted me to move out and to separate and as much as it hurt me to leave, I felt a little relief too.

We had made so many mistakes, so many times we had broken up and got back together, fought, argued, screwed up and it wasn't just about us anymore, we had managed to drag our friends and family through the shit too. Our children, Harrison not even four and Freyer, a few weeks old, they would never realize how hard I fought to hold us together, they would see me as the absent father, the one who left their mum.

I dialled Sebastian's number and waited for him to answer.

"Hey," he said, "how did it go?"

"The christening? Yeah, good." I frowned.

"Glad to hear it."

"Can we meet up?" I asked.

"I have just got out of the bath, why don't you come over?" he offered.

"I'm a mess, I uh, I don't know what I am going to do." I sniffed as my sore eyes filled with tears again.

"Jez? What's happened?"

"We're spitting up." I said. "She doesn't want to be married to me anymore. I don't… I can't take this…" I began to sob again, pathetic I know, but I couldn't help it.

"Come over, Jez." He said in my ear.

"I can't, I've been drinking." I sniffed and wiped my eyes. "I just thought we could meet up somewhere round here, that's all."

"Fuck, Jez, I am so sorry, I never thought this would happen."

"I think I have been expecting it, not right now, maybe a few more months down the line." I explained and looked at the house.

The pain in my chest began to writhe again. "Look, I'll see you tomorrow."

"I'm getting dressed, I'll be there in about half an hour, just don't do anything stupid." He ended the call and I sat there staring at my phone. I had a few text messages I hadn't read, so began opening them up. One from my dad, wishing us well on the christening, one from Elle and Julian to say they were home safe and one from Hermione, checking that I was okay and telling me she loved me no matter what. Had Kelsey told her before me? Why would my sister, the one who only cared about herself, seem so worried about me? I dialled her number,

"Hello?"

"Did she tell you?" I demanded angrily.

"What are you talking about?" she sighed.

"Did Kelsey tell you she was going to tell me to leave, that she wants to separate?"

"She may have mentioned something," she replied cautiously.

"Great," I snapped, "so she told you before she told me."

"Does it really matter, Jez? She admitted her feelings for you had changed, she never said she was going to ask you to leave, not today anyway." She explained. "I am so sorry. Are you okay?"

"Of course, I am not fucking okay." I ranted.

"I thought you might take it badly." She sighed. "Come home tonight, don't be there alone."

"I can't, I've been drinking."

"You only had a few pints." She reasoned.

"Well, I have work tomorrow, I was going to come up Wednesday, but I might leave tomorrow night instead. I think I need to."

"All right, we'll be here for you, okay?"

"Okay." I sniffed and wiped away the few tears that had fallen. "Thanks, Hermie. I'll phone you tomorrow."

"Love you, big brother."

"Love you too." I replied and ended the call. I was about to get out of the car when Seb tapped my window.

I opened the door and climbed out, he said nothing as he folded his arms around me and gave me a much-needed hug.

"Let's go and get a pint." He said and pulled me towards his car.

I sat at a table as he brought over two pints, he placed one in front of me and sat down.

"Mine's just a shandy." He explained. "I have to drive back."

"Thanks for coming over." I muttered.

"I couldn't leave you in that state on your own." He frowned. "So, what brought this on?"

"Nothing, we had a great day, and then she came down after putting Freyer to bed and said she didn't want me to come back from Canterbury."

"So…" he pointed to my eye, "…that was nothing to do with it?"

"No," I frowned and rubbed the sore patch of skin and bone, it felt bruised. "Harry through a major tantrum when we got back because he wanted to open his gifts and because I said no, he through a car at my face." I explained.

"Ooh, feisty little bugger." Seb smiled.

"He's turned into a little brat since Freyer was born, seriously, Kelsey can't see it, but I can."

"Wow, maybe he has picked up on what's been going on between you two." He suggested.

It hit me then, of course he had, he was an intelligent kid, he would see the damage we were doing to each other, that's when I realized that she was right and all the tears in the world would not change the fact that we were destroying each other, slowly but surely, that would never be right.

Seb and I had talked for the best part of an hour or so, when I decided it was time to go home, that running away from this was only going to make things worse. She had put the wheels in motion and all I had to do was walk away.

He dropped me at home and hugged me again before he left, I watched his lights fade in the darkness and walked up our drive. Kelsey was sat in the living room watching television. My heart fluttered as I caught a glimpse of a tear on her cheek but turned and walked out to the kitchen. I filled the kettle and put it on to boil.

"Are you alright?" she asked quietly.

"Yes," I replied keeping my back to her. "Tea?"

"Please." She said and pulled out a chair. "What did Sebastian have to say about it all?" she asked. I turned to face her. "I saw him pick you up."

"Actually, he was quite good about it, I hadn't realized how far down we had dragged everyone around us, he also said that Harry's behaviour could be to do with how things have been lately."

"The tornado of Jez and Kelse is certainly destructive." She agreed.

"We had some good times though, it wasn't all bad."

A small smile crept across her face, "Yes, we did. Can I ask you something?"

"Sure," I shrugged as I turned around and began preparing some cups.

"If you meet someone you like, please tell me." I spun around to face her again. "I couldn't stand to be the last to know."

Her eyes filled with tears once more and my heart twisted in my chest.

"Kelsey, there won't be anyone else, not for a long time. How could I give my heart to someone else when it still belongs to you and will do for the foreseeable future?" I fought hard to hold it in but couldn't stop myself. "Will you do the same for me though, when the time comes?"

"If it happens, then yes. But it won't, I'll be too busy with the kids and everything else." I finished making her drink and placed it in front of her. "Thank you, Jeremy, thank you for loving me, for giving me two beautiful children and thank you for showing me that no matter how bad a person is, you don't give up on them."

"You are not a bad person, Kelsey, you never have been. You may have a few hang ups, but so does everyone. We're just not good together, not when you strip us away, we're toxic and that's not a good thing to be." I stated. "I've decided to head up to Canterbury tomorrow night. I think in light of the situation, staying until Wednesday is only going to drag it out."

"Okay." She said and lifted her tea to her lips. "I think I am going to take this to bed, I am exhausted."

"Sure, I'll sleep on the couch."

"You don't have to."

"I think it's best." I insisted. She stood from the table and left the kitchen.

I didn't sleep much at all, but I woke with my alarm, crept up to our room and found a clean shirt for work. She slept soundly as I headed to the bathroom, took a shower and got dressed.

I didn't even make a coffee, I just lifted my bag and my keys and went to work.

I spoke with Mark before everyone else arrived and explained about how Kelsey and I had decided to separate. I felt he had a right to know and he said how sorry he was. Sebastian came to work as normal and we headed out to lunch, I couldn't eat, but it was nice to get away from the office for a bit.

Upon returning to the office, Amanda, my assistant, greeted me with a smile, a smile that said she knew and felt sorry for me, a smile only a girl could give and not anger you. I guessed Seb had told her because I felt sure Mark wouldn't have.

"I have finished these for you," she said placing three manuscripts on my desk. "Oh, and John Smithey called, he wants to meet with you this week."

"I can't," I frowned, John was one of the writers for a local magazine we edited. "I have annual leave, so I will meet with him when I get back."

"So, you are coming back then?" she checked.

"Why wouldn't I?"

"Well, um, your wife and… It's none of my business."

"No, it isn't." I snapped.

"I'm sorry. I'll um…" she turned to leave.

"Amanda," she turned to face me, glowing almost with her blush, "my leave has been booked since I got back after the wedding." I explained.

"I know, but Kelsey and… I'm sorry. I just hate to see this happen. You are such a nice guy and the last person who should have to go through something like this."

"Thank you." I nodded.

"Have a nice break."

"I plan to." I sighed. She left my office and I glared at the manuscripts. I couldn't sit and read through them again, I trusted Amanda so lifted them and took them to Mark.

I knocked on his door, "Mark, Amanda has finished these, I trust her work, can you sign them off for me?"

"Sure," he smiled and tapped his desk for me to put them down. "What time are you heading off?"

"Now, if it's okay, I can't concentrate on anything." I explained.

"I am not surprised. You get going, have a safe trip and take care of yourself, mate."

"Thanks, Mark, see you next Monday." I promised and left. I waved at Seb as I passed his desk and headed out to my car.

I didn't want to go home, I didn't want to see her and then say goodbye, and as I drove the busy roads back to the home that would no longer be mine, my heart began to hurt again. By the time I pulled onto the drive, my insides were tearing at each other. Okay, last night it seemed we were doing the right thing, but as I stared at the house that was meant to be our new start, the ache inside erupted and I felt that familiar prickle in my eyes.

This was it, no more hugs from my son as he ran up to greet me after a long day at work, no more smiles from my daughter as I put her to bed at night. No more whispers from my wife when we turned off the lights. It was all over, as of now, everything we had was gone.

I turned my key in the lock and the house exploded in noise, Harry was running around bottom half naked and Kelsey was yelling from the downstairs bathroom. Freyer was screaming in her bouncy chair in the living room and there were toys and nappies all over the floor.

"Harrison James Buxton, get your butt back here now." Kelsey roared as she marched out of the bathroom. "Oh, you're home early." She said to me.

"Yeah, finished what I needed to do." I lied. "Is everything all right?"

"Actually, no. Harrison has been so naughty today and he has just wet himself again." She explained. "Hang on, let me get Freyer's bottle, she's hungry."

"I'll feed her, you sort Harry out." I said and put my bag on the floor in the hall. I hurried to the kitchen and found her bottle sat there waiting. I lifted her from her chair and into my arms, "Hey, what's all this noise?" I said to her as we sat in the arm chair. I held the bottle to her mouth and she began to drink. I watched as a little tear dripped down the side of her face. "I am so sorry, sweetheart." I muttered. "Sorry this is happening, you haven't had much time with me. I am sorry I will miss so much of your life, how you will laugh and crawl for the first time and Daddy will not be here to see it. I tried, I really tried, and I suppose it's just not meant to be. But I do love you very much, besides your mother, you are the only girl in the world who I would die for, never forget that." I pecked her forehead and inhaled her beautiful, baby scent and it made my eyes tingle with tears. Leaving Kelsey was going to be tough, but I actually believed that leaving Freyer and Harry would just about kill me.

As I winded a more settle Freyer, Harry returned to the living room and sat on the floor in front of the TV like he had been an angel. I could hear Kelsey upstairs, so after strapping Freyer into her seat, I went up to see her.

    She was sat on our bed staring at her hands, the pain on her face made me doubt our actions, but as soon as she realized I was there, she looked up.

    "She took all six ounces," I said trying to be casual.

    "Great, thank you."

    "Kelsey, are you having second thoughts?" I asked hopeful. She frowned. "It's just that if this is so right, why do I feel like my life is ending?"

"It's not easy for me either." She admitted. "But say we try again, in a few months, I'll be doubting us again and we'll be back to square one."

"You can't love me as much as you say you do then." I frowned. "If you did, then you would keep trying, you wouldn't give up on us."

"You say that and yet you were so ready to leave me the day Freyer was born. You came back, but you never told me why, okay, you didn't have a chance to, but still, if you loved me as much as you claim to, then why would we treat each other that way? Aren't you tired? Aren't you sick of all the fighting?" her eyes filled with tears. "I am, I am tired of fighting for us, love should never be about that, it should be as easy as breathing and it was once. When we first met, I fell for you instantly, I knew you were the one I wanted and there would never be another." She explained. "I felt so proud to be your wife, I changed when I had Harrison, I know that it hasn't been easy for you. We make up, we have sex and then within a few days we are at war again. These past few months, it has been an up-hill struggle and I don't have the energy for that anymore. I should trust you, but I don't, I should believe in us, but I don't."

"Just say the words and I will stay, I won't even go home for this visit. I'll stay with you and the kids and we can work this out, just please, Kelsey, I am begging you to not give up on us..." My eyes filled with tears and my body ached for her, how could she do this to us, we were amazing together? I fell to my knees and crawled over to her. Taking her trembling hands in mine I gazed into her eyes. "I love you, I love you as much today as I did the day I made you my wife. I have messed up so much in my life, don't take away the only thing that keeps me going, that's you and our children." She placed her hands either side of my face and blinked as tears fell from her eyes. She wiped my tears with her thumbs and pressed her lips to mine. I could taste her salty tears mixed with mine as we kissed, tenderly at first, as her lips softened, she pushed her tongue into my mouth, kissing me deeply, the first real kiss we had shared since before Sebastian's wedding.

My heart filled with hope, I had done it, I had talked her round. But as quickly as the kiss happened, it ended, and she moved from my lips.

"I love you, Jeremy, I always have, and I always will." She declared. I almost smiled, but noticed her lip quivering, "But I can't change my mind, not this time." She stood from the bed and left me alone in the room. My heart, only seconds ago filled with hope, exploded in my chest, we were over. Done.

Twenty-Three

Kelsey

I hated what I was doing to him, to us, but I had to be strong. In my head, I knew we were doing the right thing, but my heart told a different story. Without rhyme or reason, I did love him, implicitly. He was my Yang, the other half of me, but how many times were we to try and try again?

I wanted so much to just say yes, *let's try again*, but we were becoming a cracked record and I suppose the fear that we would only make things worse got the better of me. I'd already had such a hard day, Harrison had been a little sod, he really had. He got up not long after Jeremy left for work and that was it. Freyer had suffered with colic all day and by the time Jeremy walked through the door at two, I was at my whit's end.

He went in to 'fix it' mode and took control of the situation and this was one of the reasons I knew I couldn't go on with him. I chased Harrison up to his room and managed to get him washed and dressed in clean clothes. I couldn't believe he had wet himself three times that day, though my mum had mentioned that he might be picking up on what was going on between Jeremy and I. I hadn't thought about it, but I suppose with the move and Freyer, he had gone through a lot and he was coming down with a cold, so I guess, the strained vibes from Jeremy and me wouldn't have helped matters.

Hearing him beg broke my heart, I won't lie and after kissing him for the last time, I left him kneeling on our floor crying. I walked away, and he sobbed in our room for a good twenty minutes after. How could I be so heartless, so cruel? What the hell was wrong with me, he was perfect, well, perfect for me.

    I sat on Harrison's bed and listened as he began to pack his things. Petrified of going back to our room and watching him walk away from us. I almost did, I almost ran in there and told him to stay, but my head had taken over and as hard as it was for me to allow him to leave, I knew I had to, there was no turning back now.

For weeks, I had contemplated life alone. I had even spoken with my uncle regarding my inheritance from my father, because if Jeremy left, I would need to find the money to cover the mortgage and bills. Thank God, Harrison had free nursery now, because that was an expense I could no longer afford. I had told my mum and Dave that we were separating and sat there while she called me all of the selfish idiots to ever live and I suppose she was right, I was an idiot because I had this wonderful man who would do anything for me and I was making him leave.

Was I punishing him for what happened that day? I don't know, I only knew that after I told him what I wanted, I began to feel better. That was until he came home, begged me to change my mind and then began to pack.

I stood and walked towards the door, but he came out onto the landing and into the main bathroom, collecting his shaving stuff and toothbrush, I waited until he went back to our bedroom and walked towards it.

On the bed sat his case, a huge black thing that he seemed to carry his life around in before we met. Oh, how I wished I could go back to that summer, when we were about us and hot sex, before Tara and his almost wedding, when we would walk the lanes through Winterbourne Kingston, skipping through puddles and hiding under trees as the heavens opened up. How we would watch movies and scoff popcorn, spending the afternoons making love as the rain pelted against the window. We were that simple once and I missed that. Then Tara drama, we got back together, I lost the baby and we both changed. Finding our way back together after months of torture, that was the hardest time in my life and now I was about to walk back into that world freely, was I out of my mind?

We were Jez and Kelsey, doomed from the start. Nobody ever said love was easy, not after the wedding, not after having children, life was a struggle for everyone in the real world, but happy ever afters were reserved for fairy-tales, weren't they? He gets the girl of his dreams, she gets the guy of hers, that was fiction and I stopped believing in those stories when I saw my husband in his car with another woman, the same woman who had groped him and made him ejaculate, the same woman who tried to destroy our relationship and very nearly did.

Was I playing into her hands, was that what this was all about? Because for a millisecond as I watched him pack, I wanted to tell him to stop. Then we could make up and be happy again for a little while, that's when my hackles raised again, I didn't want happiness for a little while, I wanted it always. I didn't want to question where he had been and who he had been with, but I felt like I would want to and that's what the problem was. I didn't trust him or his feelings for me, even after him begging to give him a chance, I still couldn't trust him and that was wrong, that was why this had to be the end.

He flashed his tear-filled eyes at me, a frown creased his forehead and he swept his hand over his hair.

Clearing his throat before he spoke, "I'll come for the rest when I get back, if that's alright."

"Yes," I nodded, "of course, it is."

"Right, well, um, I had better go and say goodbye to my children." He muttered and lifted his bags from the bed. My heart skipped a beat as he walked towards me, he was broken hearted, any fool could see that. I tried so hard to hold my tears in my eyes, but they fell. He stopped at the door, leaned in and pecked my cheek softly. "Take care of yourself, Kelsey." He said and walked down the stairs.

I followed him and sat on the third stair as he went into the living room.

"Harry," he said lifting Freyer from her chair, "Daddy has to go away for a while, will you promise me something?"

"Uh-ha," he said walking towards him.

"You are going to be the man of the house now and I want you to promise Daddy that you will look after my girls for me, can you do that?" Jeremy asked.

"Yes, Daddy." Jeremy bent down and picked him up in his other arm.

"I love you both so much, okay?" he sniffed.

"Daddy is sad." Harrison said.

"I am, that's because I am going away, and I will miss you both."

"I miss you too, Daddy." Harrison said and hugged Jeremy tightly. He put him down and held Freyer up in front of him.

"You are such a beautiful little girl, no man will ever be good enough for you and though I won't always be around, if anyone ever hurts even a hair on your head, I will destroy them." He kissed her cheeks and then her head before placing her back in the chair. "I'll phone you on Mummy's mobile tonight from Auntie Hermie's, okay?"

"Kay-Kay," Harrison nodded. Jeremy hugged him again. "Bye-Bye, Daddy."

"Bye-Bye, Harry," Jeremy croaked and turned to face me. He walked towards me and handed me his wedding ring. "I don't want this anymore." He dropped it into my palm and it may as well have been a grenade for the amount of pain it caused.

"Oh," I sniffed and began removing my rings.

"No, keep them." He said.

"But this one was your mum's." I said pointing to the eternity ring he gave me at our wedding.

"And it didn't bring her much luck, either." He sighed, turned from me and lifted his bags. He walked to the door and opened it. My heart was pounding in my chest as I glanced down at his wedding ring, tears blurred my vision and dripped into my hand, the breeze from the open door caught me by surprise, I looked up and gazed into his eyes one last time.

"I'm sorry." I choked out with emotion tearing at my throat.

"I know, but it doesn't matter anymore, does it?" He stated and closed the front door. I honestly don't think I had ever seen him so hurt, so distraught, I couldn't take it, I ran up the stairs knowing Harrison and Freyer were okay and fell to pieces.

The hours ticked slowly by and all I could think about was him, if he was alright, if he got to his sister's safely, if he hated me now. I couldn't blame him if he did, I did this, I split us up and as much as I believed I was doing the right thing, to actually watch him walk out of my life crippled me.

I fed the kids and bathed Harrison ready for him to go to bed. Jeremy called just after eight and asked to speak to *'his son'*. When Harrison Handed my phone back to me, I was hoping to speak with him, but he had already hung up. Thinking that Harrison had accidentally cut him off, I tried to call him back.

"Kelsey," Hermione said. "Jeremy doesn't want to talk to you at the moment," she added coolly.

"Oh, I just wanted to make sure he was all right?"

"Of course, he isn't all right, he is devastated. I love you like a sister, but even I can't talk to you right now. Goodbye, Kelsey." The phone clicked on the other end and I was crushed. I don't know what I was expecting, to be able to hurt him like this and expect him to be okay with it.

Mum and Dave arrived the following day, I hadn't slept a wink, Freyer had screamed all night and woke Harrison three or four times. They probably hated me too, even I hated myself that day. I let them in just after nine, I still hadn't dressed or anything. My mother went off on one at me and Dave tried to calm us down.

"Well, how can she just kick her husband out?"

"It wasn't like that," I protested feebly. "Jeremy and I haven't been right for a long time and it's no one's business anyway."

"Did you know his sisters were on suicide watch last night? He actually threatened to kill himself because of this. He said he'd rather die than live without you. Oh, Kelsey, how could you?"

"How could I? How could he?" I demanded angrily. "He told me he was leaving, he is not completely innocent, Mum, so stop sticking up for him. If you are only here to have a go and make me feel bad, believe me, no one can make me feel any worse than I already do. I did this, I know, I ended it because we were destroying each other, and I won't raise my children around that."

"I came to see if you were all right," she frowned.

"Well, I'm not, I haven't slept for two nights."

"Let us take the children out for a couple of hours, love." Dave offered.

"Harrison should be in school and Freyer has the health visitor coming." I sighed. "I'll phone the school and tell them he's not right, which he isn't, he has a cold and then, if you don't mind watching them for half an hour, I'll take a shower."

"Why did you go ahead with the move? You have a bigger mortgage now and everything." Mum asked, she was not going to let up.

"I can pay my mortgage because of the money Dad left me, I will use that. My maternity pay covers the bills and food, I will be fine, I just need a few days to get my head around things." I explained. "So, can you stay and help or not?"

"Yes, love." Dave smiled. "You go and take a shower."

"Thank you." I smiled slightly and left them in the kitchen.

As the warm water pelted against my body I couldn't stop thinking about Jeremy, I knew that I would never be able to cope if he killed himself over me. My eyes hurt as yet more tears fell, fell for my kids and for my mother who thought the sun shone out of Jeremy's arse, but I couldn't cry for myself. I got what I wanted, no matter how much it hurt, this was all me. I lifted my phone from the bedside table and checked for messages, but there were none.

'Hope you are okay.' I texted Jeremy.

'I just need some time.' He texted back immediately.

"My mum told me about last night, what you said. Please, promise me you will never do that over me, I am not worth that.'

'I disagree, you are worth that and more, but I have two kids to think of, so no more drunk-talk for me. I'm sorry.'

'Sorry??'

'Sorry I wasn't enough, sorry I couldn't be your one, just sorry.' My eyes filled with more tears.

'You have nothing to be sorry for. This is all me!' I texted. 'I am sorry, okay?'

A few seconds passed before he replied. 'Okay'.

Things at home improved, Freyer got over her bout of colic and Harrison's behaviour changed with his cold ending. By the weekend things at home were more settled than they had been for weeks. I knew Jeremy would be back in Dorset, so expected him to come over any time he wanted. We hadn't discussed what would happen with the children, if he would want to see them and it was a conversation I was dreading, or maybe it was the fact that I would have to see him.

We hadn't shared a word since we texted each other the previous Tuesday. I missed him with every beat of my heart, when I did manage to sleep I dreamt of better times, happier times we shared. I was afraid to see him because I was weak, I knew if he asked to come back, I would probably agree, and all of this would have been for nothing. I had to stay strong, staying strong with him out of the picture was by far the easiest though.

He called to say he would pop round the following weekend, by the time he actually came to the house, we had been apart almost two weeks. I was anxious at the thought of seeing him, but it had to be done, I had to prove to myself that I could stay strong and show him that we could get along even though we weren't together.

He knocked on the door and I suppose it surprised me, I expected him to come in by using his key. His hair had grown, and he had lost a bit of weight, I could see by the belt on his jeans, he had moved to the next hole along. He smelled incredible, I had missed his aftershave, I knew that much.

"Hi." He said coolly.

"Come in," I smiled slightly. Harrison came running up to him.

"Hello, Harry." Jeremy chimed and lifted him from the floor, hugging him so tightly. "Have you been a good boy?"

"Yes." Harrison replied. "I miss you, Daddy."

"I missed you too." Jeremy croaked. "Where is your sister?" he asked putting Harrison back on the floor.

"This way." Harrison said towing Jeremy by the hand.

"Would you like a drink?" I asked.

"No, thanks." He said over his shoulder. I don't know what I was expecting, but his frosty tone hurt more than I thought it would.

"Wow, look at you," he said as I followed them to the living room. "Can I hold her?" he asked.

"You don't have to ask." I frowned.

"Thanks," he unclipped Freyer's straps and lifted her out of her seat. "You have grown so much." He said to her, she gave him such a beautiful smile. "Your hair is getting lighter too." He grinned and kissed her. He obviously hadn't come to talk so I drifted away from them and left them in the living room. This was how it would be now, what we had was broken, but the one thing that connected us was our children and the only reason I would see him now was because he wanted to see them and why wouldn't he? After all, this was what I wanted, right?

After a good half of an hour or so he finally came out to the kitchen.

"Do you mind if I get the rest of my shirts and suits for work?" he asked.

"This is still your house, Jeremy, you don't have to ask." I frowned.

"My name may still be on the deeds, but this was never my house, was it? You chose it, the sale of your flat paid for the other house and this was bought with the sale of that, this is your house." He corrected.

"Does it matter?" I asked.

"It did to me once, though not anymore." He added and left the kitchen. He had a right to be angry with me, but I would not let this happen in front of the children, so I followed him up the stairs.

"If you are here for a fight, I suggest you come back Monday when Harrison is at school." I stated.

"I am only here for my stuff and my kids." He retorted.

"Fine." I frowned.

"I'm back at the Manor, my uncle has allowed me to rent the guest house. It has two bedrooms, so as soon as I can get a cot and a small bed, I want to start having the kids every other weekend." He said as he placed his shirts into a holdall.

"I see." I swallowed.

"Yes, I have an appointment with a solicitor at the end of the month, they are organising an access agreement to be drawn up for you to sign."

"You are seeing a solicitor?" I questioned shocked.

"Well, like you said, there will be no going back, no reconciliations, so I thought we might as well go the whole hog and get a divorce, we're only delaying the inevitable." He replied flatly and stopped loading his clothes. "What, you thought you'd keep me dangling for a couple of years before *you* decide you want to divorce me?"

"I just thought… Okay. If that's what you want." I folded my arms. "I thought we could be amicable, I thought that the last thing you wanted was to drag this through courts and… okay. I'll get a solicitor and you can have your access." I turned to leave the room.

"I can't be friends, Kelsey, I either have you or I don't have you, if I don't have you, then we are completely over. I can't be friends with you, not even for the sake of the kids."

"Fine." I said hurrying down the stairs.

I had hoped after everything we had been through; the least we would remain is friends. I suppose I had burned that bridge and this was my punishment, I had truly lost everything, my husband, lover, soul mate and best friend.

He left after playing some more with the children, he asked if he could see them again on Wednesday and I was not about to refuse. I watched as he loaded his car and then reverse out of the drive, driving away with music thudding from his stereo taking the last of my heart with him. Then he was gone, his remaining things were gone, his hangers lay bare on the bed and on the dressing table, he had left his house keys.

A month had passed, and I was surprised at how fast it had gone. Jeremy had called a few times and only really spoke with to Harrison. He had seemed to cut me completely out of his life and that's how it should have been. I still loved him, and I still missed him, it was just when he came over, my hackles would raise and it took everything I had in me to bite my tongue.

I was so relieved to be driving now and on the first Saturday that Jeremy came for the children, after only seeing them at the house or taking them out after school on a Wednesday evening, I took myself down to Poole shopping. He wasn't sleeping them yet, but it did give me a break and I was grateful for some me time.

I sat in Starbucks on the High Street sipping a latte and staring at my rings. I still hadn't had the heart to remove them. Jeremy's wedding ring sat on my dresser at home, but I had kept my rings on.

Someone appeared at my side. I looked up to see Jude, with a huge bump in front of her, she looked amazing.

"Hey." She said cautiously.

"Hey." I replied.

"Kelsey, I um, I have… I'm a bitch, but you knew that… I uh…"

"Not like you to struggle for words." I smiled.

"It's fucking baby brain. I swear, it's like I am stupid or something." She explained.

"Please, sit down." I stated, and she sat on the chair opposite. "You look good."

"So, do you, well, except for your eyes." I frowned. "I can see the loneliness."

I heaved a sigh, "I owe you an apology."

"I owe you one, I have been so stubborn again, I am sorry I didn't come and see you when you had Freyer. I am so glad you are okay, and she is beautiful by the way."

"Thank you, she is like her daddy." I smiled.

"Actually, she is the double of you." She disagreed.

"So, you have seen her?"

"Jeremy brought them over the other night. Wednesday, McDonald's wouldn't heat her bottle up, so he came to us. Both of your kids are amazing, Kelse."

"Considering the all of shit I have put them through, I am surprised." I replied frankly.

"It's not all your fault, I know that. I could see what was happening, you two are destructive. I think he sees that now."

"He won't even talk to me so…" I pulled my purse from my bag. "What do you want to drink?"

"I am craving their Frappe's at the moment, they have a raspberry one out and its lush."

When I returned with the drinks she sat rubbing her side.

"This kid likes giving me stitch." She complained.

"I remember those days well."

"Can I ask why?" she frowned.

"Why?"

"Divorcing Jeremy."

"I just wanted to separate, the divorce thing, all his idea." I replied. "You saw what we were doing, Jude. I nearly died having Freyer, it made me realise that all the fighting was not healthy. We are always going to fight, there is just something about him that no matter how much I love him, he just manages to get my back up and I am not talking about the whole protecting me thing. I didn't like the way the relationship made me feel, I dreaded when he was home.

Frightened of saying the wrong thing, of triggering off another fight or row. It just got so toxic, I think it was making me ill."

"Do you miss him?"

"Yes. I still love him, I will always love him, but I can't be with him." I replied. "I honestly don't know if I will ever get over him, I don't know if I want either."

"Look at us, four years ago in July, we were getting ready to go to a party where I met my old man and you met yours, well soon to be ex-old man. We have kids, we have mortgages, life has dealt us one blow after another, but we survived. I have to ask you though, if you could go back to that night, would you have given Jeremy the time of day knowing all you know now?"

"Loving Jeremy brought me so much, he showed me how to be loved, how to be treated as the most precious person in the world. He gave me two beautiful children and for a while, we were happy. I would give anything to have that time again, I truly would. But that feels like a million years ago and I know we will never be able to find our way back to that again."

"So, what happens now?" she asked.

"I don't know. I admit the concept of life alone petrifies me, but I have gone a month and survived, I am sure I will continue to survive."

"Bloody hell, isn't there a song about that?" she then started humming Gloria Gaynor's *I will survive*. I had missed her so much, I smiled as she burst into song, I believed from that morning on that I would survive, I had cheated death and with or without Jeremy in my life, I was capable of anything.

Twenty-Four

Jeremy

This was the third time I had been asked to be a best man, though this time I was sharing the job. There were two grooms, Stuart had asked me, and Elliott had asked Sebastian, so the speeches were going to be interesting.

This time though, the speech wasn't the thing concerning me, I knew Kelsey was going to be there too. We had only seen each other when I went over to collect the kids and had as little contact as possible. We had been divorced six months and apart for just over a year. Ending our marriage cut me in two, but as the strain of the legal side was lifted once it was granted, we became the amicable adults she wanted us to be. Despite the fact that we had both moved on with our lives, we would always have something between us. It wasn't easy, but then where Kelsey was concerned, nothing ever was.

Arriving at Sandbanks hotel, ready for the wedding, I climbed out of Jude's car. She lifted the car seat carrying their son, Oliver, out of the back. He was the double of Sebastian in looks and had Jude's feistiness. He had made Seb grow up and become the man I had always hoped he would be. Jude looked stunning in her dark blue gown, Sebastian took the car seat from her and they held hands on the way in, still deliriously in love and I was happy for them.

I took a deep breath as we entered the ceremony room, Stuart and Elliott, who had been at the hotel all night, were stood at the front of the rows of chairs. There would be no walking down the aisle and although we had joked about Elliott wearing a dress, this was certainly the first gay wedding I had been too and until the rehearsal, I had no idea of what would happen.

The four of us wore royal blue suits with black ties and white shirts. I had Elliott's ring in my pocket and Seb had Stuart's. As we stood at the front of the room, the guests took their seats ready for the ceremony.

The ceremony was actually over quite quickly and as the registrar pronounced them as a married couple, the room erupted in applause. I turned to see Kelsey stood there, she looked radiant in a cream dress and high heeled shoes. I knew the kids wouldn't be there because no children were invited, Jane and Dave had them for the day.

My heart hardened when I saw him stood with her though, Chase, the American guy she had befriended when she went over there. Apparently, he came over with her uncle and they hit it off. I didn't like the man, but maybe I was looking for a reason not to. Either way, she got with him way before I even considered looking for someone else.

We stood on the patio surrounding the swimming pool and watched the photographer as she snapped pictures of the happy couple on the beach.

"You look nice," Kelsey said as she appeared next to me.

"Thank you, you do too." I replied and glared over at Chase. "He is here again then." I added sourly.

"For a few weeks," she nodded. "Where is she then?"

"Oh, she's here somewhere, I think she is at the bar." She turned around and glared at my once assistant, Amanda. "I knew you'd end up with her."

"You know it wasn't like that. I never even thought of her as anything more than a colleague and friend." I explained myself needlessly.

"I am just winding you up." She smiled. "She's nice and the kids love her. Don't forget Harrison has hospital this week."

"I know, Wednesday at four. I, as always, will be there." I said.

"Thank you. I just don't know if I could handle it very well if it's bad news." She admitted.

"You would, Kelsey, have faith in yourself." I stated. The silence became awkward. "Well, have a good day." I said.

She smiled, "You too. See you Wednesday." She added and walked away.

I walked over to Amanda holding out two glasses of wine. She looked stunning in her tight fitted pink and black dress, showing her slim body and long legs. She had become my rock, she was my go-to friend when I didn't want to whine to Seb again. We talked for hours and when I had the kids, she'd come out with us to help. It's not easy controlling a toddler and a baby at the same time.

Things developed eventually and then she finally admitted that she liked me and more than just a friend. I suppose I had grown to like her also. We had only been seeing each other since my divorce was finalised and that's when I felt that maybe I could allow someone into my heart again.

She was funny and intriguing, she had travelled the world and we shared so many stories about food we had tried and places we had seen. Life became easier with her around and though I never thought I would be able to trust another woman, Amanda filled my once bruised and battered heart with hope.

"Are you okay?" she asked.

"I will be after the speech is out of the way." I admitted taking a glass and sipping it.

"An old hand like you, this must be easy." She smiled.

"Nothing is ever easy for me, you should know that by now." I sighed.

"You look gorgeous, by the way."

"Really? How can anyone look more gorgeous than you?" I grinned. She laughed lightly and placed her hand in mine.

"Jez Buxton, you keep talking like that and we might have to go to our room early."

"Well, no one would miss us for at least half an hour, would they?" I gleamed squeezing her hand.

"I don't suppose they would." She muttered. "See you up there?" she smiled warmly, the sun twinkling in her beautiful eyes.

"You go first." I nodded and let her hand go, watching as she walked towards the open doors.

I looked over to Kelsey, she raised her glass and smiled, I did the same and headed back inside. I had thirty precious minutes and planned on making every one of them count.

It had taken a long time and a lot of soul searching to get to where Kelsey and I were now. Losing her almost killed me and I'll be honest, in the first few weeks, I would have happily just ceased to exist. She was my world, my everything and to walk away after all we had been through left me feeling soulless. Going home helped, although my sisters were worried and sat outside my room most nights, I was grateful to not face the emptiness in my life right away. I hadn't been home for such a long time and to be honest, with Kelsey only going there a couple of times, it helped.

After consuming a ridiculous amount of Jack Daniels in the first couple of days, I decided that wallowing and hiding were not the answer. I went riding with Hermie, I helped out in their clothes boutique, I did everything I could to avoid thinking about Kelsey. I phoned Harry a couple of times and he kept asking when I was coming home, that caused pain to run through my veins, lying to my son cut me in half.

I spoke with Seb and he told me that my aunt and uncle said that I could move into the summer house. It made perfect sense, though the last thing I really wanted was to be back at Buxton Manor. I supposed it was better than finding a flat somewhere suitable enough for my children to come to. That hit me hard, I would become the 'MacDonald's Dad', you know the ones, you see them in there on a Wednesday night feeding their kids because maybe where they live isn't suitable enough for them to go to, or perhaps they could only rent a room in a house.

Renting the summer house was my best and only option really. Kelsey and I had to decide how things would work, finances, how much would she need of my pay to survive, she had a mortgage to pay and with only being on maternity pay herself, I knew she would need more than half of what I earned.

I returned to Buxton Manor and made my aunt and uncle accept an offer of rent before I would agree to move in. I think I offended them, but I had to pay my way, it was only right. Being back in

Dorset hurt more than I expected, the first night in the summer house I cried myself to sleep.

I missed her with every aching beat of my heart, I missed my children, I missed my bed, going to the fridge and finding a beer, I missed the scent of the freshener in the downstairs loo, how Kelsey would iron my shirts. I missed putting Harry to bed and lying beside him making shadow puppets on his ceiling while making up stories. I missed my two-a.m. feed with Freyer, how she would gaze at me with her beautiful blue eyes, her soft hair rubbing against my face as I winded her over my shoulder. I missed that stupid clock ticking in the hall, it was my lullaby and I wanted it all back, I wanted it and Kelsey had taken it away from me.

By Monday, my pain and heartbreak began to change. Sebastian was showing off his latest scan pictures to the office as I entered and all of them turned to look at me. Eyes full of pity and uncertainty. I hated it, I hated that Kelsey made me look weak and pathetic, I hated that I was made to look a victim. I was a bloody man for Christ sake and I was going to darn well act like one.

"Alright, Jez?" Seb asked cautiously.

"Yeah, do you want to go for a pint lunch time?" I asked.

"Sure," he frowned.

"Nice week off?" Amanda asked.

"Fantastic." I smiled. It was forced, but I think it worked. I hurried to my office and closed the door.

As the week progressed and the weekend approached, the angst I had against my wife grew. I knew it was wrong, but I couldn't help how I felt. I called and bluntly asked if I could see the kids and she said yes.

Before I drove to my house, I parked the car and calmed myself. I needed to stop my hands shaking and I needed to try and keep a lid on my temper. I was going to see my kids and get some more work clothes, that's all. I didn't want to argue or fight, I wanted to show her I was capable of living outside of the bubble of Kelsey and Jez. We were no more, I had to get over that and in time I knew I would learn to accept that we would be better off.

Our children had to come first now, they didn't ask for this, they didn't deserve it, so for them and only them, I fought very hard to not let Kelsey know what I was beginning to think about her.

She looked tired and afraid, I suppose facing me for the first time since she said she wanted me to leave was also tough on her. I saw her, for the first time, as a strong and in control woman she had so clearly become since we had met. The young and naïve virgin I met was gone, truly gone and standing in the hall was the mother of my children. That's all she was to me now, I mean, my feelings for her were still as strong though I knew in time they would fade, but from now on it wasn't about us, it was about providing for my children, giving them as much of me as I could without getting in the way of whatever life my now ex-wife was going to make for them.

I am not proud of how I acted, in fact, I am bloody ashamed. I wanted to hurt her, to shock her. I wanted her to know what it was like to not be in control of something. So, I lied about making an appointment to see a solicitor, I had googled some and thought about the concept of a divorce, the ending of us, the piece of paper that would release her from me. I knew it had to be done, I just didn't know if I was ready to let her go completely yet.

After a month or so, I managed to arrange to have my children with me during the weekend. It was something I looked forward to and as the weeks passed leading up to it, my angst against her dulled as did the ache in my heart. We agreed to Wednesday evening visits, where I could take them out to dinner, just as I thought, 'MacDonald's Dad', then I hoped she'd agree to me having them every other weekend. Though, I had to see if I could cope with them alone. So, I didn't sleep them at first.

It's amazing how fast the months passed us by. Kelsey and I tried very hard to be amicable for the sake of the children, it was the least we could do. The formalities of separation were ironed out, she was able to manage her mortgage with her inheritance, so it meant that she was happy with some money for the children each month and the rest of my pay was mine.

Losing Kelsey made me grow up fast. The spoiled brat I had become had gone, I had my own bills and worries. I had my own life again and as more weeks passed, I began to enjoy life again. I also began to see that Kelsey letting me go meant that I got the better end of the deal, she worked hard with our children, they were clean and fed, they had everything they could possibly need and were well looked after. She had always been an incredible mother and doing it seventy-five percent of the time alone, was astounding. I started to see her through new eyes, eyes that could now see how amazing she really was. My love for her changed, it hadn't ended completely, I doubted that it ever would, she would always be the mother of my children and for a while we had an amazing time.

Learning she had a friend in the states, Chase, didn't hurt as much as I thought it would. I will not lie and say I was happy she had got together with someone else and as my relationship with Amanda bloomed, I hardly had any room to talk. I suppose I was afraid he would steal my family away. She promised me that she would never move to America and I had to trust her on that. Harry liked Chase and so did Freyer, as long as he was good to them, I didn't have a problem. So, I would be there for when she needed me, sort of like before, only now we had an understanding, I had my life and she had hers. We had separate lives with a connection that would live with us forever, two amazing children and although we had been down this long and sometimes arduous road, we had survived, maybe not together, to get here, we had to take different paths, I see that now.

Twenty-Five

Kelsey

If it wasn't for the fact that I knew Stuart would never have forgiven me, I wouldn't have considered going to the wedding. Stuart had insisted I bring Chase, and though we only saw each other when he came over to visit, I thought it would show everyone that I wasn't bitter.

Divorcing Jeremy was easier than I thought it was going to be. I am not saying it was easy to sign a piece of paper that would end our marriage and walk away. I meant the process. We met at some solicitors, I agreed to Jeremy's terms, his access order and his offer of child maintenance. I signed some paperwork and within a few weeks, I was sent my decree nisi. Three months later a decree absolute came through the letterbox, that was it, Jeremy and I were no longer married.

Mum and Dave had gone to America during the summer after Jeremy moved out. I phoned to speak to them one day and Chase answered the phone. We talked for almost an hour and he said if I ever needed to talk about anything, I was to call him. He came to visit with my aunt and uncle the following March, a week before what would have been my fifth wedding anniversary. I would never have been able to get through it without him there.

Nothing happened, nothing. I wasn't ready for anything and though Jeremy didn't believe me when I said we were only friends, nothing had happened, not on Chase's first or second visit to the UK. We remained friends and spoke almost every day over the phone and through Skype. He adored the children and it was nice to know that he was there for me.

Nicki and Felix had moved away to Winchester, he had been offered a Head Chef's position in a top hotel there and they had to go. Their twins, a little girl called Brenna and a boy called Braden, were almost nine months old when they left. Jude and I remained close friends, in fact, she wanted me there when she had her son, Oliver, I was one of the first people to see him.

Life was improving. Jeremy and I were able to talk without arguing and even though I knew he had started seeing Amanda, his ex-assistant from his office, it didn't bother me, I was happy for him. Well, I tried to be happy for him. I think he began to see that we were right to separate our lives. That the destruction we caused by being together was not good and we came to a silent agreement that for the sake of Harrison and Freyer, who were completely innocent in all of this, we had to get along and make more of an effort for them.

I'd be lying if I said it was easy. It was things like the first's that hurt the most. Harrison's first birthday since our split, where Jeremy came to his party and we barely shared a word. Our first Christmas apart was almost unbearable, I set the children's gifts out Christmas eve, which happened to also be my first birthday without Jeremy in my life. I sat on the floor in front of the fire with a glass of wine crying.

When Jeremy arrived Christmas morning to watch the kids open their presents, I was surprised that he greeted me with a gift he had got me, luckily, I had bought one for him too, but never imagined he'd ever give me anything again. He pecked my cheek and asked if I had a good birthday, I couldn't lie, and I told him the truth. It was miserable, and I had never felt more alone.

I think that's when things changed for us, we had turned a much-needed corner. Things between us continued to improve and I honestly believe that for the first time, he actually respected me and my decision. I admitted that divorcing him was a tough decision, but we mutually agreed it was the right decision.

I knew Jeremy had heard that Chase and I were talking, though he never challenged me or accused me of anything, I felt things tighten between us for a little while. He admitted that he was afraid Chase would come over and push him out, even asking me to more to the states, something I would never do.

When Chase came over for a third visit since we had been friends, it was just before my absolute arrived. I had continued to talk to him and I was open with Jeremy about it all, I had nothing to hide. He deserved to know the truth even though there was nothing to really tell until Chase and I actually went out on a date. It took me another three weeks before I allowed him to spend the night and we had been together since.

It's hard when he has to return to Boston, but we couldn't do it any other way. Chase wanted me to go over and see him for a few weeks, but I still have to persuade Jeremy into letting me take the children first. I could not go without them. Still, for now I am happier than I have been in a long time, partly because I have made peace with myself for deciding to end our marriage, but also because I truly believe now that I deserve to be loved, Chase is a wonderful man and he made me smile again, he pulled me through the darkness and became a beacon of light. He understands that my feelings for Jeremy are still there, though, it's more of a family love than a love that a couple would share, after all, he is and always will be the father of our children.

I watched as Jeremy and Seb approached the grooms, all four of them wearing the same blue suit and looking like a bloody boy band. After the ceremony, I approached him as he watched the photographer take pictures of our friends.

We spoke, and I tried to keep it polite, I couldn't help but remark on his relationship with Amanda, but only after he made it known he was displeased at seeing Chase there. After a brief conversation, we parted, and I returned to Chase,

"Hello, beautiful." He grinned. "This beer is good."

"I am glad you have finally found one you like." I smiled.

He glanced around at the many guests, also Jeremy, now speaking with Amanda. "So, your mother has the children, we have time to ourselves for the first time since I got here, and, where are we? At a wedding." He handed me a glass of wine.

"Well," I grinned. "We can leave early, if you want to."

"I want to." He nodded.

"I should warn you though, I have a bad habit at leaving early, especially when there has been a fight or an argument."

"Yes, well, I bet you haven't left early to have the most amazing, incredible love making session you have ever had." He bragged.

"No, not yet, anyway." I pressed my body against his. "So, what time were you thinking of leaving?" I asked waring as I thought about his proposition.

"Oh, in about, five minutes. I doubt anyone will notice."

I watched as Amanda left Jeremy standing alone, he looked at me, I raised my glass and smiled slightly. He did the same and followed her. I stared briefly, wondering what was going on, then Chase's hand pressed against the small of my back.

"Let's get out of here." I said, drained my glass and took his warm hand in mine. An afternoon making love to Chase without the risk of Harrison coming into our room, that was too good an opportunity to miss.

I found the grooms and pulled them aside while Chase headed out to see if he could find us a taxi,

"Chase has a touch of jet-lag," I lied. "We're going to pop back to mine, so he can get some rest, maybe we'll pop back tonight."

Stuart smiled warmly, "You still can't lie to me."

"Okay, well, we have no children at home, so um…"

"I knew it, you are going home to shag that gorgeous looking Yank." He grinned and pecked my cheek. "Have fun, babes."

"I plan to." I grinned.

"Thank you for being here, Kelsey."

"I wouldn't have missed it," I smiled again and hugged him. "Elliott, you have a wonderful husband here, you make sure you look after him."

"I promise," Elliott grinned. "Thank you for coming today, I know with Jez and everything…"

I shook my head, "We're okay, we spoke earlier. I think he has gone up to his room with Amanda," I admitted raising my eyebrows. "Harrison has hospital this week and we're going together."

"Text us how he gets on." Stuart said.

"Uh, you will be on honeymoon, I am sure you can wait until you get back."

"Nonsense," he grinned. "A quick text won't distract me too much." He then winked his eye. "I can multi-task, right, Elliott."

"Oh yes." He grinned proudly.

"Enough," I chuckled. "I will try and come back tonight."

"Well, if you don't, we'll pop over when we get back." Stuart promised. I hugged them both and joined Chase at the door. He took my hand and led me out to a waiting cab.

Wednesday, Harrison sat beside me in the waiting room of Martin's new clinic at Poole hospital playing on my phone. I hadn't been there since Freyer was born, so it seemed strange being there again. At least we didn't have to travel to Southampton this time. Harrison was almost five now and doing well at school. He was the image of his father and just as intelligent. Jeremy had hinted at putting him through a private school, but he had been through so much, I felt taking him away from his school friends would have done more harm than good.

"Sorry I am late," Jeremy muttered sitting beside Harrison. "Traffic was terrible."

"We still have a few minutes." I smiled nervously.

"Are you alright?" he asked.

"Well, no, not really."

"It'll be fine, Kelsey, I am sure of it." He smiled slightly. "You okay, Harry?"

"Yep," Harrison replied not taking his eyes off the screen.

"Guess what came on the radio on the way over," Jeremy grinned. "Bruno Mars, Marry Me, remember at our wedding how they all got up and danced to it with us?"

"I do," I nodded and smiled. I remembered watching almost the whole guest list joining us on the dance floor.

"It was a good day, wasn't it?"

"It was, is, and always will be one of the best days of my life." I agreed. "If you ever want your mother's ring, you only have to ask."

"I gave that to you, Kelsey, I won't take it back. It can be passed down to Freyer when she is older enough if you don't want to keep it." He stated. "How is Chase?" he asked. "I didn't see you at the wedding reception, Stuart said he was jet lagged or something." I blushed slightly, or something was certainly right.

"Yes, he was exhausted, the flight over was delayed and… actually, we uh, we went home to make the most of an empty house." I admitted truthfully.

He smiled slightly, "I see." He said clearing his throat.

"Sorry, that's was um…, forget it." I felt my cheeks warm.

"It's okay," he nodded. "You uh, you still blush like a beetroot when you talk about sex."

"Jeremy," I chuckled and shifted in my seat. "Little ears have big mouths too, you know."

"He's not even listening, right Harry?"

"Huh?"

"See." He smiled.

"So, you left the wedding early too." I accused.

"Yes, Amanda wanted to show me the room."

"Liar." I smiled. Jeremy grinned, his blue eyes began to twinkle.

"Harrison Buxton?" a nurse called out.

"Oh, my God." I sighed and stood heaving a shaky breath.

"It'll be fine," Jeremy assured. "Come on, mate." He said taking my phone from Harry. "Time to see the doctor." He added handing it to me.

Martin stood and greeted us with a friendly smile, he shook Jeremy's hand and then mine before we sat. We hadn't seen him for three months, then out of the blue, Harry had to have some tests, we were here for the results.

"So, Harrison, how are you?"

"Good." He replied. I rolled my eyes, he could talk really well.

"He's been really good." I added.

"Well, I have some news about the last tests we ran." Martin said. "Harrison's heart has improved. I can confirm that according to his last scan, his ASD has closed."

"His hole has closed?" I queried. "Can that happen?"

"Yes, it can. It is quite common and means that Harrison is now a healthy little boy and will continue to have a normal, happy life."

"So, he doesn't need the operation to close it?" Jeremy asked.

"No, it closed by itself."

Tears filled my eyes, "That's amazing news." I sniffed. Harrison looked up at me. "You are all better." I told him.

"So, can I start swimming now?" he asked, something he had wanted to do for months.

"You can do anything you want to, Harry." Jeremy replied ruffling his hair. "Thanks, Martin, for everything."

"It's my pleasure."

"I can't thank you enough." I said as I stood.

"Honestly, Harrison's body did all the hard work." He insisted. "He's a good lad and a real credit to you both."

"Thank you." Jeremy and I said together and smiled.

"Can we go to Sprinkles now?" Harrison asked referring to the new ice-cream parlour in town.

"Sure." I sniffed again and wiped the tears from my eyes. We said goodbye to Martin and left the hospital feeling ten feet tall. He said he would see us in a year and that was the longest Harrison would go without having to make a visit to the hospital.

Jeremy said he would meet us down in Poole and while I went and ordered at the counter of the new restaurant, Harrison sat at a table waiting for his dad. I ordered him a huge ice-cream sundae topped with cream and chocolate sauce. While I waited, I phoned my mum and told her the good news and as I promised, I texted Stuart.

When I got to the table, Jeremy was sat with Harrison, they were video chatting to Hermione and Elle who were screaming when I arrived.

"That's amazing news, Harrison." Hermione said.

"I know, mummy is getting me a sundae to celebrate." He repeated my words.

"Ahh, well, you enjoy it and remember, I will be down soon, we are going to Adventureland like I promised." They talked for a few more moments and then he handed the phone back to his dad. Jeremy spoke with them briefly and then ended the call. Still using the same phone, I had bought him for the last Christmas we were together and on a black leather chain, dangling from his neck, was his wedding ring. When we started talking properly again, I gave it back to him and told him it was his to sell or whatever he wanted to do with it. I liked that he decided to keep it after all.

"I ordered you an Americano."

"Thank you." He smiled.

"I can't believe it, he is really going to be okay."

"I know," he agreed. "Best news all year."

"I'd say." I nodded.

"I told Amanda on the way here, she is ecstatic for us." He muttered.

"That's sweet of her." I smiled, I meant it too. "I called mum and texted Stuart, he asked me to."

"I need the toilet." Harrison said.

"I'll take him." Jeremy went to stand.

"I know where it is," Harrison insisted. "I can go by myself."

"Are you sure?" Jeremy checked. I nodded, and we watched as he walked away. "He's an amazing boy."

"He is. God, I feel so light, like his heart condition was weighing me down." I smiled again.

"I know what you mean." He grinned. "Look at us. If you had told me when we parted that we would be here, celebrating the most amazing news ever, together, I would have called you a liar."

"We have come a long way," I nodded and smiled.

"We have. I know I said I would never forgive you for what happened that day, but I want you to know that I have, Kelsey, I did a long time ago. I had always been a failure, admitting that I failed as a husband, that hurt."

"You didn't fail me, Jeremy. We weren't good together, you are still one of the most important people in my life."

"I feel the same," he nodded. "I like Amanda a lot, I don't know what will happen with her, but I do know that I will always be here for you and the kids, whenever you need me."

"That means so much." I said as Harrison headed towards us. "Thank you."

"Thank you, Kelsey, even though we are not together and have both moved on, I will always be grateful for what we had while we had it."

"Any regrets?" I checked.

"Too many regrets, but I can live with them." He smiled slightly.

"Same." I admitted.

Our coffees arrived, and we marvelled as Harrison tackled a mountain of ice-cream, grateful that he was going to be alright and so happy that Jeremy was there to share it with us. Yes, we had come a long way and we still had a way to go. But I knew that apart, we could still be good parents to our children. No matter what we did or who we were with, nothing would change that.

The End

The Season Series

Set in the beautiful county of Dorset, the Season Series is a story dear to my heart. It's home for me and Jeremy and Kelsey have been the best characters I have ever worked with. Bringing this story to an end has felt slightly bittersweet, but I am happy that the story has ended the way it did, and you never know, you might just hear from this amazing couple again.

Summer Rain

Cruel Winter

Autumn Fires

Spring Fever

Thank you for joining me on this incredible journey, and remember, keep reading!

Please find all of my other work on Amazon all sites.

Follow me on Twitter @MelissaJRutter

Facebook, AuthorMelissaJRutter

Website: millyrutter.wixsite.com/authormjrutter

Printed in Great Britain
by Amazon